UNDER CONSTRUCTION

A WOMEN IN TRADES ROMANCE®

KATE COLE

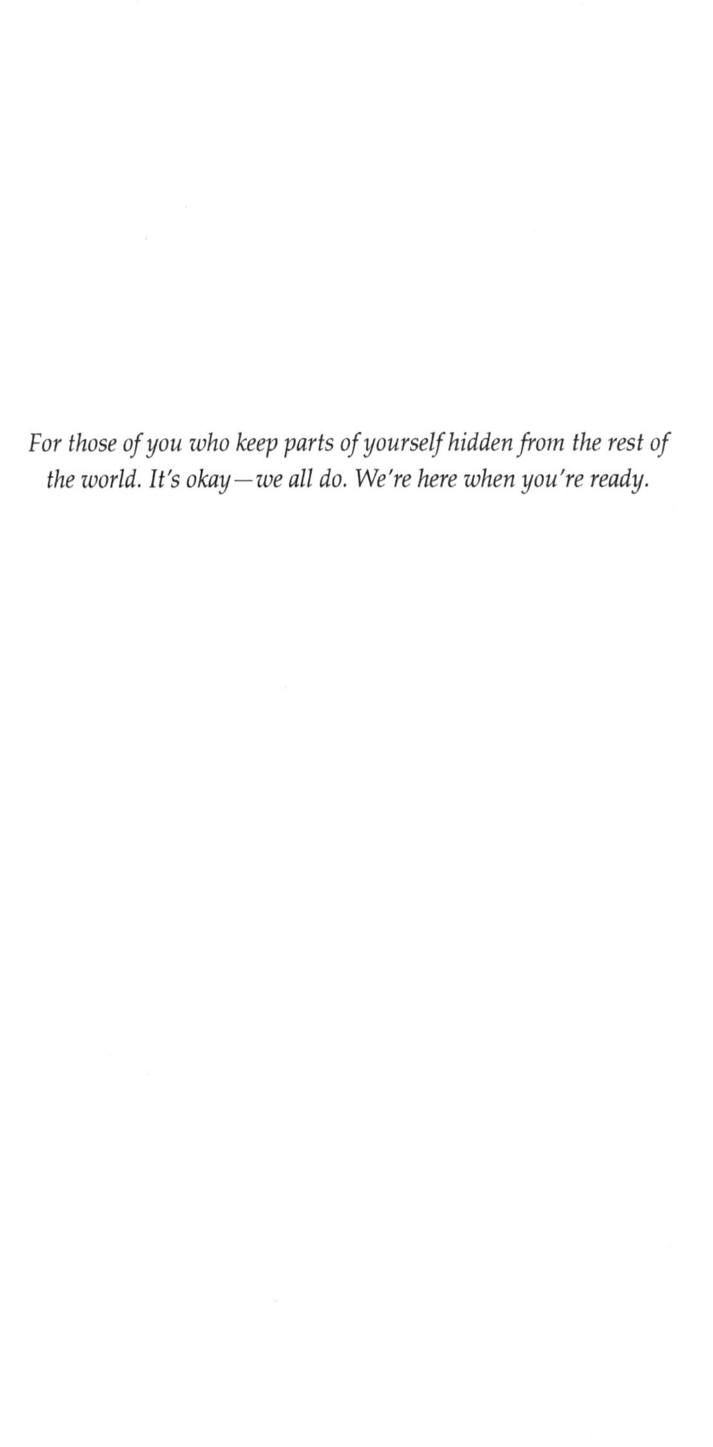

For those of you who keep parts of yourself hidden from the rest of the world. It's okay—we all do. We're here when you're ready.

CHAPTER 1

"Oh my god, if this guy highlights one more mortar patch I'm going to lose my shit," I mutter, rubbing my face in exasperation.

Two years of hard physical work. Raking, repointing, dutchman repairs and meticulous stone replacements, and this dude rips it all apart in a thirty-minute site review.

"Is this mortar recipe one that was approved? Because it doesn't look like the proper colour match." Kent adjusts his safety glasses and frowns.

Of course it's an approved mix, but this guy wouldn't know his sedimentary from his igneous and certainly couldn't appreciate the inherent colour variations of the materials if he tried. I don't bother to explain. I've worked in this business long enough to not engage. It just leads to more frustration, and—if I'm particularly unlucky—mansplaining from a guy with zero subject matter expertise.

Larry, my site supervisor, steps forward on the scaffold.

"I assure you, it's an approved recipe, Kent. We've been using the four approved colours the best we can, but in some cases the variations in the historic stone and the patina make the colour-matching tricky."

Kent's frown deepens.

It's seven thirty a.m. and we're assembled on the scaffold to do one final walk-through of the exterior façade of the Taylor Building, the most recent heritage rehabilitation project contracted to Fleming Stone Services. We've been at it since seven a.m. and the coffee is wearing off fast. The building summer heat, combined with layers of personal protective equipment, is working to kill any enthusiasm the team may have had about reaching this key project milestone.

It doesn't help that Project Manager Kent Armstrong is outdoing even himself in terms of scrutiny. Just shy of pulling out a magnifying glass, he carefully examines each repair, each stone, and seems to find countless defects in the work. *Count. Less.*

He stands with self-assurance and authority, elevation drawings in one hand, orange highlighter in the other. I want to choke him. Instead, I stay off to the side of the group and bite my tongue, taking cleansing breaths. Larry has this under control. For now.

Kent hums and rubs his impeccably shaved chin. He marks a star at the exact location of the mortar patch on the drawing. He hesitates, adds a question mark, and then moves farther down the scaffold.

We carry on like this for another hour. My internal body temperature continues to climb under my high-visibility vest and the increasing annoyance I feel as my work is ruthlessly picked apart.

Fleming has been working for Kent for two years. Two hellish years. Okay, maybe I'm exaggerating. The rest of the crew seem to like Kent just fine and show him nothing but the respect that a project manager and client deserves. But these last twenty-four months, it's been awfully difficult not to take Kent's criticisms personally. Particularly when they seem rather pointed. At me.

We've had a few run-ins, and each of those has left me with a growing level of scepticism and the aforementioned frustration. I've basically given up. Sort of. Except maybe when emotions run a little high, and frustration tips over into angry fits of rage and I can't control myself. Like today. Like it's about to. *Right. Now.*

"This repair…what's going on here?" Kent asks, pointing his obnoxious orange highlighter in the general direction of a complex dutchman stone repair.

"Avery, can you come up here?" Larry hollers over to me.

I wince. *Get. Me. Out. Of. Here.*

I put on a brave face and make my way to the front of the small pack.

"What's up?" I keep my gaze focussed on the building's stone façade and slowly breathe in, breathe out. More cleansing breaths.

"What's happening here?" Kent asks me.

"Could you perhaps be more specific?" I am actually trying to not sound abrupt or irritated. I may or may not be succeeding.

"Well, the stone match isn't great and the tool marks on the replacement are too pronounced. They just stand out too much," Kent states bluntly.

I lean forward and put on my best Team Player face and dig deep for patience.

"The host stone was quite heavily soiled, and that makes matching it with new repair materials challenging, even after laser cleaning." No one else is speaking, so I fill the awkward gap. "But we want to keep as much of the original stone as possible, and we accept that while the repair may be more visible now, with the passage of time it will become less discernible."

Kent thinks about what I've said, scratches his chin as he already has several times this morning, deepens his furrowed brow. "And the tool marks?"

"The tool marks on the repair are made to mimic the original patterning from the mason, but with time those too will erode and soften with age."

"They're too visible," he asserts.

I press on. "We are up on the sixth level, Kent. Once we're at ground level no one will even notice."

"Well, that's a weak argument, if I've ever heard one," he retorts.

I'm digging deep now. Really deep.

"I want it redone."

And I feel it. The tip over of emotions into something darker. It starts deep and travels up my body. I don't hesitate before stepping closer, instinctively.

"I'd advise against it," I say, equally firm. "Replacing it will require a full stone removal and put the original material at risk. We will likely have to remove even more of the original stone as we take out the repair. It's high risk and low reward, considering no one will ever see it from typical viewing distance."

Now Kent's face flushes. "What ever happened to the old saying that 'the client is always right'?"

I snort. It isn't pretty, but I can't help myself. Larry peers over Kent's left shoulder and gives me a look of warning. He's a dear friend, but he's also my boss. I weigh my options. Short-term pleasure with a side of mortar shack clean-up pain? Or spare my own feelings and toe the company line?

Just as everyone believes I will remain silent, I strike.

"Didn't you already view the dutchman repairs and sign off, Kent?"

Oh, snap. Kent slowly turns his hard hat-covered head and throws daggers at me with his eyes. I pull up my tablet and open the right folder. Kent thinks HE is the one who's organized and has his shit together. Well, not today, Kent!

It takes me a few awkward moments, but I retrieve the sign-off sheet dated March 25th. *Bingo!* I hand the tablet over to Kent and gloat quietly, "Highlight THAT, mother trucker."

Larry nudges me, eyes the size of saucers, likely terrified of the fallout of my retort.

Kent angles his sharp gaze at my tablet, sees his initials, and shakes his head in denial.

"I don't care; I'll cover the cost. Replace it."

I can tell he's only doing this out of spite now, and my stomach boils with rage. I stand firmly in place.

"Sure, boss," Larry answers, just a little louder than typical for emphasis. He hopes the matter will be dropped. He is about to be disappointed.

"Stone conservation adheres to a code of ethics and guidance for practice," I state firmly, chin high in defiance. "What you're suggesting is contrary to those ethics. No heritage stone mason—myself or otherwise—will perform the risky and invasive work you're requesting willingly."

The rest of the crew avert their eyes, the wooden floor on the scaffold suddenly very interesting. *Cowards.*

"Avery, why don't you head down to the mortar shack, maybe help with clean-up?" Larry suggests gently. "We can handle things up here."

Here it is. Penalty for my frank speech. I knew it was coming, but my cheeks flush hot, skin slapped by the betrayal. Kent smirks and turns back to his work, pulls out the orange highlighter and emphatically circles the stone in question. I fantasize about where I'd like to stick that orange highlighter right now.

I turn decisively and head directly down the scaffold steps, heavy safety boots clanging on the steel mesh stairs. By the time I get to the mortar shack, my mood is as dark as a hundred years of accumulated stone soot and atmospheric soiling. I slam the door shut and start throwing tools into our tool crates, thankful to be alone with my thoughts and free to exorcize my rage.

This meeting was meant to close out the project, one final walk-through and rubber stamp on a work site that has been plagued by stress and stumbling blocks. Cursed from the start, the Taylor Building project has been nothing but cost overruns and delays, and while I'm not the business owner, it reflects poorly on the entire team when the Fleming Stone Services sign lingers too long on a construction hoarding. Everyone just wants to pack up and move on.

I'm alone long enough to dial down my internal thermostat and begin breathing normally again when there's a knock on the shack door. I look up just as Kent is pushing the plywood hatch open. My stomach drops. He's the last person I expected to see, and I'm completely unprepared.

"Something urgent has come up at head office and I need to get over there to sort it out," Kent explains. "I've left the list of deficiencies with Larry and the boys. That should leave you with enough to get started. I'll come back tomorrow to finish our site walk."

I resist his bait and instead barely grunt in response. I keep my head down and pretend to be otherwise occupied. After a lengthy pause, I spot Kent's movement in my periphery. I look up as he's turning toward the door, but he hangs mid-stride.

"You know—" he stops.

I look in his general direction but avoid making eye contact.

"You really need to stop taking things so personally. You're a competent heritage stone mason, Avery. Not every criticism is a personal attack."

"Next you'll be telling me to smile more," I mutter.

"Pardon?" he asks. "You also need to stop muttering retorts under your breath. Quite frankly, it's unprofessional."

My response is physical. I stop moving and look straight in his eyes. He takes a step back. I think he's about to backpedal, but he surprises me again and steps forward.

"No one doubts that you're capable. It's just business. I'm not going to pay for inferior work, and—news flash—it's literally my job to highlight the deficiencies. Stop making it personal, Avery."

I inch forward as well.

"*News flash*, Kent," I say sharply, altering the pronunciation of his name just slightly so it might sound like a female body part. "I don't actually work for you."

"I'm the client, and I sign off on the work for payment, so really *everyone* works for me." He adds a satisfied smirk.

God, he's such a dick.

"Who's the unprofessional one now?" I return my attention to the work bench.

He shifts, standing up straighter, like he's been caught ogling the secretary. Mr. Integrity looks horrified, so I'm clearly making progress. I persist.

"Look, Fleming Stone Service wants the client to be happy, but it just seems like we're working to an unattainable standard and ever-changing targets and priorities." I drop a trowel in a tool bin for emphasis. "It's unproductive and yes, *unprofessional*, to approve work only to turn around and insist it's deficient. Not to mention that we all just want to move the hell on to the next job."

I really shouldn't be abusing good tools. They don't deserve it, and it's bad form, but Kent brings out the worst in me.

I pause and look up at him. His angled features look sharp. He scratches that closely shaved chin, giving me his standard pensive expression. I can practically see the wheels turning in his head. I take advantage of his hesitation and strike again.

"It's clear you don't know the work, the physical aspects of the job, or the materials. Let's face it, Kent... you're a box-checker."

My comment lands. The nostrils on his straight nose flare and colour rushes to his face.

"If anyone is checking boxes, it's you, Avery. Taylor Building, check; next job, check. You're cutting corners to move on to the next box *you* want to check."

"You don't know anything about that box." As the double meaning dawns on me, my face heats. *Damn.*

I'm hoping my orange high-visibility vest can be blamed for casting the glow on my cheeks.

I adjust my PPE, hiding behind my hard hat and safety glasses. As the only female heritage stone mason on my team, I've mastered the art of blending in and flying under the radar. Sweat beads on my makeup-less face, so I wipe my brow.

"Maybe you should focus on the box-checking that still needs doing here before you move on to the next?" His voice dropping an octave lower.

Wait...what did he just say?

I glance up at him in surprise. His meets mine with an unreadable, steely gaze.

Did he just carry on the euphemism? Am I going crazy?

"Larry has the list. See you tomorrow."

He turns to leave, but behind his usual implacable expression I catch a twinkle in his ice-blue eyes. It's gone in a flash but lingered long enough for me to realize that this asshole is enjoying it. He's enjoying seeing me squirm and spar.

But most unsettling is the sudden shock, the skip of a heartbeat, and the realization that I'm enjoying it too.

CHAPTER 2

I trudge up to my second-story flat and hesitate for a moment when I reach the door. It's been an exhausting day. I stayed late on the scaffold to make a decent start on the mortar patch deficiencies, then laid out a work plan to address the "problem" repairs. Tonight is what I call a triple B night: Bath, Beverage, and Bed.

When I open the door, Gherkin greets me. (I name all my pets after food products; it's just what I do.) His little feline face rubs against my filthy work pants and he forgives the late dinner time with my affectionate pats. Thank goodness for pets who never highlight your deficiencies.

I fill Gherkin's food dish, top up my wine glass, and start for the bathtub when my Peter Gabriel "Sledgehammer" ring tone sounds. It's Dad.

"Hey Bella, my beautiful. How was work?"

"Aw, Dad, how did you know that I needed to hear from you?" He always knows.

"That bad?"

"The worst. But I don't want to talk about it."

"Lemme guess, it's the project manager from Hell, making your life miserable, as always?"

I've talked about Kent enough that he's now legendary at Sunday family dinners. He's assumed many monikers, including *PM from Hell, The Torturer, Control Freak,* and when I'm really pissed, *Foreman Fuckface.* (Admittedly, not my finest moments.)

I love how my parents defend my honour in each story I tell. My relationship with them is an incredibly healthy one. I'm one of few people my age who are actually friends with their parents. They're dear to me and I know I can truly be myself with them.

At work, I assume a persona. As a woman in a male-dominated field, I find I have to abandon many aspects of my personality to feel comfortable among the crowd. I need to check myself to blend in physically, to be just one of the guys. Don't get me wrong, I work with an incredible group of people. Larry and the guys would never expect me to be anything other than my true self, and they'd likely be pissed if they knew the extent of my duplicity.

I know it's not right. Just considering the stereotypes and toxic cisgender crap this line of thinking supports infuriates me, but I suppose I'm only human. This shit is complicated.

"Well, you can blow off plenty of steam on Saturday," Dad reminds me.

Saturday is my cousin Sarah's wedding. She's marrying her college sweetheart here in town and all my favourite people will be there. I've been looking forward to this for months. I love weddings and I love my family. I can't wait to celebrate with them. To dress up, have a few drinks, and dance to the delightfully cheesy boy-band hits the DJ is sure to spin.

"Think I can catch a ride?"

"No plus-one?"

"Not this time, Dad. Just me."

"The men in this town don't know what they're missing. So smart, so strong, so successful," he gushes. My heart swells.

"Oh, Dad. I'm perfectly fine on my own."

Except maybe sometimes. Like certain specific times.

"Yeah, yeah, strong independent woman and all that crap. You don't have to pretend with me, Bella. There's no weakness in admitting you want a life partner."

Sigh. No wonder I can't find my mate. My father has set the bar immeasurably high, not only by providing me with such love and support, but also by treating my mother as his true equal in all respects. It's #swoonworthy.

"Dad, at the risk of sounding like a nineties cliché, I'm not 'all that and a bag of chips.'"

"Isabella Jane Avery, you're all that, a bag of chips AND a chocolate cookie."

Like a sitcom dad, mine always uses my entire name whenever he feels the need to emphasize a point. My first name is Isabella, but I never use it at work. On my first day with Fleming Stone Services, someone misread a human resources document and called me by my last name, Avery. I never bothered to correct them, and it stuck. Sure, folks like Larry—those who issue my paycheques—know my real name, but even they don't bother calling me anything else.

After years of being on the team, Avery feels like my workplace persona. Avery; a short and concise name, right to the point. No meandering or extraneous syllables. Avery has become a character I play every day on the scaffold. No frills, just a stone mason among other stone masons, and certainly not one who has a soft spot for boy-bands, names her cats after pickles, and goes by Isabella Jane.

"Okay, Dad, I've gotta wash this grime off and get some dinner. See you on Saturday?"

"We'll pick you up at two. See you then, hon."

I hit the red button on the screen and look down at Gherkin, who has joined me tub-side. As I turn on the water and drop in my lavender bath bomb and watch it fizz, he offers up a generous *"Meow."*

"What do you think, Gherkin? Do you think I'm all that, a bag of chips, and a chocolate cookie?"

Gherkin jumps onto the side of the tub as I sink into the soothing bath and try not to think too much about the day that's passed, the hard work that awaits, and a pesky PM who'll return to complete his walk-through first thing tomorrow morning.

Yep, I'm perfectly fine on my own.

Morning comes a little too quickly, and before you can say *all that and a bag of chips*, I'm back in my safety gear, coffee in hand, bracing myself for what the day is about to dispense.

I hate those mornings when it feels like I haven't left work, and this is one of them. I run my hands through my short, dark pixie cut before putting on my hard hat and pushing my way through the gate.

Kent's the first person I spot. He leans casually against the side of the site trailer with his clipboard and dreaded orange highlighter in hand. He's preoccupied with something on his phone, and it grants me a rare opportunity to examine him without detection. I've never seen a guy more put together. Not a button missed, never a hint of stubble, not an errant wrinkle in sight. He must iron his underwear. Does he shave his chest? Maybe he's one of those naturally buff-chested men with just a touch of hair, leaving a smooth, strong torso...

Whoa! Back that truck up. Snap out of it, Avery!

What's particularly annoying about Kent Armstrong is how he seems to endear himself to the others. He's a paradox in PPE: precise, but not stiff. Buttoned up, but still stylish. No-nonsense, but still approachable. Despite his "resting bitch face," he still manages to be likeable and one of "the guys." Jerk.

I'm clearly not one of the guys.

Kent puts his iPhone in the back pocket of his black jeans. His denim shirt hitches up to reveal a carefully tucked undershirt over a trim waist. I move my eyes to Kent's feet. He's wearing black Blundstone safety boots with just enough dust and dirt on them to retain credibility with a team that works with their hands.

My inspection has taken only a moment, but long enough that several team members have now arrived and begun to congregate alongside us just inside the gate. Larry gives me a curious look, then pans back over to Kent, an eyebrow raised as if to ask a question. I pretend not to notice, picking at a callus on my hand nonchalantly.

"Shall we get started?" Larry asks as the group begins to move.

"Let's take another quick look at what we reviewed yesterday," Kent suggests.

There are audible sighs. I emit a tortured groan, and just like that, we're back to our usual arrangement: opposing sides and little hope for middle ground.

I guess that twinkle was just a figment of my imagination.

CHAPTER 3

The planets have aligned today and granted me perfect layered locks, lipstick-free teeth and even a chef's-kiss smoky eye. I've chosen a blush-coloured, empire-waisted halter dress with a distinct ethereal vibe, and the full skirt is making me feel like a goddess.

I'm part pinup girl, part girl-next-door, and all here for it. The dress emphasizes what I do have (muscular arms and shoulders from working them hard every day) but also masks what I don't have (thank you, strapless push-up bra).

My buzzer sounds and I strap on my rose-gold heels before heading for the door. As I approach the car, the catcalls begin. The hooting and hollering continues as I enter the car.

Yes, my parents think they're very funny.

"Wow, Bella! Look at you! I wouldn't rule out finding a date just yet," Dad says from the front passenger seat.

"Daniel, leave her alone. She doesn't need a date, and she certainly doesn't need her parents pressuring her about her love life."

Bless my mother. Mom—Victoria Avery—is the original feisty female, never one to put up with much in terms of societal pressure or conformity. Her lived experiences have shaped my own views of a woman's role in a family and helped form my expectations about partnerships and what I want from my relationships, romantic and otherwise.

I'm the baby of the family—my brother Gerard is married with children but lives on the other side of the country, and we rarely see him in the flesh. He's a busy registered nurse who plans his holidays months in advance. It's no surprise that he and his family couldn't make it to the wedding.

Is it wrong to admit that I like all the alone-time I get with my parents? Family dinners, game nights, day trips— we do it all. My friends are surprised by how frequently we talk and how much fun we seem to have together.

We arrive at the church right on time and are ushered to the bride's side of the centre aisle. It's a beautiful ceremony. Sarah looks positively radiant in her strapless chiffon dress. They kiss, we cry. They swoon, we sigh. All is right in the world in this snapshot in time.

We head to the reception, but Google Maps sends us in the wrong direction and one right turn instead of left sends us through a detour of a construction site. Our scenic tour entangles us in traffic delays and by the time we get to the venue—a trendy barn conversion on the outskirts of town —everyone is moving to their seats for dinner.

Thankfully, we spot our place cards quickly and there's plenty of wine on our table. It doesn't take long for us to get settled with a glass and begin to chat with the members of our extended family.

Clink, clink, clink.

The best man stands at a podium set up next to the head table.

"Hello everyone, and welcome. We're so glad you can

all be here to celebrate the marriage of Sarah and Tom—two of the best human beings on the planet."

Applause and cheers from the crowd.

"My name is Noah, and I'm the lucky bugger who gets to be best man to the groom, as well as your master of ceremonies this evening. As you all know, it's customary for there to be some sort of activity associated with getting the bride and groom to kiss."

More applause from the crowd as the bride and groom giggle sheepishly at each other at the head table.

"To get our happy couple to kiss tonight, you will need to tell us a short and perhaps previously untold story or memory about Sarah or Tom." Noah looks back to the head table and adds slyly, "Bonus points—and kisses—if they're embarrassing."

I immediately start running through my mental scrapbook of memories with Sarah, trying to find the most embarrassing one. Sarah and I are only three years apart in age and the two of us have admittedly gotten into all sorts of mischief over the years. The later teenage years alone are a treasure trove from which I could mine a dozen bride/groom kisses.

It doesn't take long for glasses to clink. Hilarious stories begin to flow along with the champagne. Several family members stand to tell stories about things caught in Tom's braces, one cringe-inducing "shitcident" (thanks, awkward Uncle George), and Sarah's embarrassing DIY haircuts.

Our bride and groom are taking it all in stride and seem to be having a wonderful time, considering that most are taking the piss. Wedding attendees seem to be showing enough restraint to ensure that it remains a class act, which is a relief.

Dinner is served and we all dive into plates of delicious food. I'm reaching for another dinner roll when a dapper gentleman in a charcoal suit stands, clinking his glass to get the room's attention. He's several tables over and has his back to me, but I can still hear him speak.

"Hello, everyone. I'm an old college friend of Tom's, and while many of the stories I could divulge might not be appropriate for tonight's crowd, I do have one I'd like to share."

His voice seems familiar, but I can't place it. It must be one of the many friends of Sarah and Tom I've met over the years.

"It seems only fair that I select a slightly self-deprecating one, to share in my dear friend's embarrassment," he continues.

The crowd is captivated, hanging on each of his words. I sip my wine and wait for the story to unfold.

"After our first year of college, the guys decided to take a weekend road trip to cottage country. We'd been riding Tom about needing to relax and be more spontaneous. Somehow, we managed to convince him to throw caution to the wind and go for a skinny dip at a local beach.

"We loosened him up with a few beers at the nearby bar and I guess caught him at a weak moment. He negotiated an underwear dip, since abandoning ALL clothing just seemed—in his words—to be taking it too far. Well, Tom has always been smarter than the rest of us, and in this instance it was definitely the case, because his good choices would serve us all in the end. Some local teenagers had spotted us going into the water and moved in stealthily to steal all our clothes.

"By the time we emerged from Lake Indiscretion, the kids and our clothes were long gone. We ended up walking two kilometres along a busy road, all the way back to our rental, wearing nothing but our wet undies and our shame. It may have been the last spontaneous thing Tom ever did, but in his defence, he fared well in this scenario: unlike me, he wasn't going through a tighty-whitey phase."

Laughter erupts across the room.

The gentleman turns to study the crowd, clearly enjoying the audience's response and enthusiasm. He pans the crowd, pivoting to see the reaction from our side of the reception. He stops short when he catches my gaze.

Oh, fuck.

CHAPTER 4

Kent Fucking Armstrong.

It takes a moment for him to recognize me, but I know the second it registers. As his face falls, my stomach drops. He seems as jarred as I am by the discovery, and quickly returns to his seat, head down.

I look away and keep my eyes on my unfinished meal. Sheer panic sets in as I consider what he's seen: my makeup, my pretty pink dress, my naked shoulders. I feel completely laid bare.

Could I make a run for it? Maybe fake an illness? Get an urgent phone call?

I consider things more carefully, and my gut flops in resignation. If only this were some inconsequential event—one where my departure would go unnoticed—I would be out the door and into an Uber before anyone said "Chicken Dance". But this is my dear cousin, a best friend, and leaving isn't an option.

So I do what any person in my position would: I drink.

I'm at the bar, collecting another medicinal Limoncello spritz (*oh lord, even my drinks are killing my street cred*) when Kent enters my orbit. I feel his gravitational pull before I see him. At this moment, he's like a black hole, pulling me in when I so desperately want to run.

"Avery, fancy meeting you here," he states dryly.

I avoid looking at him. It's a childish move, pretending that if I can't see him, he can't see me. *Fuuuuuuck.*

"Can I buy you a drink?" he quips.

"It's open bar, smartass."

The bartender passes me my drink order and turns to Kent to take his.

"Bourbon, please. Neat."

I pretend I don't find the man's drink order even remotely alluring, then finally capitulate and look at him.

Big. Mistake.

He's wearing a classic charcoal suit, and shoes that shine. That damn suit is perfect. It's tailored to accentuate his trim waist and broad shoulders—meant to turn heads and melt panties. *Shit.* Sure, Kent has always struck me as aesthetically appealing in a superficial way, and certainly well put together. Seeing him impeccably dressed at a wedding should not surprise me. But seeing him polished like this makes my breath hitch and forces me to look away again.

Maybe he's not a black hole…maybe he's the sun.

I nervously sip my drink and that's when he takes his turn. I feel his gaze as it passes over me. Without a table to hide behind, I'm even more exposed to his scrutiny. He can see my delicate, strapped heels, my toned leg along a generous split, and the gauzy fabric of my flowing skirt.

His eyes catch my dress where it cinches at my waist before joining in a halter at my neck, leaving the pronounced musculature of my shoulders and arms exposed. Trapezius, deltoid and triceps muscles all on frankly pornographic display.

Oh god, where's my shawl?

Relief comes in the form of an elegant bride and her handsome groom. Like archangels, they join us near the bar and break the strained silence. It's then that I realize how little Kent and I have actually said to each other. Our glances have written tomes, but we've spoken fewer than a dozen words.

"Hi, guys!"

Sarah positively buzzes with energy and radiates love. If not for the existential crisis beside me in a charcoal suit, I'd probably find it adorable. I plaster on my very best I'm So Incredibly Happy for You™ smile and pretend my worlds aren't colliding in this trendy hipster barn conversion on a Saturday night.

"Well, hello, happy couple!" *You're overcompensating. Chill the fuck out.*

"Have you two met already?" Tom asks.

"Oh yes, we work together, actually," Kent replies. I grimace slightly at the reminder, but take a cleansing breath and pretend this is just a normal conversation.

"So, you two went to college together?" I direct my question to Tom, since looking at Kent in that damn suit again would be inadvisable.

"Kent and Tom graduated the same year," Sarah answers on his behalf.

This confirms that Kent is probably three years older than me. I'd always kind of wondered how old he is, but it's not come up in our conversations about how terrible I am at my job or how he's an obstinate ass.

Sarah chuckles. "Funny that we've never put this all

together before. Gosh, it's such a small world, isn't it? We'll have to coordinate a pub night once we're back from the honeymoon. Wouldn't that be fun?" She looks to Tom for support.

"Absolutely!" he concurs. "We can all get caught up."

Sarah and Tom are so engrossed in their own brilliance that they don't seem to notice Kent and I aren't participating in the conversation.

Sarah leans in for a warm hug. "Listen, we need to mingle, but I'll find you again later."

I hold her tighter in a desperate attempt to keep her here —a shield protecting me from the Savile Row smoke-show beside me.

I wince as she pulls away, then take a fortifying gulp of my drink. I decide to make a run for it and head for my table. I assume Kent will read the situation appropriately and head off in his own direction, but the man never does what I want him to. Instead, he follows behind—I can feel his eyes on my bare shoulders as I round my table and take a seat.

My family is off working the room, so I'm unexpectedly alone at the table. *Traitors.* Kent hangs mid-stride and pauses before impulsively pulling out the chair beside mine. *Oh god, no.*

"Look," he begins. "I know this is a bit awkward, so let's just try to make the best of the situation."

"*The best* would be pretending our little meet-cute today never happened."

"Meet-cute?"

"Sorry, did I say meet-cute? I should have said meet-*boot*. As in, get away from my table, Kent." I lean on my drink again to provide emotional support.

"Wow, harsh. Although it's more in keeping with what I've come to expect from you... unlike what I've seen tonight."

He dares to go there, not even trying to conceal his perusal of my thigh where it peeks out from my skirt's generous slit. I adjust my dress and place a hand on my leg self-consciously.

"Listen…" I begin, stopping short as his eyes fix on something on the table. I follow his gaze to the place card sitting in front of me. Confusion shows on his face as he reads the impeccably calligraphed name on the card: Isabella Avery.

There it goes…the last of my dignity.

CHAPTER 5

"Isabella?" Kent murmurs, trying to piece things together.

My face flushes hearing him say my name. My body responds in a manner which is most unsettling. I can't place it. Is it embarrassment? Fear? Anger? Some sort of fight-or-flight reflex, perhaps. Whatever it is, it's a bizarre cocktail of feelings that has been shaken or stirred by being "outed" by Kent.

Instinctively, I get defensive. *I've not set out to deceive my colleagues, I've just never corrected their mistake. It's a lie by omission at worst, a miscommunication at best.*

"Avery is my last name," I explain. "On my first day at Fleming, someone misread a form and just called me by my last name, and it stuck. It's not a big deal."

"No, no, it's not a big deal," Kent adamantly agrees. He seems unsettled too, like his world has been tipped on its axis.

"I prefer Avery at work." It's part statement, part question.

"Yeah, sure. No problem." He nods. "I couldn't imagine calling you anything else." But his face sort of looks like he's doing just that—imagining calling me something else. I shrug it off.

"I don't know how to say this without opening myself up to misinterpretation..." he starts.

"Then maybe you shouldn't say anything." I look down at my drink, wiping some of the condensation from the glass.

"You're surprising me tonight."

His comment stops me abruptly. I look directly at him for perhaps the first time. His face is intense, his symmetrical features disarming. I don't linger on his eyes, but I don't need to look at them to know they're ice blue. I've noticed them before—through sneers, scowls and safety glasses.

"What is that supposed to mean?"

"Nothing." He looks down at his bourbon, then takes a long drink.

I shouldn't be taken aback by his comment. It's no wonder he's surprised. For the last two years I've curated a work identity that's completely inconsistent with what Kent is seeing today. But owning up to that right now isn't something I'm ready to do.

"If you mean I don't look like I normally do, it's only because personal protective equipment is not exactly wedding-appropriate," I state. "It's not like I see you in impeccable suits every day, either."

"Impeccable?" His eyebrows raise, one side of his mouth lifting in a smirk.

"Don't let that go to your head, Mister Tighty-Whitey."

His cheeks flush.

Looks like I'm not the only one who feels exposed.

The party kicks up about twenty decibels and the dance floor shifts into full party mode. The DJ has just pressed play on the boy band classic "Bye, Bye, Bye" and several of my cousins jump up and down in excitement.

This is precisely when Isabella—lover of catchy boy band tunes—would normally join the party enthusiastically and unreservedly. Instead, Avery is in control. She has to be. I stay glued to my seat and refuse to let my mask slip. Not a hip wiggle, not a toe tap.

"Not a dancer?" Kent asks, following the direction of my gaze.

"To this? No way. I'm more of a Grunge girl."

"Yeah, this New Kids stuff sucks."

"NSYNC."

"Oh yeah, not a fan at all then…"

He leaves with a smirk.

Dammit.

I manage to avoid Kent for most of the night. I field a dozen exhausting questions from friends and relatives: *Why aren't you dancing? Why are you so quiet? Why are you so antisocial?* I consider faking a headache to go home early, but guilt forces me to reconsider. I decide to pull a "Baby" and find myself a corner.

I'm alone with my thoughts and my umpteenth drink when the news begins to spread that it's time for the dreaded bouquet toss. I try to dissolve into the wall, but Cousin Emily spots me.

No, no, please no.

"Oh, no you don't," she scolds. "No running from this!"

I'm dragged to the dance floor before I can come up with a legitimate defence, and pushed into the crowd of young singletons. I assess the potential risks and decide my best strategy is to feign indifference. I will stick to the fringes of the pack and fail to use my arms in any way, thus preventing me from appearing the least bit interested—or worse, actually catching the wretched thing.

I shift off to the far side stealthily; I'm home free—there is no way that floral contrivance can find me here. The house lights go up, the music kicks in, and Sarah turns her back. She pauses.

There's a scramble as the more eager parties jockey for position. They seem to think they know where it's going. I take two steps back and fade into a shadow. I'm practically invisible now. Sarah winds up, and with the flex of her triceps, the bouquet is tossed.

Her months of upper-body work in preparation for today's strapless gown is on full display as the bouquet flies. It goes long, hurdling the pack, rotating mid-air and defying the laws of physics to veer off in an unexpected direction.

Is there a wind gust in here?

Panic sets in when the sudden realization hits me: it's coming. I'm practically hugging the far wall of the venue and there's nowhere for me to go. The jig is up. I turn, resigned to my fate as the bouquet smacks me directly in the face and then tumbles to the floor.

I find myself at the centre of the crowd's attention. Normally, this wouldn't be a problem. Normally, I'd take this all in stride—maybe even have a good chuckle. But tonight Avery is in the crowd. Avery, who needs to fade into the background. Avery, who can't stand out. *Avery is failing, epically.* The floodlight that shines on my face is only marginally warmer than the heat I feel from Kent's gaze as he watches me from across the room.

Thankfully, attention quickly shifts elsewhere. Sarah and Tom hate the traditional garter ritual and have opted for a more contemporary alternative. Dozens of silver balloons are to be released from the ceiling, with one containing a special prize.

A large group moves under the bundle and awaits their turn to clamber for a trophy. More lights, more music, and the balloons fall. It's a mess of latex and limbs as men battle for the winning balloon. Feet stomp and hands pop and the participants check their balloons. It goes on for several minutes and no winner is immediately found. Finally, cheers erupt and arms raise in celebration among a cluster of men at the far edge of the crowd. As the circle opens, a man in a charcoal suit steps forward.

Kent is holding the prize.

A chant starts to build from a murmur.

"Dance, dance, dance, dance…"

Eyes shift between Kent and me.

No, no, no, no. With each chant, my heart screams *NO!*

This can't be happening. End this hellish nightmare. I would dance with any other guest right now—even Tom's old roommate "Handsy Harry", or "Kinky Karl" from high school. Anyone who would spare me from the awkward forced proximity with my workplace nemesis.

I expect Kent will want nothing to do with this either, expect he will laugh it off and run for the hills…

I should know better than to expect *anything* from Kent.

He steps forward, and the crowd cheers. My stomach drops.

"Let's just give them what they want and get this over with," he says with a shrug.

It's becoming clear that I can't avoid this without drawing even more attention to myself.

"Oh god," I groan.

The house lights go down and the DJ hits *play*. It feels like the floor tilts, just slightly.

A cover version of Elvis Presley's "Can't Help Falling in Love" booms from the venue's sound system. It's the quintessential wedding reception song, but this version has a bit of grit to it, a sultry edge.

"May I?" Kent asks, holding out his hand.

The gesture is unexpectedly gentleman-like and I hate that it pleases me. I hesitate, but then step forward to take it. The warmth and strength of it surprises me, and I find it relaxes me enough to allow him to place the other on my waist.

Then it hits me. Scent. Warm and musky. Wrapping around me like a blanket and drawing me closer. My chest tightens, but I force myself to settle in and move to the music. Breathe in, breathe out.

It's just one dance. I can do this.

But then I remember who I am, who he is, and who we're supposed to be. I go rigid in his arms. Kent's grip tightens.

"Relax, Avery. It's just over three-minutes long—it'll be over soon."

"How do you know how long it is?"

"It's Beck. I know all of Beck's songs. He's a musical genius." He leans into my ear and adds, "But he's not Grunge. Does he meet with your approval?"

His voice vibrates in my ear and my eyes close instinctively. I almost pull away, but I override my urge to run, holding steady.

There's a long, awkward silence.

"So, you're a Beck fan. Any other interests or hobbies?" I fill the dead air with small talk. "Knitting, maybe? Correcting grammar on public signage? No! I've got it: measuring the distance between cars in parking lots!"

"You're hilarious, Avery."

I snicker a little.

"We're going to have this banal conversation, are we?" He pauses. "I have all sorts of interests. Reading, chess, running..."

His sentence hangs as he settles in closer, his entire body making contact with mine. His breath warms my ear.

"…and of course, box-checking. But you already know that I like box-checking, right, Avery?"

The last few notes of the song fade out and I find my body following his when he pulls away. His hand drops mine but his other skims my bare shoulder as he leaves. Before it fully registers, it's over.

The music shifts to the intro chords of David Bowie's "Let's Dance" and people flood the dance floor. With broken balloons underfoot, I stand there in a daze. The scent of him lingers along with the phantom traces of where he touched me.

CHAPTER 6

"I'd like a large blonde roast, black." I hear Kent's voice.

I could never mistake the sound of it now. Not when the hum of it still lingers on the skin of my ear.

I'm parked at a back table at Urban Roasters early on Monday morning, in a futile attempt to seek solace in a fortifying brew before heading to the work site. I thought I'd be safe here, to ponder my predicament before facing him and having my worlds collide all over again.

Despite my best efforts, the last twenty-four hours have been spent in silent crisis, rehashing what took place at the wedding on Saturday night. I may have also spent a good part of my Sunday convincing myself that I did not, in fact, enjoy any part of that three-minute and thirteen-second song (yes, I looked it up) or the warm buzz that stayed with me for hours.

The large coffee Kent ordered is passed over the counter in a to-go cup. He slips his phone into the back pocket of his perfectly worn dark-wash jeans and adjusts the front of his black and white plaid work shirt. He turns to leave and

I think I'm home free, but apparently he feels someone watching him, and looks in my direction.

Shit.

He spots me in an instant. It feels like an important moment, like a test. What will he do?

Please walk away, please walk away.

He hesitates for only a few seconds, then heads straight for my table. My stomach twists. I look for an exit.

It's way too early for this shit.

"Good morning."

Fuck.

"Um, hi…" *Smooth, real smooth.*

"Beautiful morning." Kent gestures to the entrance.

"Who's making banal conversation now?" Has someone commandeered my tongue? It seems I'm diving head-first into Saturday night.

Kent smirks, taking a seat. *Now I've done it.*

I hurriedly pile my belongings, stashing my book—the latest epic romance by Josie Juniper—and hiding my pink lipgloss. I avoid looking in his direction, definitely not noticing his freshly shaved chin, or damp, dark hair.

"You disappeared on Saturday night."

"I was with my mom and dad—we had to get going," I reply coolly.

You panicked and had to get the hell out of there.

"Are you sure that's what it was?"

Looks like someone's feeling bold this morning.

"What else could it possibly be?" I casually run my hand through my short hair.

I thought Kent would be as eager as I am to pretend the entire evening never happened. He can revert to obstinate ass, and I can return to the manual labour—the end.

"It's just that…" He hesitates, taking a drink. "Nothing."

His hands are smooth and tanned, nails neatly trimmed.

I place a hand on the table, boldly exposing my own, rough, calloused palms in juxtaposition. I'm proud of my rugged hands. They make me feel powerful and capable.

I am powerful. I am capable. I silently chant my affirming mantra.

We sit together for a moment in excruciating silence.

"Well, I have plenty of work to do today—guess I better get moving." I crumple a napkin and turn to slip my phone in my bag. "*Someone* seems to think the work I do is substandard and requires improvement."

*Ahh...*it's satisfying slipping back into our adversarial positions. More certainty and familiarity here.

"So we're doing this, then?" Kent asks, sighing.

"What's *this*?"

"Going back to your script where I play the unreasonable nemesis when really, you're being hyper-sensitive."

"You *are* unreasonable, Kent. That's not an opinion. And I'm not *hyper-sensitive,* I'm just a subject matter expert who expects to be treated like one."

Cough. "*Ahem...*hyper-sensitive..." *Cough.*

"Would it kill you to defer to the SMEs on occasion? Or is it just *this* SME that you have trouble with?" I stop short of calling him a chauvinist, worried the accusation might be too consequential.

He turns from playful to serious. "I know what you're suggesting, Avery, and I don't like it."

He leans forward and takes up space around our small bistro table.

"Oh, contain your manspreading, Kent. You know that I'm the only one on the team you seem to have trouble with. You carefully select only the work *I* perform to pick apart."

"That's ridiculous. Even if I *tried* to do that, I couldn't. You're one member of a large team, all doing the same work on the scaffold." He leans back, takes another sip of coffee. "Unless I stand there carefully reviewing each item against the as-built documentation and sign-off sheets, there's no way to know which patches or repairs are yours."

"You mean like…carefully reviewing them against the marked-up elevation plans with an orange highlighter? You're right, that would be CRAY-ZY." I emphasize sarcastically for full effect as I zip up my tote.

"I'm thorough, but I'm not singling you out. I'm not some misogynistic asshole." His expression is earnest. "There is no way I could do what you do every day. You're an artist with stone."

Well, that's unexpected.

I'm hanging on his every word now. His irritatingly symmetrical features are precariously close, his eyes precision-focused on me. My traitorous body goosebumps as I take in the warmth of him, the smell of his freshly showered skin.

His voice is low.

"For the record, I'm smart enough to know when a woman knows better than me—which is often—and man enough to let a woman take charge when the situation warrants it."

He stands and walks out the door.

There's a mysterious swoop in my belly and I shift in my seat. I close my mouth hastily when I realize it's been hanging open. I accidentally bite my tongue and wince.

Well, shit. Who's powerful now?

I push through the gate of the storage compound an hour later, on the hunt for stone to use for replacement repairs.

I'm cursing under my breath, angry that I need to be doing this work at all, and feeling unsettled after the coffee shop.

When I don't immediately locate our pallet of stone, I chalk it up to my lack of focus and retrace my steps. I take another look in the small, fenced area but the materials are not where we left them.

I spot Trevor, a fellow mason, and call out through the chain link fence.

"Hey T, has the extra stone been moved somewhere? I can't find it here in the yard."

"Not that I'm aware of. Maybe Larry knows?"

"Thanks. I'll check in with him." I'm sceptical. Larry knows we still need those materials. He's seen the cursed orange highlights and lengthy deficiencies list.

I head to the trailer.

Larry's seated at a boardroom table that's been set up at the far end of the large trailer. That table has been the site of many heated disagreements between Kent and me over the past several months; home to arguments about mortar colours, conservation philosophies, project scope and budgets. You name the topic, we've disagreed on it. There isn't one item Kent has capitulated on since we shook hands over the same table almost two years ago.

"Lar, has the team started moving things out of the stone yard?"

Larry looks up from his laptop and runs a hand through his cropped ginger hair. "No, are you kidding me? We still have tons of work to do."

"I can't find the pallet of stone. We need it for the replacement repairs."

"That stuff is valuable; everyone knows to keep it locked up. We'll have to ask around to make sure someone didn't move it." He stands and reaches for his phone.

As Larry starts to make calls, I check my own phone. I have a new text from Sarah.

> Sarah: Tom and I are sipping wine at a
> Paris bistro, it's heaven.

She sends an adorable selfie of the two of them looking well-rested and sated, Eiffel Tower in the background. Lucky buggers.

> Me: Dear god, look at the two of you.
> #bliss

> Sarah: We're trying to push through the
> jet lag.

> Me: Interesting choice of words...

> Sarah: HAH!

> Me: Have an amazing honeymoon,
> lovebirds.

> Sarah: Oh we will. Tom and I were already
> talking about getting the four of us together
> for something fun when we get back.

> Me: The four of us???

> Sarah: You, me, Tom, and Kent.

Oh god.

> Me: Gotta run, Sarah...duty calls. Have fun,
> love you!

> Sarah: Love you too.

I put my phone away and say a silent prayer that by the time they're back from France and settled into married life, Sarah's suggestion will be long forgotten.

Larry returns to the table, shaking his head, locks now slightly rumpled from repeated handling. Back to my work-life problems.

"No one admits to moving the materials or to seeing where they've gone. This isn't good, Avery."

"No kidding. Time is money."

"I just called the client to let them know too."

The client.

"This pallet is the last of the original stone, Larry. They don't even quarry this stuff anymore. If we can't find it, we can't do the work. Kent is going to be pissed." My stomach flutters.

Is it wrong to be so excited about this?

"Maybe he'll finally see the light about those dutchman repair deficiencies and let them go?"

"Larry, there is better chance of mortar setting up in January than Kent dropping those repairs."

"Drop what?" Kent asks as he enters the trailer.

Here we go.

Several team members join us and take a seat at the table. By the time I've thought to sit down, the only available spot is the one next to Kent. I suck it up, take my place at the table, and get ready for World War Three.

"Kent, the remaining stone we had for repairs has gone missing." Larry glances over at me nervously.

"Missing?" Kent's brow furrows.

"Yeah, Avery went to the compound this morning to find it, and it wasn't there."

Kent looks over at me.

"We've checked with everyone," Larry continues. "No one has any knowledge of where it's gone."

"This is crazy!" Kent declares, sitting up taller in his seat.

I have an unobstructed view of his lap, and as he shifts, his jeans tighten around his muscular thighs.

"Surely we have more materials stored elsewhere?" he asks.

"What we had in the compound is all there is left," Larry explains. "As you know, the stone's not available anymore. We did our best to procure what we could—some remainders from previous projects and whatnot—but it's been extremely difficult to get what we need."

"What are our options, then?"

"The way I see it, we have two: wait to see if the stone turns up—which is unlikely and will cost the project money in work delays—or keep the dutchman repairs as-is."

Larry sits back in his chair, bracing for the response.

"We've been through this. We need to do the work, Larry. Those repairs just aren't sufficient."

Kent leans back, matching Larry's posture. He unbuttons the cuff of each sleeve, then slowly rolls them to his elbows. As he leans forward, he rests his forearms on the table in front of him, each beautifully tanned and roped-vein specimen on display. My throat tightens.

Oh no, not the dreaded forearm maneuver...I'm a romcom cliché!

Larry looks surprised I'm remaining silent. He doesn't know about the inner struggle taking place four chairs away.

"What about using another material?" Kent suggests.

This is when I must step in.

"When stone has to be replaced on a heritage building, you need to use the geological equivalent. Anything else would be inappropriate."

"What if we find one that's a close match? It might even

make sense for the repairs to be discernible from the original, from an ethical standpoint."

He makes a fair point, but I'm sure as hell not going to admit that.

"Using non-geologically similar stones can be very tricky," I explain. "Differences in weathering can make the two stones quite distinguishable over time, particularly when you have hardness differences."

"Avery is right—it just isn't a good idea," Larry agrees. It pisses me off that Larry needs to add anything to give what I've said extra weight.

Kent scratches his chin. "There must be a solution."

"You could leave the repairs alone," I mutter.

Sitting next to him, my quiet muttering might as well be a scream. Kent glares at me.

"There is one more option," Larry offers.

I don't know where this is going, and I raise a brow in concern.

"When we visited the old quarry two years ago," he continues, "they said they wouldn't reopen the pit without ridiculously expensive initiation costs. We ruled that out immediately, due to budget constraints. But we did spot an old, quarried slab left discarded from century-old projects that may have small amounts of quality material in it. We could salvage it for use."

Kent raises a brow in interest. "I wasn't aware."

Neither was I.

"Yeah, there's a small chance we could salvage enough from that discarded slab to leave you with attic stock for future repair work, too. But it would cost you."

"That's an attractive solution," Kent admits. "But we need to make sure the material is decent before we proceed."

"A visit to the quarry would confirm. It's only a few hours away." Larry pulls up Google Maps on his phone.

"Budget is limited—we can only send a couple of people," Kent notes. "Can you suggest someone?"

"Avery is our most knowledgeable mason," Larry declares without a moment's hesitation.

I'm proud of his assertion and can't help but smile.

"Then it's settled. Avery and I will go to the quarry as soon as possible to review the slab."

Wait…what?

Larry gives a terse nod. "Sounds good."

Everyone begins to stand, like the conversation is over, but I'm still back at Google Maps. *What the fuck?*

Kent slips his phone in his back pocket. "I'll get our project administrators to sort out the details. Thanks, Larry."

Cold panic washes over me and I feel the blood leave my face. The moment is over before I can even respond. Kent takes my conviction with him as he strides out the door.

CHAPTER 7

"For the record, *Kent*, we're not going *'back'* to anything…we never left. I'm still here, working my ass off, trying to prove myself as a woman in a male-dominated profession, and you're an intolerable ass."

I'm ranting to Gherkin while I pack my overnight bag, saying all the things I wish I'd said yesterday to Kent, to Larry, even to the barista who got my drink order wrong. I may be exceeding the healthy recommended dosage of pet talk today, but my frustration has reached fever pitch.

Gherkin looks up at me, clearly passing judgement.

Even the cat thinks I'm a bloody idiot.

The administrators on the project are inconveniently efficient and manage to have our trip organized in record time. They have us booked at a hotel less than an hour from the quarry for one night, but thankfully we are expected to take separate vehicles for insurance reasons. This spares me the torture of hours of travel time trapped in the same vehicle as *Foreman Fuckface.*

Yep—I'm pulling out the big words.

At this point, I'm forcing myself to take things one hour

at a time so I don't panic at the thought of what's ahead of me—long days spent with a man who infuriates me, and no one else there to provide a buffer.

By lunchtime I'm pulling into the hotel parking lot. We've arranged an early check-in so we can drop our bags, get our safety gear on, and head over to the quarry.

There are no problems with the reservation, and I book into my room without incident.

Thank god this isn't an "only one bed" trope.

I'm hoping to fly under the radar, avoid Kent, and just leave a note at the front desk to meet me there, but we cross paths in the hotel lobby.

"Glad I caught you." Kent adjusts his duffel over his shoulder. "We should drive over together. The location of the quarry is a bit tricky—hard to find by apps."

I wince. Hard. My physical discomfort must be noticeable, because Kent continues.

"Listen, I've been there before. I know where I'm going. We'll lose valuable time if you get lost."

"I have a great sense of direction."

"Oh yes, you always find your way to a snide remark."

Zing!

"Such a funny guy. I thought we had to take separate vehicles for insurance purposes?"

I don't get it. Kent should be as uncomfortable with the idea of being trapped in a small car together as I am. "Can't I just follow?"

"Surely one short drive isn't a big deal? We can take my car. I'll take on the liability."

His insistence gives me pause.

Does he actually want to be with me right now?

I concede and agree to meet him out front in twenty minutes. Nineteen minutes later Kent pulls up at the hotel entrance in a black Tesla Model S.

Of course he does.

I'm clearly in the wrong line of work if this is what a senior project manager can afford. It makes my Prius look like a bloody clown car.

Kent steps out of the vehicle and leans against the sleek top.

He's a goddamn movie star.

"All set?" he asks, looking at me from behind stylish sunglasses.

Something is different about him and I can't place it. Then it dawns on me…he has one extra denim shirt button undone and seems slightly wrinkled from the drive. It annoys me that I find this version of him appealing.

I shake it off, yank the door open, and take my place in the passenger seat.

Two things strike me immediately. The first is that the car is immaculately kept—not a spot of dirt in its beautiful interior. Then there's the scent. Kent's musky scent washes over me, set to maximum intoxication. A mix of patchouli, warm hints of tobacco leaf and something sweeter fills my nose entirely and transports me back to the dance floor. A flashback to hands touching, cheek against cheek, the hum of his voice in my ear.

I look out my side window and give myself a mental pep talk.

Come on, woman. Get your shit together.

I've composed myself by the time I turn to face him, but then catch sight of his strong hands at the wheel. Those beckoning forearms—denim shirt sleeves casually rolled up to expose tanned, smooth skin…

Say something. Anything.

"Are we going to have to listen to Beck the entire drive there?"

Oh fuck, not that.

"No, I downloaded some of your favourites to a playlist," he replies with a smirk as he turns out of the parking lot. "You know...lots of NSYNC and other poppy boy bands."

I roll my eyes and mentally kick myself for misdirecting our conversation. I change the subject to avoid any wedding-adjacent topics.

"You visited this quarry before?"

"A few of us visited back at the outset of the project to explore whether reopening the quarry was a viable option, but we quickly dismissed it due to expense."

"Ah, I must've been still finishing at McKinnon House."

"Larry and a couple of the other guys made the trip for Fleming." He glances in the rearview mirror before changing lanes and merging onto the highway.

"Speaking of Larry, he called ahead and had them move the unprocessed slab we're interested in over to the cutting facility." I take a sip from my ubiquitous stainless steel water bottle.

Why is my throat so dry?

"Okay, walk me through this, Avery. How will things work?" He steals a glimpse of me.

"Wait, you're asking me for direction?"

"I've already told you that I have no problem taking direction."

His pointed comment makes me pause.

"We need to look at the stone, but reviewing the exterior isn't enough. We'll have them make an exploratory cut with the wire saw to see the inside of it. With any luck, they'll have already made the initial cut before we get there, but that may not be the case."

"Why would that be lucky?" Kent asks.

"The cutting can be time-consuming. It's slow cutting with a diamond wire and plenty of water to keep things cool. Think reciprocating saw but blown up to massive scale."

"Ah, yes. I noticed those machines when we visited. Quite a production facility."

"Yeah, it's incredible what these processing facilities can do now. Cut multiple sheets at a time with multiple diamond wires, dice up slabs the size of your car like it's gouda. All fully automated too. It's impressive."

"Have you always been so interested in stone? What made you decide to be a stone mason?"

I can tell his interest is genuine, and it surprises me. I've always gotten the sense that he doesn't take me seriously, that he thinks I'm in over my head—a small fish in a big pond. Shifting to this dynamic of equals is unexpected, but not off-putting.

"I've always been a bit of a heritage building junkie," I begin. "I found myself collecting coffee table books in high school and being drawn to architecture sections in libraries."

"Pardon the pun," Kent jokes.

It makes me chuckle.

"Hah, yes."

The joke loosens me up a bit more, so I continue.

"I considered a career as an architect, but really prefer to work with my hands. I like the idea of making other people's visions a reality."

"Where did you train?"

"Well, first I got a geology degree, thinking that would give me my stone fix. Just turned out to be a gateway drug. I ended up going to the UK to a Heritage Stone Masonry program."

"Wow, you really know your stuff, then."

"I guess you could say that."

I'm expecting an unkind comment, a little dig, but it never comes. I let us sit in silence for a few minutes and then return his gesture of interest.

"So…have you always been a scope-cost-schedule junkie?"

"You mean, have I always been a project manager?"

"Yeah."

"I'm actually a conservation architect."

No way.

I'm shocked by this revelation. What an unexpected turn. I had Kent pegged as a buttoned-up bean counter, a spreadsheet soldier, a regular budget boy. I did not see him as a creative type with a love for things heritage.

I'm rendered speechless, and Kent can't help but notice.

"You're surprised by that?"

"Yes, I am," I admit. "Based on the conversations we've had, this surprises me immensely."

Kent stops at a red light. He turns to look at me, wearing a grin.

"You call them conversations, I call them character assassinations."

"Don't be so dramatic." I roll my eyes.

"You think I'm some sort of arch nemesis—the evil villain to the Taylor Building."

"I just think you need to brush up on your code of ethics and guidance for practice, that's all."

The light turns green and Kent makes a left-hand turn onto a gravel road. We're getting close to our destination and it's a relief. Any more bombshells and I'm going to unravel in Kent's leather seat.

"Hey, I'm a stickler. I'm the best thing that's ever happened to that building," he asserts. "I don't settle for anything less than the best."

"Why are you project managing and not working as an architect?"

"I'm what you call a *knowledgeable client*. Lots of archi-tects end up working as PMs."

We pull up to a large, nondescript building in the

middle of nowhere. Kent wasn't kidding about it being off the beaten path. As he puts the car in park, I realize I've been completely distracted by our conversation. I'd thought the drive would feel endless, but here we are already.

Kent powers off the car and unbuckles. He hesitates before getting out and turns to face me. His eyes are bright and striking. They'd seemed ice cold before, but now they're refreshing pools of blue. A cool drink of water after a hot summer run.

"I guess there's more to both of us than meets the eye."

This is the first real acknowledgement Kent has made of the paradox that is Isabella Avery, and it's a lot to take in. But what's distracting me more is the idea that he's also carefully selected only parts of himself to be seen.

While attempting to conceal so many parts of myself in my professional world, it's never occurred to me that Kent might be doing the same.

It seems he has a few surprises in store for me too.

CHAPTER 8

 Kent's Tesla is incongruous with the construction equipment and dirty pickup trucks that line the quarry's parking lot. It stands out like his refined appearance often does on the scaffold. But just like the dirt on his steel-toed boots lends him credibility, the stylish car also works. Instead of looking out of place, it seems to grant him authority.

We grab our hard hats and reference samples and head to the entrance, kicking up dirt as our feet hit the gravel. We're met at the door by a burly guy in a plaid shirt.

He eagerly greets us. "Hello, Mr. Armstrong. Welcome back."

Correction: he greets *Kent.* He doesn't seem to even notice me standing beside him. I shrug it off, assuming that his enthusiasm for Kent is based on an existing relationship. Kent's been here before, met all the players.

I take it in stride and extend a hand to introduce myself. "Thanks for agreeing to host us with such short notice."

"Oh yeah. Hi." His hand is weak and barely touches me.

He never mentions his name or asks for mine. "Come on in."

He leads us through a reception area and into a noisy, busy processing room. Massive stone slabs are in place near equally massive diamond wire saws and are being sliced like bread via computer-operated machines.

Kent eyes the expanse of machinery. "These facilities never cease to amaze me, Rick."

I guess his name is Rick.

"A lot going on here today—we're prepping a large order of granite countertop materials for a commercial project," Rick explains.

I admit it is quite impressive, but I want to get to the point of our visit. Where's our precious slab? As if intuiting my eagerness, Kent keeps things moving on our behalf.

"We're eager to see the stone for our own project," he prompts.

"Come on back; we've got that in our smaller processing area."

We follow closely behind, into an adjacent space, and find a heavily soiled slab about the size of a Mini Cooper that's clearly just been moved here from outside. It's coated with biological growth but has one freshly exposed face from an exploratory diamond saw cut.

The stone is beautiful. Its sedimentary layers of buff, grey, browns and subtle reds are muted and indistinguishable from a distance, but come to life upon close examination.

"We went ahead and made one cut, so you can see the interior of the slab." Rick directs his comments to Kent—apparently, I'm still invisible.

I'm annoyed, but rather than engage with the business operator, I keep busy carefully examining the stone and assessing its quality and condition. I pull out a small sample of stone I brought from the Taylor building and hold it up against the slab. It seems to be a perfect match, but what I see concerns me: fissures.

"As you can see, the stone is a perfect match," Rick continues.

"Avery, what do you think?" Kent asks me from across the room where he stands with our charming host.

"Hmmm. I think we might want to make another cut, further down the slab."

"We can get that stone cut to any size you'd like, Mr. Armstrong, and have it delivered by truck to you right away."

Yep, he's still ignoring me.

"It's Avery you need to convince, Rick." Kent gestures in my direction and offers a polite smile.

Rick's face sours. He doesn't want to convince me.

Kent joins me at the slab and leans in to study the stone more closely.

"What's up?" he asks.

"I'm seeing fissures. The quality could be compromised from quarrying with explosives." I point at the subtle but lengthy lines that run the width of the stone. "It could be only superficial, but it could also continue deeper into the slab. We won't know if we don't make another cut."

"We don't use explosives," Rick dismisses. *Looks like he's hearing me just fine after all.* "We use wedging and channeling to extract our stone."

"That might be the case today, but this slab was extracted many years ago and it may have been impacted by less than ideal quarrying practices," I explain, more to Kent than Rick.

"A little explosive isn't going to cause problems for a slab that size." Rick shakes his head.

He's still only talking to Kent.

I straighten and place my hands on my hips. "I assure

you, explosives can destroy stone, particularly with softer materials like these."

Rick looks at me like I'm an idiot. "It's *stone*. Stone isn't soft."

"Stones have relative hardness. Haven't you heard of the Mohs scale?" It's a bit troubling that I'm having to explain this to someone who has built a career around the material. "Granite is a six; it can probably withstand explosive extraction. This stone has a hardness of only a two or three."

Rick flashes a sly grin at Kent before turning back to face me. "I'm sure you know all about hardness."

His remark hits like a slap in the face. I turn and look at Kent, making sure he's heard it too.

Surely this asshole can't mean…

I opt to ignore the comment and change tacks.

"Look, if we can just get another cut, we can make sure it's in good condition and let you get back to your other important work."

"All of the guys are busy and can't be spared to make the cut right now. We can make the cut and send you photos." His tone suggests that he'd be doing us a big favour giving us what we don't want.

"We've come a long way to see the materials," Kent insists. "We'd really like to see them in person."

Rick turns his back to me before he speaks.

"Listen, the materials are fine and they match the sample. Are you really going to delay this based on some woman's opinion about a few flaws on the stone face?"

"That *person* you're referring to has a geology degree and is a professional stone mason." Kent's voice rises and his face colours.

"*You* listen," I step in front of Rick and deliver a fair amount of sass. "We need that stone and are willing to pay good money for it, but we also need to make sure it's not

Swiss cheese. We can wait patiently while you find someone to fire up the saw."

Rick turns to face me, clearly pissed.

"I'm sure you're used to throwing on the hard hat and playing foreman back where you come from, but around here I'm the one in charge. We can't make any more cuts today."

"Whoa, *playing foreman*?" Kent asks.

"Whatever, *Rick*, I'm not here to question your authority. I'm just a customer who wants to buy a product." I step in closer, make myself bigger.

Rick the Dick steps away, slow to turn his steely glare, and walks over to another machine operator in the adjacent workspace.

Kent approaches me.

"Avery, I don't like this guy. I don't like his tone or attitude one bit."

"Yeah, but we need the stone. It'll be over soon enough." I shrug.

"I don't want to make decisions for you, but one more questionable comment from him and we're out of here, okay?" Kent looks to me for support.

"Yeah, yeah…"

Two long hours are wasted watching the sloth-like operator fire up the saw and make one more cut at Kent's specified location. (It had to be Kent's instructions, of course.) When the cut is finally made, a team removes the extraneous material, revealing the face of the stone, and more fissures.

Folks, we have Swiss cheese.

Kent looks to me and I shake my head to the negative. He nods in agreement and approaches Rick.

"Looks like we've got more fissures, Rick. I don't think we're going to be able to take the materials. It's just not worth the cost to transport them if we can't make full use of the slab."

Rick's face darkens. "My employees have just used hours of their valuable time and you're not going to take it?"

"You know how expensive the handling and transport costs are, Rick. It's not worth it if we can't use the stone."

"All because that woman decided to play stone mason today and thinks she knows best?" Rick points a finger in my direction.

I'm not even fazed. I've been down this road so many times that I've become immune to it. Unless I'm feeling my safety is at risk—which sadly happens more often than it should—this type of harassment tends to just roll right off me.

"Dude. Check your chauvinism," Kent remarks.

I hate that he feels he needs to defend me—it makes me feel small and not in control.

"Oh, I see what's going on here." Rick crosses his arms in front of himself and cracks a slimy smile. "Has she been checking to see where *you* fit on the 'hardness scale' too?"

Kent's shock and disgust are palpable. He stands tall and catches my eyes.

"We're leaving," he snaps.

I can barely keep up with his stride as he marches out the door.

CHAPTER 9

"Kent, wait," I call out.

He's made it all the way to the car by the time I catch him.

"The repairs! That stone might as well be a unicorn—this could be the only chance we'll get to find a match. We could have negotiated some smaller pieces, or a better price."

"Fuck the repairs." His nostrils flare and there's a heat in his eyes I've never seen before, even through the worst of our verbal sparring matches. "I'd sooner let every repair stand than buy one cubic foot of stone from that asshole."

I never thought I'd hear him back down on those repairs, so his proclamation blindsides me.

"What? Why? Because some guy can't handle being challenged by a woman? It happens every day, Kent. If I let that shit get to me, I'd never work in this profession."

"It's bullshit, Avery. He didn't just insult you, he insulted me too. I'll never do business with that company again." He opens the passenger-side door. "Get in the car."

He angrily marches to his side of the vehicle and takes

his seat behind the wheel. I do as I'm told and climb inside. This may be the first time I've ever done what he tells me.

We drive back in silence. Emotions are high and neither of us seems to know what to say. It's a completely wasted trip. Wasted time, wasted money, wasted energy. All spent so some quarry operator could knock us both down a few pegs and suggest that my advice is being taken only because I'm sleeping with the client.

Fuck you, Rick the Dick.

By the time we get back to the hotel I'm wishing we'd just opted to drive home tonight. I practically make a run for the elevator once the car is parked and yell goodnight over my shoulder. I don't linger long enough to even hear Kent's response.

I opt for room service and a therapeutic romcom back in my cozy king-sized bed. If I need to stay the night, I might as well make the most of the heavenly bed and use some of the amenities.

I get halfway through an uninspiring pizza and *The Hating Game* before my frustration returns. I get antsy, and even Josh and Lucy's witty banter can't help me relax.

Maybe a drink would settle my nerves?

I make myself decent, opting for an oversized Carhartt crew neck sweatshirt over my sports bra with my favourite cropped leggings. I grab some pomade and tussle my short locks, which have flattened after spending the afternoon under my hard hat, then apply some pink lip gloss before heading down to the lobby bar.

It's a Wednesday night, and I'm happy to see that only a

few people are here enjoying quiet drinks alone. I take a seat at the bar and contemplate my drink order.

"An Old Fashioned, please."

My handsome bartender winks at me and starts to pour.

"Great choice," I hear over my shoulder.

I turn to find Kent behind me. He's freshly showered, his dark hair still damp, and he's as casual as I've ever seen him, wearing distressed jeans and a worn grey T-shirt.

The bartender returns with my drink and Kent moves in beside me and orders his bourbon, neat with water back.

"Do you mind if I sit?" he asks.

"No, that's fine."

My crew neck slips over my shoulder, revealing my fair skin. Kent's eye catches it, but he looks away. I take this opportunity to look back at him. I've never seen his upper arms before—he always wears long sleeves at work—and I can't help but notice how the short sleeves of his shirt cling to his unexpectedly defined biceps.

I turn back to my drink, take a sip, and sigh.

"Rough day, wasn't it?" he asks.

"Totally frustrating."

"No wonder we're drinking." Kent's drink arrives and he leans to take it, resting his elbows on the bar. His T-shirt strains against the involuntary flex of his muscles. "You ran away so quickly, I didn't even get a chance to make sure you're alright."

"Alright? Why wouldn't I be alright?"

"Um, because you were sexually harassed today?" He takes a generous drink of his bourbon, then swirls the glass.

"I'm not kidding when I say that this stuff happens all the time." I take another fortifying drink myself.

"That's fucked up, Avery."

"Maybe it is, but it's the reality of the situation. Of *my* situation."

"It shouldn't be that way."

"I knew it would be part of the job when I chose to be a mason. I can handle it."

"You shouldn't have to handle it."

His voice is harsh, and it forces me to look at him. His clear blue eyes grow intense as they linger. He glances again at my shoulder, and I instinctively adjust my top to cover it. Nothing makes you straighten up like a conversation about sexual harassment and a dude suggesting you're railing the boss.

"Too bad all men aren't taught to know and do better." He takes another sip and looks down at his glass. "My mother would have kicked my ass if I'd pulled anything even remotely like what that dick did today."

It occurs to me that I've accused Kent of doing exactly what this asshole did today: treating me differently because of my gender. The realization makes me go cold, stomach twisting with regret.

"Kent, I owe you an apology."

"No, stop. I know you razz me for giving you a hard time, but I know that even *you* don't lump me in with that asshole."

I take a deep breath, unexpectedly relieved by what he's said. A silent moment hangs between us. Only the sounds of hotel jazz and ice clinking in my glass fill the gap. I shift the drink nervously, making it louder.

Kent turns slightly on his stool to face me and leans in. At this proximity I can feel his warmth and smell his freshly showered skin—his usual musk, mixed with hotel soap. I try not to breathe him in, but it's so tempting.

He smells so good.

"Please tell me that no one working on the Taylor Building has pulled any of this misogynistic shit."

"No, the team is great."

Kent examines my face, looking for evidence of truth.

"I'm serious," I insist. One more delicious sip.

This drink is going down a little too easily.

He seems convinced and relaxes in his seat.

"Aside from the whiteboard incident," I confess.

Kent's brow furrows.

"I once was in a meeting at the trailer and one notoriously difficult team member—who shall remain nameless—didn't like that I was winning an argument. I'd been sketching out an idea on the whiteboard, and it was clear he'd run out of arguments to refute me. He got up from his seat, walked over to where I was standing, and took the whiteboard marker right out of my hands."

I tip back the last drink of my cocktail. The ice falls to the bottom of the glass, punctuating the sentence. At the sound, the bartender glances over and I motion for another.

Why the hell not?

"That's some seriously passive-aggressive shit." Kent shakes his head in disbelief.

"Yep, I was so pissed. I had to leave the jobsite to cool off. I fantasized about wrapping my hands around his throat for about two weeks." I chuckle. "Since then, we've developed a great working relationship, but there's absolutely no question that he had a hard time adjusting to my being on the project."

"Why do you think that is?" Kent suppresses a smile. He thinks he knows the answer.

"Why do *you* think that is?"

My next drink arrives; Kent asks for another.

"I'm not going to answer that. I know better than to answer that."

"Oh come on, Kent. I know I'm a whole lotta business."

A smile crosses his face that's as bright as the fucking sun. White, perfect teeth set against tanned skin, and one beautiful dimple on his left cheek. I've never seen him smile like this—so genuine and unreserved—and it forces a smile of my own.

We stay like this for a moment, just admiring these new faces in front of us. The heat of his eyes and almost two ounces of bourbon hits my cheeks. We're interrupted by the sound of Kent's second drink being set on the bar for him.

It's really Kent's turn to talk, but I feel an urge to fill the space. I push it away, letting the moment hang. A rare concession for me, allowing someone else to take the lead.

"Am I a whole lotta business too? Is that why we clash?" He takes a large drink of his bourbon, one inquisitive brow raised, dimple still there, just slightly.

"Maybe? But I don't really know your business enough to make that judgement," I admit. "Despite my best attempt to compartmentalize my life, you know a lot more about me than I do about you,"

"What do you want to know?" he asks casually.

Like he's not just handed me the map to some other universe. I don't even know where to start. When I don't take the bait, he continues.

"Would it make you feel better if I told you more about myself?"

"Maybe?"

Yes.

"Well for starters, I'm a conservation architect who just happens to be the son of a PhD chemist mother who raised me *not* to be a misogynistic asshole, and a father who taught me how to tie a Windsor knot, play chess, and treat a woman with respect."

I pretend his words didn't just melt my panties.

Feminism is my new kink.

"I need to meet this smart woman—she sounds pretty badass." I contemplate pressing my icy glass to my pulse points to cool myself down.

"Unfortunately, we lost her seven years ago." He looks down at his drink with regret.

My stomach drops with my social gaffe. I worry I've

turned the conversation sad, when what I so desperately want is to put the beautiful smile back on his face.

"I'm so sorry, Kent." I grab his arm without thinking.

The contact startles us both. Skin on skin. Heat against heat.

Kent looks down to where my hand meets his arm and his muscles tighten. I pull my hand back, reflexively, the sudden movement dropping my shirtsleeve again. This time something makes me decide to leave my shoulder exposed. Kent's eyes find my skin. I feel them trace the line of my shoulder and up my neck, as plainly as fingers. My eyes lock onto his handsome face.

"We should probably call it a night." His voice brings me back to this time, this place.

I cling to my glass like a life preserver. We both quickly finish our drinks, charging them to our respective rooms, and make our way to the elevator.

We step inside without considering the implications of close proximity and enclosed space. I select the seventh floor; Kent pushes the number six. We each take a corner and wait for the doors to close.

Surrounded by mirrors, the effect is surreal—nowhere to hide and no safe place to look. I stare at my feet until the elevator stops at the third floor. The doors open and another man gets on. I glance up at the buttons, reading fire safety signs to occupy myself as the elevator slowly climbs.

My eyes accidentally catch Kent's in the mirror, and hold. The intensity of his gaze is both glorious and frightening and sends a warm buzz to the apex of my thighs.

A bell sounds for floor six, and Kent moves to exit as the doors slide open. He steps around the man between us and sweeps past me, allowing his hand to brush mine.

"Goodnight, Avery."

The doors close before I realize the moment is gone.

Once I'm at my floor, I find my room and scan the key to

make my way inside. I peel off my sweatshirt and pants and head to the bathroom where I take a long look at myself in the mirror, dazed.

What just happened?

I wash up and brush my teeth before taking off my restrictive sports bra and slipping into an oversized T-shirt for sleeping. I slide between the sheets and sink into the comfortable mattress, but after several minutes I'm still tossing and turning. The evening has left me unsettled and the bourbon from my drinks isn't relaxing me as it should.

I shift to my side and close my eyes tight, but all I see is him looking back at me from the elevator mirror. I move on to my back but feel the ghost of his hand against mine. Heat builds, so I pull down my sheets.

The memory of his touch brings a buzz to my skin and warmth between my legs. I shift my hips. I need pressure. One hand moves down and finds my slick heat, the other moves up to grasp a small breast. I sigh with relief.

Fingers circle and slide, twist and tug as images flash across my mental screen. His hand on a wet glass, denim straining across his thighs, biceps tightening his shirt.

Ice blue eyes find me in the elevator mirror.

Oh, god.

The sensation floods over me as my pace picks up and I wonder if he's doing the same in his room below mine. Is his naked body tanned, like his arms? Warm and strong, like his hands? Would his heat intensify his delicious, musky scent?

Oh god, his smell.

It's enough to tip me over the edge. Aftershocks hit with a shudder.

I lay still, letting myself imagine he's here with me, until I drift off to sleep.

CHAPTER 10

I had the best sleep in weeks last night. I'm afraid to admit to myself that my best sleep in weeks was likely the direct result of a mind-blowing orgasm credited to Kent Armstrong.

I mean, did he give me said orgasm? No. But let's be frank—he *gave* me said orgasm. And, if I'm being honest, it's a bit of a mindfuck.

Literally.

In spite of the generous mix of denial and willful disregard I'm arming myself with to face the day, I still fuss in front of the bathroom mirror before heading down for breakfast. Just a little more time on my hair, a little more makeup, a few extra minutes to choose between construction equipment T-shirt one and construction equipment T-shirt two.

I really need to pack better.

By the time I'm downstairs with my wheelie suitcase, I've worked myself into a bit of a state. (In my defence, I may have found the elevator slightly triggering after last night's *moment*.) I expect to see him at each turn, but he never materializes.

I shake it off and grab myself a plate of food from the breakfast buffet. I manage two strong cups of coffee but just a few scant bites before I give up and head to the lobby.

"Good morning! I'd like to settle up and check out."

"Good morning. What room, please?" asks the cheerful woman at the reservation desk.

"Room 709." I hand over the keys.

"Oh, yes… you were here for work related to the Taylor Building, correct? Mr. Armstrong already settled the bills before he left this morning, so there's nothing owing. I hope you had a satisfying stay?"

Now there's a loaded question.

I should be relieved, having managed to avoid facing him after everything that happened last night. Instead, I'm flooded with the strangest mix of emotions. Confusion certainly, gratitude for covering the hotel bill, and anger for being ditched without so much as a middle finger.

I tell myself it's ridiculous—it's not like we're friends. Kent doing his own thing is his default setting—why wouldn't everything go back to the status quo? But another emotion battles for supremacy: disappointment at having not seen him before he left town.

The drive home is torture. I analyze all our recent conversations, pick apart every intense look, and second-guess every shared smile. By the time I'm pulling into my parking spot, I'm finally willing to admit something: I've clearly got a thing for Kent Armstrong.

So what. Who cares?

A woman can be attracted to someone, even if they work with her; it doesn't have to mean anything. It doesn't mean I need to do a single thing about it. What happened privately last night will never happen again. I'm a professional woman who can maintain ethical work boundaries and not act like some weak-kneed schoolgirl when faced with an attractive colleague.

No more lingering glances, no more exposed shoulders, no more drinks alone in hotel bars. The end, moving on.

After my little pep talk, I'm feeling better and decide the best course of action is to stay busy. Very busy. I use the rest of the workday to answer emails, prepare estimates for a couple of small side projects, and finish some reports.

I'm an efficient, capable woman.

Once the work is done, I close my laptop and attend to domestic affairs. When that's done, not a single garment is left unlaundered or a single surface left unclean.

One of the pros of having a one-bedroom apartment is that it doesn't take long to clean it. One of the cons of having a one-bedroom apartment is that it doesn't take long to clean it when having an existential crisis.

Sonofabitch…

An incoming text makes me laugh.

> Sarah: I think I just ate my body weight in cheese.

> Me: I'm sorry, is this some sort of kinky Paris honeymoon dirty talk? (You know how I feel about cheese)

> Sarah: Tom is already snoring beside me. We're an old married couple already.

> Me: Lemme guess, too many museums in one day?

> Sarah: 25,000 steps!!!!

Me: I don't think you're supposed to use all your energy BEFORE arriving back at the hotel room. #honeymoonfail

Sarah: IKR?

Me: Are you having the best time, though?

Sarah: THE BEST

Me: Aww, I'm so happy for you guys. When do you get back?

Sarah: Back to reality on Saturday.

Me: But then you get to see me!

Sarah: I'm going to need some serious gym time to work off all this cheese. I officially have Brie butt.

Me: We'll kick that Brie butt back into shape!

My fitness is important to me and helps me to perform better at work. My line of work is quite physical and requires a great deal of strength and stamina. I need to move stone every day, climb the scaffold, lift heavy bags of materials. If the team is to take me seriously, I need to literally pull my weight. This makes me a consistent gym-goer and trainer. Pride really is the ultimate accountability.

When Sarah wanted to get into shape for the wedding, she came to me for help. Weight training and workouts can be intimidating when you're not familiar with it all, so I was happy to take her under my wing and help her feel confident on her special day. It seemed like the ultimate wedding gift. We've both found having a workout buddy helpful on those days when the siren song of the couch and a bag of Doritos proves almost irresistible.

Sarah: Dear god…

Me: I promise to be gentle. (Evil laugh.)

Sarah: Ok, but can we start off slowly? How about some yoga?

Me: Fine, fine. But let's at least make it count, make it a Power Flow.

Sarah: I might die.

Me: Get back on that horse, girl!

Sarah: I might puke.

Sarah: Speaking of getting back on, Tom is stirring…

Me: Whose turn is it to puke now!??

Sarah: LOL

Me: Power Flow, 7:30 on Sunday. Book it on the app, I will too.

Sarah: KK Gnight.

Me: xo

I pull up the yoga studio's app and book in for the Power Flow class at seven thirty p.m. on Sunday night. Then I grab my latest romance novel and settle in for an escape.

CHAPTER 11

Kent is conspicuously absent at work on Friday, which is frankly a relief. It grants me the freedom to focus on work and chip away at the dreaded deficiency list in peace.

By the time the workday ends, I've finished almost all the mortar patch replacements and only those last few orange-circled dutchman repairs are left to be dealt with, once we've resolved the missing stone issue.

With any luck, the stone supply problems will have convinced Kent to leave the repairs as-is and those deficiencies will be removed from the list. If this is the case, the work could be completed as early as Monday, and we can finally move on from the project.

Hallelujah.

After a long Friday night spent alone with Gherkin, over-analyzing every detail of the quarry visit, I decide that

Saturday brunch would be a great mid-day distraction. I invite Mom and Dad to Urban Roasters for a weekend treat.

I grab my favourite quiet corner table with a coffee and wait for them to arrive before ordering. Daniel and Victoria Avery turn up in style, making the millennials with their laptops look dowdy. With matching sunglasses and pressed cotton shirts, they look like they came from the Hamptons instead of suburbia. Hello #aginggoals.

"Ah, here's our dancer." Dad chuckles, pulling off his Ray-Bans and sliding into a seat.

Mom gives him a playful swat. "Daniel, stop it."

It's the first time we've seen each other since the wedding, and my busy week has helped me to avoid any playful teasing I normally would have been subjected to because of *The Dance.* Until now.

"Go ahead, get it all out of your system." I roll my eyes.

"I just think it's *quite* interesting that the only dance Bella decided to share at the wedding was with that handsome friend of Tom's." Dad flashes a Cheshire cat smile.

Oh yes, he really thinks he's being clever now.

"Dad, that's Kent. PM from Hell."

"What?"

"Yes, so put our wedding plans on hold—he's my client."

Dad looks like he's trying to work out some complex math problem.

"Foreman Fuckface knows Tom?"

"Daniel—language!" Mom glances over her shoulder, self-consciously.

"Wow, didn't see that coming." Dad looks down at the menu, shaking his head.

"I must say, when you described him previously, I imagined horns and warts, *not* what we saw last weekend." Mom rolls both lips between her teeth mischievously.

"Appreciate what you saw, Vic?" Dad teases.

"Regardless," I jump in, "the man is, for most intents and purposes, *my boss*, which puts him solidly in the friend zone."

Mom and Dad exchange knowing glances, then shift their eyes back to their menus.

The moment passes and I'm just thankful to move on to other subjects and be spared from further interrogation. The rest of the visit is spent eating, laughing, and doing my level best to avoid any conversation about Kent Armstrong.

The Zen Den is hopping when I meet up with Sarah at seven fifteen on Sunday night. Nicole at the front desk tells us there's a special Latinx theme for tonight's class, which has attracted quite a crowd. This news excites me; I already love Power Flow, and the contemporary playlist classes always have a fun and fresh vibe.

"How's the jet lag?" I ask Sarah.

She's clearly worse for wear, but trying to push through it.

"I don't want to talk about it. Let's just get this shit over with."

"Where's the enthusiasm? Brie butt is already winning, woman! We need to show it who's boss." I flex an arm in a sign of strength.

Tom ambles up to us, looking just as tired.

"Tom thought he'd join us too," Sarah explains.

I love Tom and never mind when he tags along. It's an unexpected but pleasant surprise.

"If I stay home, I'll just fall sleep too early and wake up at three a.m. Hope you don't mind me tagging along, Bella."

"Not at all!" I lean in to hug them both in welcome.

Tom's face lights up with recognition as he's pulling away from me. "Hey, glad you could make it, buddy."

I turn to see who Tom is speaking to and the space-time continuum glitches as my mind processes the face in front of me. The next several seconds pass in a blur as I watch a series of *bro* hand grabs, back pats, and various quintessential *dude* greetings.

No, no, no. This can't be happening.

"Hey, Avery." Kent grins. Clearly he's not as surprised to see me.

"I thought it'd be a great idea if Kent joined us," Tom states matter-of-factly. As if this is not, in fact, the worst idea to ever to be conceived of by a human being.

"Oh yeah, sure. Hi, Kent."

Remain calm. Nonchalant.

Kent adjusts the strap of his duffel as he turns to face me. I can't help but notice it's the same small duffel he used for the trip to the quarry. *Our* trip to the quarry.

The sight of it sparks something inside me, and the memories connect like falling dominos. White-toothed smiles, a dimple on a cheek, ice falling in a glass, mirrored walls, doors sliding shut, alone in my bed, hips moving, heat building.

"Let's get ready!" I state far too enthusiastically and make a beeline for the change rooms.

Sarah follows behind me faithfully, chatting about a yoga studio she saw in Paris as we settle into a spot at a bench. I make my way to a bathroom stall to buy a few contemplative moments and steel myself for what's ahead.

From my perch on the toilet I rest my head in my hands, take deep, cleansing breaths, and push the panic aside. Once I've caught my breath, it occurs to me that places like the Zen Den and the weight room are *my* domain. My physical strength is the one thing I'm most certain of. I lift stone for a living, for Christ's sake.

This is my *house, fucker.*

Kent is about to see me as he would every day at work: a strong and capable person who is confident and difficult to thwart.

I can do this.

I literally shake it off, shrugging my shoulders, limbering up and stretching out in my most dominant Wonder Woman pose.

I head back out to Sarah.

"Are you okay?" she asks. "I hope you don't mind that Tom and Kent are joining us."

"Oh no, not at all—it's fine."

I force a relaxed smile. It feels like I'm trying to convince myself as much as Sarah.

I strip off my hoodie and look down at my workout gear. I'm wearing a pair of cropped black yoga leggings and matching sports bra. They're like a second skin and rather revealing, but I never wear more than that to practice because the Zen Den is a hot yoga studio. The room starts at one hundred degrees before you've even downward dogged.

I take a quick look over at Sarah and notice she's wearing a similar outfit, but with a loose-fitting tank over her bra. I wonder for a moment if I should throw on the tank I have stashed at the bottom of my gym bag, but reconsider when I look at myself in the mirror.

I'm proud of what I see. I've worked hard to make and keep my body strong. Some of the guys at work have been known to call me GI Jane because of my short hair and muscles. I probably shouldn't like that they comment on my appearance, but it's always made me feel kind of badass and like one of the guys.

I smooth a hand over my defined abdominals.

"Let's do this."

There's just a cluster of spots remaining in the back corner of the room by the time we've made it into the studio. We've beat the guys out of the change rooms, so I have enough time to perform a nanosecond risk-assessment and determine my optimal location. I decide I'm best situated in the back, where I can practice discreetly and not feel like I'm under examination. Perfect.

Sarah and I settle into seated positions on our mats, and I let the warmth relax my tense muscles. I rest my hands facing up on my crossed legs and take slow, counted breaths while I settle in for practice. I try to close my eyes, but I'm not ready for it yet. I feel on edge, like I need my wits about me.

Tom enters first, wearing just navy-blue athletic shorts. I'm actually impressed. It looks like someone else has been getting into shape for the wedding.

I glance over at Sarah who is admiring her bare-chested husband with unreserved adoration and maybe a measure of lust. It's sweet. She spots me catching her and shrugs. I wink back at her and smile.

I take one more counted breath in, one more counted breath out. The door to the quiet studio creaks open and a man slips inside. A darkly tanned back with black athletic shorts is what I see first.

Then I die.

This isn't the Kent I know at all. The man before me is nothing I was expecting. He's certainly not the buttoned-up boss with the sunshine smile, and not even the defined biceps and muscular thighs I'd perhaps anticipated. In fact, it isn't the unquestionably beautiful shape of this man's body, or his obvious physical fitness that stuns me.

It's his full.

Fucking.

Torso.

Of.

Ink.

He quietly steps over to the spot in front of me and rolls out his mat to settle into place. From my location I see half his torso has been drawn with tattoos of architectural drafting instruments. They start along his left side and wrap around his abdomen and over one defined pectoral. At first glance I can see a protractor, a T-square, a drafting compass, and even a French curve.

Oh, that French curve.

I catch myself staring, eyes wide, and quickly look away. I check to make sure Sarah hasn't seen me looking at him. When I'm confident my cover isn't blown, I begin to feign disinterest.

Holy shit.

My mind is officially blown.

Anything I may have thought I knew about this man has been completely turned on its head.

And completely turned on.

I'd been so concerned about my own appearance just minutes ago, it never occurred to me that it was *HIS* appearance I had to worry about. Then the penny drops. I'm seated behind this tanned, muscled, deliciously inked man for the next sixty minutes through a hot Power Flow yoga class. I swallow hard.

I'm fucked.

CHAPTER 12

"I encourage you to lie flat on your back in a restful pose. Put your day aside and settle in for these next sixty minutes of strengthening and meditative practice."

Alex, my favourite yoga instructor, provides calm and confident direction. I'm feeling neither calm nor confident, but I go through the motions and take my position. If I'm going to make it through these next sixty minutes, I'll have to park my brain somewhere and try not to overthink things. I'm a master at compartmentalization. I can do this.

"This class is intended to improve both physical and mental strength through the breath-body-mind connection and foster endurance and focus," she continues. "By learning to work through the challenges on our mats, we also learn to work through the challenges we face in our everyday lives."

Woman, you have no idea.

I'm not a religious person, but I say a little prayer on my mat.

Gimme strength, gimme strength.

The opening notes of Spanish classical guitar begin to play over the studio sound system. I close my eyes and let Alex take us through several opening floor positions. I warm up and stretch my legs and hips with eyes closed, blissfully ignorant to what is happening one mat away from me.

Inches. He's inches away from me.

"Slowly roll to your right side, resting in fetal position before moving onto all fours, our table pose."

I do as she tells us, taking my time and keeping my eyes closed to preserve my inner Zen.

"Now let's work through some cat and cow movements as we transition to our contemporary Latinx playlist. Have fun and enjoy your practice, everyone."

Fun may be a stretch, Alex.

At this point I'd settle for mere survival—bonus points for preservation of dignity. I'm under-promising to myself with the hope of over-delivering.

The catchy sounds of Shawn Mendes and Camila Cabello singing "Señorita" cause an involuntary hip wiggle. I forget myself just long enough to open my eyes and catch-sight of what's in front of me. My breath hitches as I watch Kent's exposed muscular hamstrings flex with every cat and lengthen with every cow.

Dear god, are hamstrings usually this sexy?

I avert my gaze. Alex takes us through several more floor positions until we're standing at the tops of our mats. I close my eyes and place my hands together at heart center.

Another silent prayer.

"Let's work through a series of sun salutations to warm our bodies up."

Warm enough, thanks.

She demonstrates our sequence. I keep my eyes closed, pretending to be fully immersed in the experience.

I know these poses well enough to do them in my sleep, so I handle them masterfully blind. Even when Alex throws a downward facing dog and plank position into the mix, I can focus on my mat.

So far, so good.

"Really tap into your Ujjayi breath," Alex suggests, as if I've not been trying to breathe through this all along. Inhale, exhale. Grounding breaths.

Why is the air so fucking thick in here tonight?

Alex modifies the sequence once more. I'm doing fine until she prompts us to chaturanga. From a plank position, we're transitioned to upward facing dog, and I'm not sure if it's subconscious instinct or something chemical that forces my eyes open at that precise moment, but that's when I do. And I see him—hips thrust downward to the mat, strong back bent upwards and on full spectacular display. His broad, strong shoulders transition to a trim waist and those damned tattoos peek around from his rib cage, moving with every beautiful flex of his muscles.

Fucking chaturanga.

I'm temporarily saved by the next downward dog, but each time we're brought through the sequence I catch sight of him again. It's sweet torture and the seductive music and lyrics only add to my building, unadulterated lust.

Dear...sweet...lord...

Choosing to position myself behind Kent has been a gross miscalculation, possibly the worst lapse in judgement I've ever made. I'm both captive and captivated, condemned to sixty sweaty minutes of tempting and torturous movements. I whimper and bite my lower lip.

Several more minutes pass and I mindlessly follow Alex's instructions, distracted by how Kent capably manages each new, challenging position. It's pointless to pretend I'm not watching him at this point; it would be futile to even try. I'm hypnotized by lickable lats and devourable delts.

The heat builds in the room as the movements intensify, several grab towels to wipe brows or necks. I watch as two drops of my own sweat land on the mat beneath me. The air is stifling.

Alex isn't done with us yet.

Another Camila Cabello song comes on; this one is about hot and heavy "Havana" and our movements slow to adopt the beat. No one can resist moving their hips to these new sultry, sexy sounds.

My senses are already heightened, and the song's driving bass goes straight to my crotch. I can't help but clench as Alex directs us to warrior two, forcing me to face forward and I allow one little peek.

Just a peek.

He's standing strong in a lunge squat position, right foot forward and left foot back. His torso is twisted to face the side of the room and his tattooed left side is fully exposed to view. I boldly watch his naked, glistening back as a single bead of sweat slides down one smooth, tanned oblique.

He's a fucking work of art.

It's the final catalyst, my complete undoing.

I barely get through the rest of the class, distracted by fantasies of hot moments alone in dark places, sweaty skin on sweaty skin. I may have motioned with my tongue at one point, as I imagined licking his muscular back like an ice cream cone. In my erotic fantasies I'm licking him and then he's licking me. Giving and taking, scraping of teeth.

I'm wound so tightly by the time we're in our final resting pose that my eyes are wide open and I can't stay still. Sometimes I nod off and snore embarrassingly during savasana, but this time I worry I've whimpered audibly. My fatigue offers no respite from the buzzing on my skin. I feel like I'm radioactive and about to blow.

"Feel free to stay here in relaxation and meditation as long as you like—there is no rush. When you leave, please do so quietly to hold this peaceful place for others. Namaste."

There is nothing peaceful about my departure. I'm the first one up from the mat, and I quickly collect my things and run to the change room. Once there, I grab my towel and head straight for the shower. I throw on the cold water, not even waiting to peel off my sweaty clothes before setting myself beneath the stream. I gasp in shock but stay in place. I think I hear a sizzle as the water hits my skin, washing away about a dozen filthy fantasies before I need to face him again.

CHAPTER 13

"What's the matter with you?" Sarah gives me a confused look as I return to the bench wrapped in a towel.

"I just really needed to pee."

"Are you sure?"

"Yeah, I'm fine now. Great class. I'm gonna sleep like a baby tonight."

No chance in hell I'm sleeping tonight.

Sarah stifles a yawn.

"Hell yes. But Tom wants to grab a drink first. He's desperate to get back to our regular sleep schedule. I swear that man even makes type A for Avery seem laid back."

"Hey, I'm not always type A."

Wait a minute…drink?

"Nice try. Anyway, we're going to the pub up the street to grab a pint. You're coming, right?"

I rub my face with my hands.

"I know you work with Kent; does that make things weird?"

Only weird because I want to jump his bones.

I sigh. "No, it's fine."

"That doesn't sound convincing. Talk to me."

Sarah places a hand on my shoulder.

"It's just odd. Why hasn't Kent been around before? Why is he suddenly around now?"

"It's crazy we never put this connection together before, isn't it?"

Sarah chuckles like it's actually funny and not a living nightmare. This little *connection* is making it very difficult for me to cordon off the part of my life where Kent belongs, and keep Isabella Avery in her parallel universe. It's also making it very difficult to bury deep this new infatuation.

"They've just reconnected lately. You know how life is." Sarah shrugs. "Kent lost his mom a few years ago and I think it threw him for a loop. He became a bit of a playboy, which obviously wasn't where Tom was in his own life—thank god."

Kent Armstrong, a tattooed playboy?

"I have a very hard time imagining Kent Armstrong as anything other than an uptight box-checker."

Those words trigger in me a physical response, but I press on.

"Oh, he's tight alright..." Sarah says with a devilish grin.

"Sarah! You're a married woman!"

"I'm married, not dead." She saunters off toward the shower. "And you're not dead either, Bella. Don't think for a moment I didn't notice you watching him tonight."

Shit.

"Let's get a couple of pitchers—it's a better value," Tom suggests, forever the fiscally responsible friend.

"Stop managing the crowd." Sarah playfully taps his arm.

Tom is a financial comptroller at a big financial firm in town. I didn't know what this was before I met Tom, but since then, I've managed to discern that he oversees the financial reporting for various corporations. It's no wonder Kent and Tom get along so well. Kent is essentially Tom Lite.

"Bella, what do you want? Beer okay?" Tom asks.

"Oh yeah, sure. Why wouldn't it be?" I smile nervously, eyes shifting to where Kent sits. Thankfully he's distracted by a menu.

"I know you're less of a beer drinker," Sarah notes.

"I like beer just fine."

Big, tough, beer-swigging stone mason here.

Kent is staying quiet so far, in observation mode.

We're seated on a local pub's patio and it's a beautiful summer night. Unfortunately, I've only packed a floral sundress to throw on after class, so I sit in my feminine frock feeling horribly self-conscious. Had I known there was any chance I'd run into Kent, I would have packed a less delicate and revealing garment.

The server takes our drink order and leaves us in relative silence. A rowdy group of soccer fans sit inside the pub and celebrate when their team scores a goal.

"So...small world, right?" Tom opens the conversation, then looks between Kent and me.

I wait to respond, hoping Kent will address the comment. Neither of us speaks.

"Isn't she the best?" Sarah looks at me affectionately. "I love that she never let the world tell her she couldn't be a stone mason. Fuck the patriarchy, right, Bells?"

"She's extremely talented."

I spy something like pride in Kent's expression when he

says that, and it surprises me. I catch myself lingering on his face and quickly look down at my hands.

"Way to go, Bells," Tom adds.

Sarah gets up from her chair. "I need to run to the little girls' room."

Tom stands too. "I should go too, before our beer gets here."

Oh god, don't leave us.

As soon as Tom and Sarah have left the table, I nervously pick at a callus. I find a very interesting dessert menu to peruse and then check my phone for messages.

Nothing, dammit.

Kent breaks the silence.

"I'm not used to hearing people call you that."

Our eyes meet just for a second. There's a little zap when they do.

Did he feel that too?

"Bella?" I ask.

"*Bella, Bells*...I'm so used to Avery."

I don't know what to say, so I say nothing.

I wish our drinks were here, so I'd have something to do with my hands.

"So here we are back at a bar," Kent jokes. "We really need to stop meeting like this."

He seems nervous too, which I find comforting.

"Maybe we need to drink to tolerate each other." I'm trying to be funny, but the joke falls flat.

The moment the comment's left my lips, I regret it. It seems too harsh after the kindness he's just shown me, but I feel a self-preservation instinct taking over and the need to push him away.

The man is my boss. I've already told myself we can't do this: we can't flirt, we can't make lovey eyes at each other, and we shouldn't even be sitting in a bar like this right now.

"You don't really think that anymore, do you?" he asks.

It's a moment of unexpected and refreshing honesty, and I feel compelled to look at him again.

Oh shit, lovey eyes.

"Well, that's much better." Tom interrupts the moment as they rejoin our table.

As if on cue, the server delivers our beer and pours each of us our first pint.

"I propose a toast," Sarah begins, raising her glass. "To unexpected connections."

We all raise our glasses and start to clink them together with cheers.

"Don't forget to look in the eyes," Sarah reminds us. "It's bad luck if you don't."

I put off clinking Kent's glass as long as possible, knowing the moment we look at each other, it will feel like a shot to the chest or somewhere further south. Much like when I know touching something is going to give me an electrostatic shock, I avoid it as long as possible.

Yep, there it is.

I keep the eye contact as brief as is socially acceptable and then take a long drink.

"That was one hell of a workout tonight, wasn't it?" Tom asks.

Oh Tom, you have no idea.

"Yeah, it's been a while since I've done any yoga. I was a little rusty," Kent replies.

Not from where I was standing.

I compel my inner monologue to shut the fuck up.

Sarah looks over at me with a knowing grin and I kick her lightly under the table.

If I don't start talking, she's going to say something that will implicate me for ogling Kent, so I jump in.

"I've never understood the toasting thing. Why is it bad

luck to not look people in the eyes? What's supposed to happen? A lifetime of lukewarm beer?"

"In some countries there's a superstition that if you don't make eye contact while toasting, you're cursed with seven years of bad sex."

Sarah's facial expression while telling me this is one of pure delight. She didn't even have to try, and I played right into her hands.

"That's ridiculous," I huff.

"It might be, but I'm not taking any chances," Tom leans in to look Sarah in the eyes and give her a quick peck on the lips.

Kent and I watch uncomfortably and take another drink from our glasses.

Turns out it's very difficult to *not* think about sex when *trying* not to think about sex.

"How's your dad doing, Kent?" Tom asks.

I take a deep breath, relieved we've moved on to other topics.

"He's good. He's adjusted to retirement well. I never thought I'd see him enjoy this stage of his life, so I'm really happy for him."

He hasn't said much, but I'm fascinated. I know so little about Kent that I find myself listening attentively for any tiny nugget of information.

"That's great. I'm sure it's tough without your mom around," Sarah notes.

"Yeah, he never expected to retire alone, that's for sure." Kent takes a sip of his beer and then continues. "I think that's why I had such a hard time convincing him to do it. I just didn't want to see him retire too late to enjoy it."

"That would be terrible," Tom begins, then looks over to me. "How 'bout your parents, Bells? I didn't get a chance to talk to them much at the wedding. They're doing well?"

"They're great. Planning a big trip to Europe in the fall."

I take a drink and pause. I'm sad for Kent. He's lost his mom, and now dealing with the aftermath, while I talk so openly about my own two healthy parents. It feels cavalier, so I try to lighten the moment.

"Those two put my social life to shame."

I glance over at Kent, who seems unfazed.

Good.

"Well maybe if your *boss* would give you some time off, you'd get out more," Sarah teases, giving me a wink.

"I'm sorry, was that directed at me?" Kent asks, pointing toward his chest.

"Um, yeah," Sarah replies with a shrug.

"You know, I'm not exactly her boss." Kent gestures in my direction.

Hearing him say *her boss* makes me flush for some reason.

Like I'm watching a tennis match, my head swivels back and forth between them. I'm starting to feel self-conscious, so I chime in.

"Larry is my boss; Fleming is my employer."

"Yeah," Kent confirms.

"Whatever, *demanding client*." Sarah chuckles as she divulges my little secret.

"Oh, is that what you call me?" Kent looks directly at me, but instead of being annoyed by this label, he's smiling.

His smile heats me like a warm shot of bourbon and coaxes out a smile of my own.

His teasing feels familiar—almost intimate—like we share an inside joke. I like it.

"Kent's always been bossy. I've been on the receiving end plenty of times," Tom says.

"Like telling you to swim naked?" I ask, remembering the story from the wedding.

"That's just the beginning. Maybe I need to tell you a few more stories."

Tom's look is wicked, and I'm instantly curious.

Do tell.

"No thank you," Kent dismisses.

"Maybe just one? How 'bout when you *voluntold* us to break into the all-girls residence?"

Kent covers his reddening face with one hand, but he hides a smile behind it too.

Well, well, well.

"Some people like being on the receiving end of my bossiness."

Kent faces Tom when he makes the statement, insinuating that Tom was complicit, but when the married couple look at each other, he turns to me with dark eyes. The double entendre hit its mark and I shift in my seat.

My mind rewinds one hour to the yoga studio. To beautifully tanned, sweat-covered skin and all the things I imagined doing to it…

I take a generous drink from my glass. My pulse races.

"Bella, you're not saying much tonight," Sarah notes.

"Words I never thought I'd hear spoken," Kent teases. He grins, proud of his zinger.

I can't help but chuckle, and soon we're all laughing, sharing the joke. There's an unexpected group chemistry emerging and I really like it.

Then my stomach drops as it registers: this isn't supposed to be happening. I'm not supposed to be cozy with the client.

Sitting on a patio with my boss's boss feels like a betrayal. What would Larry think if he found out? It's *his* job to manage the client—not mine—and yet here we sit together, laughing and sharing a beer on a Sunday night. I need the reassuring comfort of clear professional boundaries. I panic, feeling the situation slipping out of my control. I need to extract myself.

I don't know what to do, so I revert to standard operating procedure when backed into a corner: I light a match and burn the motherfucker down.

CHAPTER 14

"Yes, I guess you do prefer it when your staff keeps their mouths shut," I deadpan.

"They can speak as much as they like as long as they're agreeing with me," Kent jokes, still playful.

"Yes sir—right away sir." I mimic a salute.

What am I even doing?

Kent's brow furrows. I take a quick look over at Tom and Sarah and they share the same confusion I see on Kent's face.

"When they're silent, they can't compromise that ego of yours," I continue.

"*Ego?*" Kent's face darkens. "What the hell are you talking about?"

It's like settling into Aunt Bettie's old couch, the way we fall back into this adversarial discourse—it's ugly as hell, but comfortable and familiar and you know you can't fuck it up.

"What else could it be, if you're not taking good advice from the experts you hire?"

"I think we've already established that I actually know a

thing or two about conservation architecture," Kent says, looking a little full of himself.

"If you were any good at it, maybe that's what you'd be doing instead of micromanaging your trades."

The moment the statement lands, I regret it, but I can't take it back. My gut wrenches, but I mask it with an apathetic expression. Kent's face shifts from dark to completely sour and he slowly gets up from his seat.

"Sarah, Tom...it's been lovely seeing you. Time to haul this monster ego of mine home. Goodnight."

He tosses a twenty-dollar bill on the table and heads for the exit without a backward glance.

I have a fitful sleep and am not in the best of moods by the time I arrive at work the next morning. Tom and Sarah gave me a proper dressing-down after Kent left, and when they asked for an explanation, I tried my best to brush them off with *"this is how it is with Kent and me,"* and *"we'll never get along,"* and even a lame *"we just don't understand each other."*

The truth is, I feel bad about what I said, and it calls for an apology, but that plan goes out the window the second I arrive on site.

"What do you mean the scaffold's been red-tagged?" I hear Larry shout the moment I open the site trailer door.

Larry's red face is rather disconcerting.

There's a small group of team members assembled around him, listening attentively to the conversation between Larry and some man I've never seen before. He looks very official, holding a clipboard and scribbling down notes on what appears to be a standardized form.

"We've done an inspection and there are concerns about

the tie-ins to the building. The scaffolding might not be safe," says the man with the clipboard.

"We've been using that scaffold for almost two years!" Larry exclaims, his voice rising another octave.

"Well, thank goodness nothing serious has happened, and you're welcome," Clipboard Dude replies, not taking his eyes off the sheet in front of him. "It's being red-tagged as a no-go zone until we can get a structural engineer in here to do a full assessment and make sure it's safe."

Clipboard Dude rips off the top portion of the document and hands it to Larry.

"We're almost done here!" Larry shouts.

At this point I'm concerned about his heart because his present complexion is neither normal nor healthy. Thus far I've remained a silent observer, but my own blood pressure is starting to rise as I process what's being said.

Since Kent had miraculously agreed last week—via official email—to let the stone repairs stand, I had only a few mortar patch replacements to complete. After finishing those and a few other small jobs today, I was ready to finally say goodbye to the Taylor Building.

I'd arrived this morning believing this was my last day on the project. My last day dealing with endless delays and difficulties. My last day dealing with Kent Armstrong.

Heavy, booted feet sound on the trailer steps before the door opens.

Speak of the devil.

"What's happening?" Kent demands.

He's all business, wearing his standard plaid work shirt and black jeans with required PPE. Black jeans have no right to look this good on a man.

He seems to have shaved extra close this morning—I swear I could cut myself on the sharpness of his chin. He emits authority like some exotic pheromone and I'm feeling the effects. I involuntarily picture the ink and muscle hiding beneath his buttoned shirt and my fingers twitch as I mentally run my hands down his stomach.

I'm starting in on an X-rated fantasy when I become lucid.

Snap out of it.

Kent spots me, but looks back at Clipboard Dude, seemingly unaffected.

I pretend this doesn't hurt.

"We've red-tagged the scaffold, I'm afraid." Clipboard Dude repeats, crossing his arms in front of him. "No one can use it until a structural engineer has assessed it and confirmed it's safe."

"Larry, how quickly do you think your engineer can get here?" Kent asks.

Larry shakes his head. "I'm not sure, but I doubt she can make it today."

"We're so close to completion, this is crazy," grumbles Reid, our youngest crew member.

"Is there a possible work-around?" Larry asks the group. "We've only got a few hours left to do."

"It doesn't matter how many hours of work you've got —rules are rules. If you enter that scaffold, you're doing so at your own risk and are liable to possible legal ramifications."

Clipboard Dude has all of the legalese down pat.

At this point, my blood is at simmer and it won't take much to push me to a full boil. I'd been hours from putting this entire building rehab—and the situation with Kent— behind me. Now I'm in project purgatory as we await the structural engineer and, possibly, scaffold modifications.

This could take weeks.

Enter, boil.

Kent has nothing to do with this, but he's going to be my scapegoat—I'm in a fighting mood now.

"Are we to believe that this 'random' inspection just

happened to take place on our *last* day of work here by pure *chance*?" I ask him.

"Yes, Avery, the health and safety regulations have conspired against you specifically," Kent retorts. "God, and you think *I'm* the one with the ego problem."

"Who said anything about ego?" Reid muffles through a mouthful of donut.

"Even *you* have to admit that something is fishy here." I point directly at Kent.

To call what I feel *frustration* would be like calling the arctic chilly or the ocean a bit wet. Prior to my arrival at work, my emotional state had already reached crisis point. If I'm to maintain any degree of professionalism I need to put the Taylor Building and Kent Armstrong in my rearview mirror as soon as possible. This scaffolding delay keeps me tethered to both of them.

I don't like how this lack of control feels, and I've proven that when rendered powerless, I don't behave well.

"Despite what *your* plans are, I don't plan on taking any chances with the safety of my trades," Kent declares. "Larry, do your best to get the engineer in here quickly."

Kent turns to leave, but I'm not done yet.

"This is bullshit, Kent."

"Avery..." Larry warns. His freckled cheeks still pink from stress.

Kent approaches, knocking me back with his signature scent. I take shallow breaths and try to make myself bigger against his wider frame. This is when I notice the tightness of his flannel sleeves and how his shirt strains across his chest. Things I'd never registered before now, before I'd really seen him.

He leans in close enough for me to see the light blue swirls of his irises and his dilated pupils.

"We all want to see the end of this, but don't be unprofessional." Kent's words are low and slow, punctuated with a jaw clench from restraint.

Heat spreads like flames across my face. He's hit me where it hurts—my reputation. And what's worse is that I know he's right.

This time it's me who walks away.

CHAPTER 15

I lick my wounds at home for the rest of the week. The more I think about how I handled Monday in the trailer and so many other situations on site, the more I realize my pride has been getting in the way. In my attempts to preserve my professional reputation, I may have, in fact, been damaging it.

It's like an out-of-body experience as I replay various conflicts with Kent over the past several months and how they may have been seen by others. I'm embarrassed.

Pride's a bitch.

Since the scaffold is a no-go and the next job isn't ready to start yet, I use my time to work on summary reports and documentation. In heritage rehabilitation projects, it's important we record all the interventions carried out throughout the course of a project and note which stones are original, which are replacements, and which have repairs. We also record mortar recipes and repair methods so the next generation of specialists, who need to care for the building in the future, have this useful information.

As much as it pains me to admit it, Kent is a top-tier

project manager. He's invested in Building Information Model (BIM) technology that provides a 3D rendering of the entire building, broken down stone by stone, so we can look at this building virtually and enter what we've done to each separate building part. It's the best possible technology for heritage recording and will aid in its long-term maintenance.

I'm up to my eyeballs in documentation updates on Wednesday when my "Sledgehammer" ring tone sounds. I look down at the screen and see it's Larry calling.

"Hey Lar, how's it going?"

"I've got an update on the scaffold situation."

Larry always cuts right to the chase.

"Good news or bad?"

"Depends on how you look at it. We had our structural engineer out to site. She notes some serious concerns. It's a good thing they caught it. It kinda makes my stomach turn just thinking about it."

"So then *don't* think about it. No one was hurt and we're working to fix it." I want to put his mind at ease.

"So…good news is that we caught it, bad news is that it's going to take a couple of days to get it sorted. Then we'll need to get that cranky inspector back out to site to review and rubber-stamp it. I doubt we'll be back in action until next week."

"Don't worry about me; I've got plenty to keep me busy here at home."

I take a sip of my third cup of coffee for the day. One of the hazards of working from home is having unlimited access to good coffee, which means I consume way too much of the stuff.

"I'm sure you do," Larry says, "I'll leave you to it and keep you posted."

"Wait, Lar, before you go…"

Maybe it's all the coffee that's made me jittery this

morning, maybe it's the restlessness that's set up residence in me since Monday, but I need to settle something with my mentor and friend.

"I'm sorry if I was unprofessional on Monday. I'm just so frustrated and eager to move on to the next project."

"No harm done, Avery. I know that you and Kent have a…unique dynamic," Larry says with a chuckle.

How is this funny?

"The last thing I'd ever want is for my words or behaviour to reflect poorly on Fleming."

"Your skills and knowledge speak for themselves, alright? So you have the odd verbal sparring match with the client—so what? The man has it coming sometimes."

"Only sometimes?" I deadpan.

"Well, *sometimes* I think you two go after each other for sport." He chuckles again.

Why does he keep laughing?

I think about what Larry's said. Is it possible he's right? That Kent and I chase the thrill a good argument can give us?

"I don't think that's the case," I respond. "At least not from my end."

I'm not comfortable with Larry thinking Kent and I are doing anything together for enjoyment. He's starting to feel like my dirty little secret.

"I think he enjoys getting under your skin."

I know Larry's comment is innocent, but the unintended connotation brings on a flood of feelings. It's embarrass-ment mixed with pleasure. I'm horrified Larry is even thinking about this, but nevertheless I smile as I ponder the notion that Kent might care enough about me to want to rattle my cage.

Cared might be a better word. Since making those terrible comments at the pub, questioning his architectural talents, he's probably pinned my picture to a dart board. I remember his emotionless expression from Monday, and my stomach drops.

I let Larry go and get back to work. I try not to think about the things I may have broken, or why I so badly want to fix them.

It takes just a few hours of silent introspection to finally admit that I need help. I do what any wise woman in my situation would: I reach out to other strong females for support. I set up a group chat with Sarah and my friend Greta, an electrician I met while working on another building project. These women never let me down when I need reinforcement.

> Me: Ladies, I need to call in the reinforcements…

> Sarah: Everything ok?

> Me: I'm fine, I just need a distraction.

> Sarah: Gee…what or WHO would you need a distraction from? I wonder????

> Sarah: Does he have a torso full of ink?

> Sarah: …and a body that won't quit?

> Sarah: …but you're just "professional colleagues"? YAWN.

> Greta: Wait, what's happening? What have I missed?

Sarah: Just Bella pretending she wasn't salivating over Tom's friend Kent during yoga class

Greta: Kent who?

Sarah: Kent from her work, Kent

Greta: Wait. Is this Foreman Fuckface? Is Foreman Fuckface saliva-worthy? Why didn't we know this?

Me: Can I get a word in here, please! For the record, I can appreciate a male body for the beautiful thing that it is. Don't hold it against me.

Greta: You mean his body? Hold his body against you?

Sarah: Air high five.

Me: I walked right into that, didn't I?

Greta: But seriously, what's up?

Me: Just a lot of crap. Work, life, drama. I need some girl time.

Sarah: GIRLS NIGHT OUT!

Greta: That's a great idea. We haven't had a proper night out in ages.

Sarah: I want to wear heels! I want pre-drinks!

Me: Out to a club? I don't know…is that even our scene anymore?

Greta: I think you need to shake your bells, Bells.

Maybe Greta's right. Maybe I'm only fixating on one

man because I've not been getting much *other* male attention lately. Maybe I need to hit a reset button and get back to my pre-Kent settings. But let's face it, my factory defaults are rather lackluster at the best of times.

If Friedrich Mohs assessed my love life like he had the relative hardness of stone, he'd likely find mine at the upper limit of his scale: hard, immovable and resistant to the mark of others. Many have tried to set me up with friends or acquaintances, to scratch my tough exterior, but nothing has ever really come of it.

Maybe I'm too busy, maybe I haven't found anyone who held my interest. Maybe it's a combination of the two. The result has been a few short-term relationships interspersed with hookups when the need warranted it. In recent months—and to be honest, until the quarry—the need just hasn't warranted it.

Getting out and blowing off some steam would be a great distraction, regardless. It's been ages since I've primped and preened and had a night on the town. I need to drink a little, flirt a lot, and dance like no one is watching.

Me: Let's do it.

Sarah: Yay! I think Tom is busy on Friday
night, want to do it then?

Greta: Yes, please!

Me: Let's meet up here at my place to get
ready, have a couple of drinks and then go.

Greta: A couple of the guys from work have
been talking about a new club downtown,
I'll get the name, we can check it out.

Sarah: Plan set.

Me: Thanks, girls!

Sarah: We've got ya, Bells. Now off you go…sweet, tattooed dreams. XX

Greta: Maybe you should have put down three XXX

A true smile is on my face for the first time in days as I settle in for sleep. I feel sad for the women who've never had these types of friends in their lives—sisters from other misters.

CHAPTER 16

I always kick myself for committing to going out on Friday evenings. It seems like a great idea at the time, but when Friday rolls around, I'm ready for loungewear, a book, and quality time with the cat.

No wonder I'm still single.

I'm an expert excuse-maker and can usually wiggle myself free of these obligations. This time things are different—I need my girls like medicine. An evening with Sarah and Greta is better than therapy. The second they walk through my door, I know I've made the right choice to push past the instinct to nest.

The Weeknd is turned up loud, drinks are poured, and before long every surface of my small apartment is covered with garments, hair products, or makeup. We take our time styling each one of us. Sarah opts for bridal white again, but this time it's a sinfully snug tank dress. We convince Greta to slide her shapely body into a blood-red cap-sleeved wrap dress that makes her already small waist look tiny and accentuates her curves.

When it's my turn, the girls have me try on about a

dozen outfits, but nothing seems right. Sarah digs deep in my closet, mining for skin-baring treasure, and finds gold. Well, not gold exactly, but the fashion equivalent: the little black dress that everyone seems to have but never has an opportunity to wear. It'd been cast aside and forgotten, lost in a wardrobe dominated by work pants and construction brand sweats and tees.

"It's too bold," I fret.

"This night calls for bold, Bells," Greta says as she pushes the hanger into my chest.

I try it on. It's a very short, backless halter dress. I tend to favour halter dresses because they show off my strong arms and shoulders. Thankfully the dress still fits after being long abandoned at the back of my closet and the fabric feels incredible against my porcelain skin. I still worry it's too much.

Sarah must spot my hesitation. "If you don't wear this dress, I'm never speaking to you again."

"Is that supposed to deter me?" I tease.

"Bells, that dress is incredible. Why haven't you ever worn it before?" Greta asks.

"Probably because it looks like *this*," I say as I gesture towards myself.

"And what exactly is *this*?" Sarah asks.

I turn in the mirror in front of me, taking it all in.

This dress feels amazing.

A smile breaks out across my face and the girls know they've won.

We each find a corner to finish our makeup and sip our drinks. When there's a lull between songs, Greta takes the opportunity to ask about the wedding. She couldn't make it, and is eager to hear all about the day.

"So, how's married life, Sarah?

"It's pretty amazing," Sarah says with a smile. She adds a little extra mascara to her lashes.

"You two lived together for years—is it really much different?"

"I guess it's mostly the same, but I feel like it's reaffirmed our commitment to each other."

Sarah blushes slightly with the statement.

"It's wonderful. I'd love to find the kind of relationship you two have. It's built on so much love and respect," I confess.

Once I've learned how to balance my fierce independence with my desire to find a mate, maybe I will.

"Well, you certainly were raised with an amazing example, Bella. Those parents of yours seriously are my relationship goal." Sarah pulls out her tube of lipstick and touches up her lips.

"You and me both, woman."

"Bella's parents are the ultimate power couple," Sarah tells Greta.

"Not quite." I roll my eyes, but in truth I'm super proud of the relationship my parents have. They've set a really high bar for my brother and me.

"What do you think is their secret?" Sarah empties her glass.

I'm surprised by the question and think before I answer.

"I think they're successful because they truly operate as equals; there's no unhealthy power dynamic between them. They're actually friends, and want to spend time together."

"But all married couples start out that way—not being able to keep their hands off each other. Why do you think they managed to make it last when so many others fail?" Sarah asks, topping up the Prosecco in her flute.

"Mom has always shown us that a woman's role in a family wasn't a one-size-fits-all prospect, and Dad showed us that respecting someone means more than just buying flowers; it meant communicating, and making no assumptions about what a person wants or needs."

"Yep—the poster couple for successful, healthy marriages," Sarah concludes, slugging back another generous gulp.

"Well, all this relationship talk is not what's going to put us into a clubbing mood," Greta warns.

"Agreed!" Sarah raises her glass and it throws off her balance. "Oops."

"I'd like to propose that Bella put all thoughts of long-term relationships aside tonight and make the most of *that* dress, and any attention it garners."

Greta looks to us both for agreement. We all laugh and clink glasses.

Time to hit reset.

The club isn't far, but in heels it might as well be on the moon, so we call ourselves an Uber and pile in. I check my makeup in the visor mirror to make sure my smoky eyes aren't all over my face, and apply more of my light pink lipstick nervously. It's been a while since I've put myself out there, so I'm feeling on edge.

The girls giggle in the back seat; they're already having a great time, and their smiles are infectious. I can't help but giggle too.

The driver pulls up in front of the club—The Stage—and we pour out and prepare ourselves for the dreaded lineup. Thankfully Greta has pulled a few strings with her colleagues and managed to get us on a VIP list to jump the queue.

The three of us step inside and try to get ourselves oriented. The bass hits me first, with a relentless beat that makes my chest vibrate. Bright lights flash in time with the sound and make it difficult to focus. Between pulses, we see a mass of bodies bouncing on the dance floor, bodies throbbing like some sort of giant organism. An adrenaline rush hits, and I instinctively start to move to the music.

Sarah and Greta head directly to a bar and order us a round of drinks. I've been sipping my drinks slowly tonight, wanting to keep my wits. A couple of drinks to relax is really all I need.

The three of us stand beside the dance floor, drinks in hand, and assess the crowd. We're a colourful display of cloth and skin: three distinct body types and complexions in bold white, red, and black.

It doesn't take much effort for us to attract attention, and before long we're all being dragged onto the dance floor to join in. It's pure joy as we dance as a group and lose ourselves in the music.

We stay on the floor for several songs, but at some point I lose track of Sarah. I lean in to Greta and ask where she's gone, but she shrugs. I try to tell her I'll go and search for her, but she shakes her head no.

"You stay here, I'll find her," Greta shouts in my ear. "I need a refill anyway."

I stay alone on the dance floor and sway to the music. A song I love comes on and I can't resist grooving when a handsome blonde joins me and starts to sway his own hips behind me. It's been a while since I've been the focus of a stranger's attention like this and at first I'm shy, but when I see his gorgeous smile it relaxes me and I get more bold with my movements. Eventually the song ends, and he's dragged away by a group of enthusiastic girls.

The stranger's attention has given me a boost of confidence and I decide to stay for another song. The music pumping from the club's oversized speakers is fabulously filthy. I can't help but grind my hips to the suggestive lyrics. It's a much-needed physical release.

The anonymity I feel in the large crowd is intoxicating. Free to move any way I want, I close my eyes and move my hips, no holds barred and completely uninhibited. It feels like an absolution and it's exactly what I need.

The raw sexuality of the song and its driving bass make my thighs hum and my nipples hard. All alone I bounce with the crowd, moving my hands along my body.

Keeping an eye out for Greta and Sarah, my eyes pan the floor. A man smiles at me seductively as he passes by, but he doesn't linger. I shuffle aside and allow him to pass.

I make one more sweep of the crowd and my eyes stop at a man in the mass. Someone who's been watching me. The familiar set of eyes shock me, and my chest tightens.

My lips move, but the sound is lost to the noise of the room.

"Kent."

CHAPTER 17

 I should be embarrassed, but I'm not.

I should leave the floor, but I don't.

The look he gives me is fixed and intense. When he doesn't look away, I turn my back to him and continue to dance.

Mr. Seductive Smile returns, looking for some attention, and I move with him again for a couple of minutes, but this time I'm doing it for Kent. I'm trying to elicit a response, but I'm not sure what that is. Push him away? Pull him closer?

I smell him before I see him. The warmth of his body comes next, leaning into me as he holds my forearm. My entire right side buzzes as he speaks into my ear.

"We need to talk."

My stomach flips.

I don't reply, but I lead us off the dance floor. I feel his eyes on me as he trails behind. A cluster of people block our path, and his hand goes to my bare back momentarily to help me navigate. It's a protective and possessive move that sends a delightful hum to my most sensitive parts.

I'm surprised to find Tom with Sarah at the bar. They're

locked in some intense discussion, wrapped up in each other. Greta looks just as surprised to see me with Kent, and offers a sly grin.

"What's going on?" I shout in her ear.

"Sarah sent a booty call text to her hubby, he and Kent were out golfing earlier and Sarah broke up their clubhouse drinks."

That's when I notice what Kent is wearing: a grey golf shirt and shorts that beautifully showcase his arm and leg muscles.

Has golfing always looked this hot?

Greta grins. "Aren't you going to introduce me?"

I turn to Kent, who hasn't taken his eyes off me yet. It's both unnerving and fucking exhilarating. I lean to speak in his ear and one nipple grazes his bare arm. It's completely unintentional, but I immediately want to do it again, particularly when I see his eyes darken in response.

"Kent, this is my friend, Greta." I gesture over to her.

Greta reaches to shake his hand. She's still wearing a smug smile, and for a moment I panic. I worry she's going to flirt, going to make her move. Maybe all my talk of us being "just colleagues" has been taken to heart. My stomach twists.

But Kent's eyes are back on me in an instant.

I relax.

Greta puts her lips near my ear.

"That gorgeous man is besotted with you. Do something about it."

I shake my head, face growing hot.

Friends always say stuff like this to make us feel good, right?

The evening falls apart as quickly as it came together. Suddenly Tom is taking his tipsy wife home, and Greta says she's called herself an Uber. Kent and I are left standing awkwardly at the bar, no drinks in hand. We both lean in to say something at the same time and end up talking over each other. We try a second time and fail again. Finally, I let Kent speak.

"Can we go somewhere to talk?"

His lips gently touch my ear, and it gives me goosebumps.

My heart breaks into a gallop as I nod.

We step into the warm summer night and find a bench on the sidewalk.

The air is thick with anticipation as he turns to face me. We look each other in the eye and the words spill out of both of us.

"I'm sorry I said you were unprofessional…"

"I'm sorry about what I said at the pub…"

We both pause, stunned to silence, then laugh.

"We can't even apologize without a competition," Kent says with a smile.

Out of nowhere, it starts to rain. I watch his shirt as small raindrops turn the fabric darker grey. Light sprinkles change to larger drops.

"Shit," I say, looking down at my tiny, thin dress.

"I live three blocks down; we can go there." He gestures down the sidewalk.

That's a terrible idea.

That's a fantastic idea.

We seek protection from buildings as we walk as quickly as my heels will permit. Two blocks down we're forced to take shelter under an awning. We squeeze together, slightly out of breath.

"I can't even offer you a jacket," Kent apologizes.

"I'm fine—it's warm."

We can't stop looking at each other and we can't stop smiling. The moment holds some sort of magic. It feels like the entire universe is conspiring to push us together.

Could it really be this easy?

"Let's make a run for it," Kent proposes.

"Okay."

He grabs my hand and we jog the last block to the entrance of his apartment building. Once there, he reluctantly drops my hand to unlock the main door with his key. We step into a historic building with a vintage elevator. It's exactly the type of place I would imagine Kent living and totally matches his aesthetic: clean, classic lines with contemporary touches.

"Watch your step on the stone floor; it can get slippery," he notes, looking at my black strappy heels.

When he places a hand on the naked small of my back to guide me into the elevator, my body erupts with goosebumps again. As it takes us to his floor, I can tell we're both thinking about our last elevator ride together, but we don't say anything. Instead we stand quietly opposite one another and I run my hands along my rain-slicked arms, warming my skin. Kent's eyes follow my movements. When we step out into the corridor it's more industrial than I expect. We're on the top floor and beautiful skylights let in the night sky along a vaulted ceiling.

He stops at a large wooden door and lets us inside. When I step over the threshold, I'm speechless. His place makes mine look like a cat-hair-covered hovel. It's small and sparse, but stylishly furnished with Danish pieces. Not a single square foot is wasted. There's a large open-concept main floor and an upper loft or mezzanine connected by an iron spiral staircase.

I say nothing and just take it all in until I notice Kent watching me.

"This place is incredible, Kent."

"Thanks," he says shyly. "Have a seat." He motions to a perfectly distressed leather couch.

"Kent, I'll ruin it."

I gesture to my wet dress, peeling the wet top from my skin in an attempt to restore some modesty.

"Oh shit, sorry. Let me get you a towel."

Kent circles up the iron staircase and is back before I even have a chance to snoop around.

"Here." He hands me a soft, plush towel which I wrap around myself. He takes a blanket and lays it out over the leather.

"Better?" he asks.

I sit, carefully positioning myself on the blanket, and wipe under my eyes with my fingers. I worry my eye makeup has run and I look like a disaster, but I'm too self-conscious to open my wristlet and take out my phone to check. I look at my fingers and am relieved when they come back clean.

I think of how he held my hand as we ran in the rain. My stomach flops. I fold my arms over my chest protectively.

"Are you cold?" he asks.

"No, I'm fine."

"Can I get you a drink?"

"Oh, god—yes please."

He goes to a small bar cart and prepares two glasses.

"Bourbon okay?"

"That would be great."

When he brings over my glass, my towel slips as I reach for it. Our fingers brush when I take it from his hand. I know he notices my hardened nipples under my damp dress, but he quickly looks away.

He sits at the opposite end of the couch and takes a fortifying drink. "Did you have fun tonight?"

"I did."

I sip from my glass. The liquid warms my throat. I'm not used to drinking it neat, but I like it.

"It looked like you were having a great time."

The loaded comment tightens my chest. Heat rushes to my cheeks.

"You're blushing." He smiles. The hint of a dimple emerges.

Kent's eyes darken, like they did in the club, and I feel locked to them. I can't answer.

"You don't need to be embarrassed." He takes another sip from his glass.

Something in this moment makes me pause and think. I've followed him here in a fog of fantasy and wanton desire without thinking of the consequences. I've held his hand and wrapped myself in his towel. We both know what's happening next if I stay.

With Kent.

My client.

What am I doing?

"So, what did you want to talk about, anyway?" I frown and look away.

Kent looks surprised by the shift in tone.

"I wanted to make sure we're okay."

"We're fine. We've apologized. Everything is fine."

Kent shifts forward in his seat, placing his drink down gently on the teak coffee table in front of us.

"Did I say something wrong?"

"No, I'm just not sure being here is a good idea."

My eyes pan the beautiful space, each incredible architectural detail. I could get so comfortable here. The thought makes my stomach drop.

I take one last burning gulp of bourbon, put the glass on the table, and stand, tossing the towel aside.

"I should go—I can grab an Uber downstairs." I make quick, determined steps toward the door.

"Stay," Kent calls out.

It stops me in my tracks.

I hear his steps behind me, but they stop short.

"Don't go," he says. "Please."

The urgency of his words causes a pang in my chest.

He moves closer. I can feel the warmth of his body behind me. I don't dare turn to face him. I don't have the courage to look at him yet. He's so close, I'd only have to lean back slightly to feel the strength of him against me. The temptation is almost irresistible.

He moves even closer; I feel his warm breath on the back of my neck. I close my eyes and breathe him in. His head tilts toward mine before his velvety voice fills my ear.

"I need to touch you. Please let me touch you."

Heat washes over me, leaving in its trail a craving to feel his hands on my skin.

It's a point of no return, but I can't say no. I don't want to say no.

I nod. I couldn't speak right now if I tried.

He doesn't touch me right away, and the seconds I wait feel like hours until his warm hands finally slide up my arms from my wrists. It's painfully slow as he crosses elbows and triceps before reaching my shoulders. They trace the muscles along the back of my neck. His nose touches my skin, and he takes a deep breath.

It's only touching, only fingers on skin, but it's the most erotic moment of my life.

"I've imagined these strong arms and shoulders so many times," he confesses. "Watching you use them has been torture."

A burst of joy happens, like a small explosion in my heart, and I lean back into his touch.

He presses slow and languid kisses all along my shoulders while running his fingers down my spine. It makes my legs slightly weak, so I walk toward the closest wall for support. Kent follows. When I finally get there, I put my hands up against the cool brick. He presses himself against my behind and I feel his hard length against me. I arch back into him and he reaches around to cradle my breasts over the fabric of my dress. A moan leaves my throat and Kent chuckles.

"You like that?" he asks.

"It feels so good…your hands feel so good."

He bites down lightly on one shoulder as he plays with each nipple, tugging on them slightly when it elicits an enthusiastic response.

I haven't even turned around yet and I'm already nearly incapacitated with lust.

He presses himself against me again and leans to whisper in my ear.

"I've wanted to touch you like this for so long."

It pains me to do it, but I extract myself from his grip and turn to face him.

We take a moment to look at each other, our breathing laboured and faces flushed. He has the most beautiful face I've ever seen. I put my hand on one cheek, needing to feel his skin. That closely-shaven jaw I've dreamt of touching feels even better than I'd imagined it would—smooth and strong.

Our first kiss isn't the rushed, hard and passionate one I've been fantasizing about. Instead, his lips are soft and tentative, almost reverent, as he takes his time testing angles and lingering at my bottom lip.

Once our lips are familiar, the urgency builds between us and I'm backed against the wall as I slip my tongue past his lips. I'm completely lost in him and press my body against his, eager to explore his body, impatient to feel more. I nip at his lips and tug at his hair. I want him to be rough. This is when *he* groans.

When I smile into his mouth, he kisses along my throat,

brushing his own teeth against my hot skin. I need to see more of him, chart every square inch. I grab the bottom of his golf shirt and pull it over his head. He moves in to kiss me again, but I stop him. He looks confused until he sees me looking at his chest, and he smiles.

"My tattoos… did they surprise you?"

"Only in the best possible way," I answer with a dreamy smile.

His beautiful dimple appears, but my eyes quickly return to the tanned, muscled, tattooed chest that has been a part of every sexual fantasy of mine since yoga class.

I'm staring now, analyzing each line and detail.

"I always imagined you'd have tattoos yourself, like the rest of the crew."

"No, I don't have any ink." I trace a black line with my finger, slightly dazed.

"You don't like them?"

"Oh no, I do…" My voice trails off as a second finger follows the first. "I just don't have any on my own skin."

"Prove it."

His eyes darken again and I watch his smile turn to something serious.

God, I want this man so much.

Almost in a trance I reach behind my neck to untie my dress. I slowly pull the fabric down and feel a heaviness in every erogenous zone as Kent licks his bottom lip. The heaviness turns to an ache as my dress falls to my waist and I peel it down my legs. I step out of it and kick it aside.

I haven't had a chance to take my shoes off yet, so I'm left wearing just my black heels and a pair of pale pink lace panties with a small bow at the front.

Based on the perceptible bulge in the front of his shorts, I assume Kent very much likes what he sees. I wait, let the moment hang and allow him to make the next move.

He brushes the tiny pink bow with his fingers and it's

like every single nerve ending is touched with this soft contact. My back arches involuntarily.

"You're never what I expect you to be," he whispers.

"Look who's talking."

And suddenly, we aren't talking anymore.

CHAPTER 18

"It won't fit," I tell him.

"Oh, it will," he insists. "One shift of that sexy foot and it's gonna slide right in."

We've kissed, groped, and pawed our way over to Kent's iron spiral staircase but pause here when I realize the thin heels of my shoes could slip through the mesh openings of the treads and potentially kill me.

"I'll just take them off."

His voice drops an octave. "They're staying on."

I'm surprised—and completely aroused—by his determination to keep me shod. Apparently this is his kink, and I'm one hundred percent in support of it.

"I'll carry you."

"Kent, I'm not some tiny doe—I work out constantly. Muscle is heavy."

"…and thank god for your muscle."

He leans back in to kiss a shoulder and fondle my ass.

"Or we stay down here," I propose.

He takes my face in his hands and kisses me so thoroughly, I may have blacked out for a few seconds.

I could kiss this man for hours. I could kiss this man like it's a full-time job.

He takes one nipple in his mouth and in the blink of an eye, my job description changes.

This. This is what I want to commit my life to.

Without warning, Kent picks me up and throws me over his shoulder like some sort of prehistoric panty-melter. He climbs the stairs two at a time and is short of breath by the time he places me on his fluffy white bed. The room is sparsely decorated: a simple bed with teak side tables and one Eames-style chair just outside what looks like a bathroom or closet.

"You could've hurt yourself," I scold.

"I'm fine. But maybe a little heavy petting for my services?"

We both giggle, but the laughing stops when he settles his hips between my legs.

There's so much I suddenly want to give and receive from this man that it makes me pause. He notices the change in me and offers a soft smile, like he feels it too.

"Everything okay?" he asks.

I nod and run my hand along his jaw.

"Has anyone ever told you that you have the most beautiful smile?" I ask.

His face flushes.

Aw, Kent's a little shy.

"Has anyone ever fucked you while you've worn these shoes?"

Okay, maybe not so shy.

I swallow hard and shake my head.

"There's your answer."

He kisses me, slow and seductive, until I'm melting into him like hot butter. His lips trail down my neck to my shoulder, the one he seems so fond of.

"What is this muscle called?" he asks unexpectedly.

"Trapezius." My voice is breathy.

"This trapezius has been keeping me up at night."

He runs his teeth along the muscle and follows with his tongue. I've never considered my neck and shoulders particularly sensitive, but the feel of his tongue on my skin lights me up inside. He notes my reaction and replicates the movements over my nipples.

My hips push into him in response, so he lingers and moves back and forth, switching from breast to breast, until I'm groaning and reaching down to touch myself for relief. He trails kisses down my stomach and watches me for a moment before sliding his thumbs under the waistband of my panties and slipping them off my legs.

"Can I do that for you?" he asks quietly.

I pull my hand away and let him take over.

He moves back up to kiss me on the mouth, biting and tugging at my bottom lip while one hand circles and strokes. I move my hips to help his rhythm. He pulls away from my lips, propping himself on one arm to watch.

Just when I think it can't get any better, he slips one long finger inside. I gasp.

"Do you like that?" he asks.

I can't speak, but I nod.

"Say it for me."

"Ohmygod, yes."

He does it again, but harder, and it elicits the same response. He slides a second finger in and the force shifts me slightly up the bed.

"Oh god," I moan, grabbing the covers for purchase.

"Too rough?" He kisses my stomach.

"No. More. Harder."

He follows my instructions and delivers sweet, repeated strokes with his hand until I'm gasping for air. He pauses and there's a coldness when he pulls away, until I see him stand to take off his shorts.

He walks to his bedside table and opens the drawer. That strong, tanned back of his nearly killed me during yoga class and it shows its lethality again as I watch those incredible muscles flex with each subtle movement. He pulls out a condom and turns back to face me. The erection he displays is a sight to behold. His dark grey boxer briefs cling to his defined thighs like a second skin and I'm slightly giddy as I realize that every hot yoga fantasy of mine is about to be realized.

Okay, maybe not every *fantasy…that would take days.*

By the time he returns to the bed I'm like a spring in tension, ready to pop.

He moves to take off his underwear, but I stand on my knees and grab his hands. He watches with smoky eyes and a sultry smile as I peel them down his legs.

When he steps out of them he's left naked and tanned, skin only slightly lighter where his swimsuit would be. His sculpted body belongs in a museum. I mentally place him on a marble pedestal as I take his hard length in my hand. It garners a hiss and his head rolls back in pleasure. I give a tentative stroke and he groans.

"I'm not going to need much encouragement tonight," he warns.

"No?" I ask, coyly.

"Just seeing you dance was nearly enough to push me over the edge."

He traces a thumb along my bottom lip, and I give him a playful bite. He kisses me and gently pushes me down on the bed. Soon it's skin on skin, hands working to touch every smooth part of each other, hips moving to rub and tease.

I decide to take charge. I roll Kent over and straddle his hips. He looks surprised when I take the condom, open it, and slide it on for him. We stare fixedly at each other as I ease him inside.

We pause and take in the moment, revelling in how it feels. There's an incredible fullness but also a sense that everything fits just right. Kent's chest rises and falls. I savour our connection and take a mental picture: his clenching abdominals, the pleasure in his face, the need in his eyes.

Kent grows impatient and starts to move. I follow his lead and slowly ride, rolling my hips and engaging my core. I place my hands on his chest for leverage and feel his smooth, hard torso under my fingers. The look of my pale hands against his darker skin and tattoos captivates me as I run them down his taut stomach.

Kent's face is intense as he holds my hips. My pace and force increase until I'm sitting at that amazing pleasure-pain threshold that makes me suck in a breath and tells me I'm close. Kent is too—I can see it in his face and hear it in his sounds. I change the angle so I rub against him each time I land.

"I'm so close," I whisper.

He thumbs my nipples as I thrust my hips. My glute muscles clench as a warmth that's begun in my lower belly starts to spread. I arch my back and push into his hands, encouraging him to move faster, rougher. I'm running out of steam and my legs are starting to shake, so Kent moves his own hips to help. He hits me in exactly the right place, and I roll my head back in ecstasy.

"It feels so good…"

"Come for me, Bella."

Hearing him say my name is the touchpaper that sets me alight. It's the last piece of the puzzle and when it clicks into place; it's pure bliss. Wave after delicious wave washes over me until I can't move anymore.

Kent drops his hands back to my hips, gripping them for leverage. He pushes upwards, three final, hard strokes and he's gone too.

"Fuck," he moans, eyes squeezing shut.

He holds me in place as he rides it out. We share a few extra rolls of our hips as we come down from our highs.

There's an intensity to the minutes that follow. I replay the sound of my name on his lips, remembering the potency of the moment. We exchange dozens of kisses between drumming heartbeats and ragged breaths, tangled up in each other and trying to stay close. I taste the salt of his sweat when I kiss his chest and feel the cool air against my own dampened skin. I run my nose along his warm neck, breathing in his intoxicating scent. Kent's hands smooth over my back, convincing me to linger.

Eventually I slide off his lap and Kent gets up to throw out the condom. I prop my head in my hand and watch as he crosses the floor to the washroom. His open nakedness is incredibly sexy, and my eyes drink him in. The surrealness of the moment stuns me—all we've seen and felt and done.

When he comes back to the bed, he kisses me once more before running a strong, warm hand down one of my smooth legs. When he reaches my foot, he carefully unbuckles and removes my shoe and places it on the floor, then repeats the ritual with the other.

He coaxes me under the soft covers, slides in to nestle against me, and clicks off the light. I lie against his warm body in the dark, calmed by the proximity of his skin and surprised by the power of my affection.

He plants a single kiss on the back of my neck. "God, you're so beautiful."

Never have I felt more adored.

CHAPTER 19

It doesn't occur to me until morning that it had been a foregone conclusion I'd stay. I wake up alone and naked in Kent's bed, the morning light casting a warm glow over the space. I stretch out, practically purring with contentment in his divine bed.

I slip out from under the sheets and step inside the ensuite bathroom to clean myself up as best I can. My makeup is a fright and I have awful bedhead—one of the pitfalls of a pixie cut—but I do the best I can to limit the scare factor.

When I come back to the bedroom, I realize my dress is still downstairs. I'm a hot mess, but there isn't time to think too much about it because Kent's at the top of the stairs as I'm slipping my panties over my hips.

He's wearing a light grey T-shirt that fits so closely over his muscles it's making me jealous—I want to *be* that T-shirt. It's paired with loose-fitting and deliciously low-riding pyjama pants that make the air thinner and temperature approximately ten degrees hotter in here.

Does he have a permit for those pants?

"You take yours with milk, right?" As he hands me a mug of coffee, I spot my dress draped over his arm.

His eyes instinctively fall to my nakedness, but I'm surprised to find I'm not uncomfortable with it.

"Yeah, I do."

I take a generous sip. I didn't drink much last night, so I've spared myself a nasty hangover, and the coffee is delicious.

Kent hands me my dress. When I reach to take it from him, he pulls it back at the last second, playfully, giving me a tentative smile.

"Hey."

He says it almost like a question: *Are you okay? Are we okay?*

I can't stop my face from spreading into a huge smile. His own widens into a dimple-inducing stunner, emerging like a sunrise to brighten the room.

We're okay.

"Good morning." I take the dress from his hand.

"Are you hungry?"

I put my coffee down so I can slip on my dress. I tie the halter behind my neck while he watches attentively.

"I could eat," I reply nonchalantly.

"You're gonna get cold in the air conditioning. Let me get you something to wear."

He walks to a closet opposite the bathroom and opens a drawer, pulling out a T-shirt.

"Here, try this. It'll at least cover your back."

I take the light blue shirt and inspect it. It's a well-worn and ridiculously soft Beck concert T-shirt. It instantly cracks me up.

"You really are a Beck fan?"

"Of course, did you think I was joking? Musical genius, Avery. Musical. Genius."

He's back to *Avery*.

Hearing it brings me straight back to last night—to the single most powerful sexual moment of my life. I consider how to proceed.

"So…you said my name last night," I begin.

"I did," he states confidently. He doesn't blush, doesn't look away. "Was that alright?" He moves in to close the gap.

"You can call me whatever you want." I shrug it off, playing it down.

"Whatever I choose, I'm sure it'll be nicer than *Foreman Fuckface*," he teases.

"You know about that?" I hide my face in my hands.

"Sarah spilled the beans when she was drunk last night."

"I'm sorry—"

He interrupts me and pulls my hands from my face. "Oh no, you're not," he says with a chuckle. "But that's okay—I'm going to get the ultimate revenge."

"Oh yeah, how's that?"

He still hasn't let go of my hands, so I hold his tighter.

He places his cheek against mine to speak softly in my ear. It feels like settling into a warm bath. You know…if a warm bath gave you orgasms.

"Now you'll have to tell her you're fucking *Foreman Fuckface*."

My chest feels too small for my heart.

*Fuck*ing, *he said. Not fuck*ed. *Interesting.*

He slides his nose along my cheek and soon our lips are touching. He drops my hands to cradle my face before delivering a knee-weakening, breath-shortening, panty-warming kiss for the ages.

Sweet Jesus. Good morning, indeed.

With one extra kiss, he pulls away.

He grabs my coffee to carry it downstairs. "Come eat."

I take a few seconds to slip on the T-shirt, which smells

like him. I'm already weak from the kiss, so the smell of the shirt makes me straight-up swoony. I grab my shoes and follow.

I like Take-Charge Morning-After Kent.

Downstairs I look at the architectural details again. I love how the designer placed a really small yet efficient open-concept kitchen off to the side of the main living area. The contemporary design works so well, juxtaposed against the heritage warehouse-style interior. No detail was overlooked.

"Did you design this space?" I ask.

"I did." He opens up the industrial-style fridge and pulls out various ingredients.

He seems a bit shy talking about it, and I worry he's still upset about the dig I made at the pub—about his talents, or lack thereof.

"It's beautiful, Kent."

He looks up with a slight smile. "Thank you. Now… how hungry are you?"

Ravenous.

"Maybe just toast and coffee? I need to get home to feed Gherkin."

"I'm sorry, feed the Gherkin?" he asks, one brow raised. "Is that a euphemism?"

I burst out laughing.

"No! God, Kent! Gherkin is my *cat*."

"Why didn't you just say that?"

"Say what? That I need to get home to feed my kitty?"

"Never mind, that would've sounded dirty too." He grins.

We drink coffee, eat our toast, and chat about all things architectural. He gives me the details on the interior fit-up and shares a few lessons learned from the project.

We seem to be avoiding the elephant in the room: what happens next?

Eventually the coffee cups empty and the reality that I *do* need to leave sets in.

"I really have to go."

I retrieve my previously abandoned wristlet from the coffee table and collect my shoes.

"I can grab an Uber downstairs," I tell him.

I open my tiny handbag to take out my phone.

"At least let me drive you home," Kent says.

"You really don't have to."

He rounds the kitchen island and approaches me. He seems eager to get between me and the door.

"Please, let me do this. Remember that mother of mine I told you about? She'd be *very* disappointed in me if I didn't."

Oh, well played, sir.

I crouch to put my shoes on and think for a moment. I'm not sure what's best. What is this between us? Just a one-night stand? Does he feel obligated to me? I don't want him thinking I have any expectations. But when I tell myself this, I notice a pang in my chest.

Maybe I *do* want more.

"You don't mind?"

His face brightens. My tension lifts.

"Just let me throw on some clothes."

He's off to the stairs and bounding two at a time before I have a moment to reconsider.

We cross the street to his car and I climb inside while he unplugs from the charging station. Once he's settled, I give him directions to my apartment.

We drive in relative quiet, just making a few comments here and there when we spot something interesting. Maybe this is it—when the chemistry runs out in the sober light of day. But I can't blame what happened last night on alcohol.

The only thing I was drunk on last night was him.

We pull up in front of my apartment and find the perfect parking spot.

There's the universe cooperating again.

Kent walks me to the door. This is when we're supposed to say goodbye and go our separate ways, but something keeps us tethered. It feels like we're in some sort of limbo: still buoyant over what we've done, but not sure where to go from here.

"This is a nice place," Kent notes, looking at my building and the pretty planters along the sidewalk.

"Thanks, I like it."

"Are you going to invite me in?" He flashes a charming smile.

My stomach flips like a giddy schoolgirl. "You want to come in?"

"I need to meet this famous Pickle."

"Gherkin, it's *Gherkin*."

"Why on earth did you name your cat after a pickle?" he asks, feigning disapproval.

His upturned mouth gives him away.

"I always name pets after food items. It's just what I do."

"That's random."

I point a finger at him. "You can't come up if you're going to judge me on my pet names."

Kent grabs at my finger and pulls me in. "I'm sure Gherkin is an absolute princess."

"Prince. Gherkin's a male."

"I've met plenty of male princesses."

"Touché."

I've forgotten about prep and pre-drinks when I open my apartment door. All events before Kent clearly swept away on a tsunami of lust. I'm horrified by the state of it. Not a single surface isn't covered by clothing, cosmetics or various other accoutrements designed to primp or preen.

"Oh god, it's a bloody disaster," I mutter.

I pre-emptively close the door, almost squashing poor Gherkin against the jamb.

"What's wrong?" Kent asks.

"You shouldn't see this."

I rub my face as heat rises to my cheeks. Kent's place is a fucking palace compared to mine—on a good day. Surely one look at this chaos will send him running for the hills. Plus he's about to see every part of me that I've kept hidden: frilly, pretty things that are incongruous with the person I've put out in front of him these many months. I'm not embarrassed by it, but maybe having a hard time taking the last step.

Kent moves to face me, pulling my hand from my face.

"I'm happy to hang out here in the hall all day, but poor Pickle is going to starve if we don't feed him."

I look up at him. The warm smile Kent gives me is one that I've never seen from him before. A calming smile. The kind that tells someone they're safe and secure. Everything is okay here.

"What kinky things are you hiding in there, Avery?" he asks, "Sex dungeon? Orgy stuff?"

I laugh and rest my head on his shoulder.

"It's all good, you just didn't find mine." Kent squeezes my hip. "Not yet, anyway."

I melt into his chest to breathe him in, and he gifts a sweet kiss on my temple. Our eyes lock. I decide it's my turn to knock him over with a mind-blowing kiss.

I take his face in my hands and feel his short stubble against my palms before I plant one that's open-mouthed and slip my tongue past his lips. I press my entire body against his as I work to—quite frankly—bring him to his knees. I change angles and test different positions and pressures.

I'm working on an A+ in seduction when I suddenly get schooled; Kent presses back, pinning me against the door and taking control. He ends up with my bottom lip between his teeth and his hands on my ass.

Wasn't last night supposed to defuse this tension? Wasn't it supposed to dilute the inebriating chemicals that have been running through my system? Instead it seems to have opened a floodgate and I might drown in the wave.

CHAPTER 20

"Have a nice day, Mrs. Allen," I say to my elderly neighbour as I wave and shut my apartment door behind us.

Kent and I suppress laughter as we fall into each other behind my door.

"Oops."

"Oh, well—a little PDA won't hurt her," I say with a shrug.

He turns to take in my apartment as Gherkin winds himself through our legs and head-bumps our shins. I rush off to the kitchen to feed him and he follows behind me, leaving a trail of "meows."

By the time I'm back in the main living area, Kent is looking at the framed photos I have lined up on a table.

"That's my brother and his wife," I tell him.

"Siblings…are they all they're cracked up to be?"

"Yeah, they are. I mean, we haven't always been close, but we are now. It's nice to know I have someone to talk to when our parents drive me nuts or I'm not sure what to get them for Christmas."

"Handy."

"What's it like being an only child?"

"Sometimes a lot of pressure. They put all their eggs in my basket," Kent says with a look of resignation.

I collect the few items that cover the couch. Kent plops down on the fluffy white cushions. It takes about ten seconds for Gherkin to prance by me and jump on his lap.

I wince. "Sorry."

Kent is so particular about his appearance, and he's about to be coated in cat hair.

"It's all good. It's nice that he's friendly."

Gherkin looks up at me with a smug expression. How quickly I've been replaced.

I drop on the couch opposite them, tuck a leg under myself, and watch the spectacle.

"So…that eggs-in-basket comment sounded a bit loaded," I venture.

He scratches Gherkin's chin and looks thoughtful.

"Ah, it's not a big deal. I've just been feeling some pressure lately where my dad is concerned. It's fine."

Judging by his face it doesn't seem fine.

"Being an only child with an aging parent must be difficult," I say, inviting him to elaborate.

"I didn't handle my mom's death very well and I made a few bad decisions in the months following."

His focus is on my spoiled cat, as he strokes Gherkin's back, inciting purrs at surprising volume.

Is it wrong to be jealous of a cat?

"I've been working hard to prove to my father that I'm solid now and he can depend on me," he adds.

There's a heaviness in his expression. It sparks a strange instinct to care for him; I can't help but wonder whose support *he* can depend on.

"Well, you certainly seem solid. You're about as steady as they come."

"I'm trying to show him that I can make good choices so he can relax and enjoy retirement."

"You're a successful PM, you designed your own flat, you seldom have a hair out of place, and you even drive an electric vehicle, for fuck's sake. I think you're keeping your shit together just fine, Kent."

He rolls his eyes but smiles at my assessment. I reach over and scratch Gherkin with him, eager to share something, to show Kent we're on the same team.

This guy must've had a pretty significant derailment if he's still worrying about things at this end of his pendulum swing. I don't dare ask. I move to a lighter subject.

"So...disregarding the beauty counter barf job, this is my humble abode." I gesture around me. "It's pretty different from your place."

My one-bedroom apartment has a fairly typical open concept plan. One large island with bar stools separates a modest kitchen from the living and dining areas. A sliding glass door opens onto a decent sized balcony that I use as much as I can.

I'm not a sparse decorator like Kent is. My numerous bookcases are loaded with architecture and technical books and packed with relics I've collected from my various built heritage projects. There's a small chunk of carved stone here, a wrought iron finial there. I love my little curiosities.

My dining table is most often used as a desk—particularly while I'm working from home—so it's covered with my laptop, papers, and work journals.

My décor is mostly white and light grey. I like a bright space, but this colour palate also helps to hide some of the tabby hair Gherkin sheds on a daily basis. My bedroom is also white, but with hits of pale pink. I love pink—it's my frilly little secret. Only my closest friends and family know this about me.

I try to make an objective assessment of my domain and

realize that—compared to Kent's dark greys, teak wood, and warm leathers—my place might best be described as a bake shop display case. Lighter on the theme cakes, but heavy on the meringue. I just hope he likes what's on offer.

"I like it. It's comfy," he says. He settles into the couch a little deeper and Gherkin clings to his lap for dear life as Kent makes his adjustments. That cat isn't going anywhere soon.

"Can I get you something to drink? Tea? Coffee?" I ask.

"I'd love another coffee."

"Okay, be right back."

I head off to the kitchen and fire up the single-serve coffee maker. I watch Kent from behind the marble-topped island as he scratches Gherkin's ear and reaches for a book on old English church interiors from my coffee table.

The sight of him so comfortable in my space both thrills and terrifies me.

I could get used to this.

I shouldn't get used to this.

I head back to the couch with his coffee, set it on the table, and return to my seat.

"You're not having one?" he asks.

"No, I really need a shower, actually."

I look down at my feet, still in my shoes. I unbuckle the straps and pull them off. I stretch out my feet, circle my ankles, and toss the shoes aside. When I look up, Kent is staring, with those delightfully dark eyes.

"I'd intended to hike those shoes over my shoulders, but you had your way with me before I got the chance."

Oh my.

Several parts of my body kick into high alert.

"Are you saying you want a do-over?" I boldly ask.

"Definitely a do-over. Although I'd happily agree to another do-under, truth be told. It was pretty spectacular."

Yep, DEFCON one.

His comment sends heat directly to my crotch.

My cheeks heat as I smile. I'm not exactly shy, but in the light of day I'm a little bashful about this, apparently.

"Up to you—things work well when you decide." He winks.

Dear god, where did this killer wink suddenly come from?

I'm stunned by his candidness. Maybe we both are, because we just smile at each other in silence for a minute. Kent continues to scratch and pet Gherkin.

"Do you mind if I have a quick shower?" I ask, standing.

"Not at all, go ahead. I'll keep Pickle company."

Damn cat.

I head off to my ensuite bathroom, quickly pee and brush my teeth before peeling off Kent's Beck T-shirt and the rest of my clothes. At the last second, something makes me decide to open the bathroom door—just an inch—before stepping into the glass shower stall.

It's a bold move, and I second-guess myself. How will it be interpreted? Will he even notice the invitation? Will he accept?

Underneath the hot water I relax and take a deep breath. I wash my face and shampoo my hair, then turn my back to the stream to rinse, shutting my eyes.

By the time I'm opening them again, I spot movement through the steam-covered glass.

My belly flips nervously.

I see him peel his top up and off, then pull his bottoms down. Efficient and decisive movements.

He opens the shower door and steps inside.

The erection he already sports makes my throat tighten. Butterflies flutter in my stomach. He's done exactly what I'd wished for, but now I'm afraid I've bitten off more than I can chew.

"Is it okay that I've come in?" he asks. Eyes focused, face serious.

"I hoped you would."

My voice is breathy as I take in what's in front of me. Kent's physique does otherworldly things to me, so I have a bit of an out-of-body experience as he approaches to step under the water. His hands rest on my waist as he tilts his head to wet his hair. He looks at me with hair slicked back from the spray. The result astounds me as the gorgeous angles of his face are emphasized and his incredible blue eyes seem to turn even bluer.

I shift back as if to make more room for him, but really I just want to take him all in and watch the water cascade over his tanned skin. Smaller trails find direct routes between muscles, a larger, steady flow washes over his tattoos.

I pull away and coax him to turn towards the spray. This is when his beautiful, bare ass is revealed in all its glory. A rush of water passes over the toned muscle, missing the pronounced hollows along each side. Its firm, curved shape —just a shade lighter than the rest of his skin—calls out to be handled. I'm powerless to the urge to fondle and squeeze.

When I do, he leans back into me. I'm only a few inches shorter, so when he does, my hard nipples graze his strong back and it drives me wild. Before long we're pressing into each other and groaning contentedly.

He breaks the connection first and turns to face me. The moment hangs as we relish the sight of each other—unexpectedly intimate and powerful seconds as we take it all in. He runs his fingers through my short, soaked hair, then takes my face in both hands before delivering a warm, wet kiss that I feel all the way to my toes.

Next it's my turn to face the spray. Kent handles me, shifting me into position in front of him to let the water run over me for a while. His assertiveness causes a pang in my lower belly and a flutter in my stomach. I tilt my head back and close my eyes against the spray while his hands smooth over my hips and stomach. He cups my breasts from his place behind me, moving up and down first, then gently squeezing my nipples between his fingers. I'm incredibly sensitive there, so his pinches make me gasp and moan.

I reach for him, but he grabs my wrists and guides my fingers to the cool, tiled wall in front of me.

Without saying a word, he's telling me to keep them there—*don't touch.*

It's torture.

It's divine.

When he returns to my breasts, I arch back into him. I need to feel as much of him as possible right now. He complies, moving his hard length against my ass.

"Is this what you wanted?" he asks.

"Um...hmm," I barely get out. I'm having trouble with words right now.

His right hand slides down my taught stomach and stops between my legs.

"What about this?" he asks.

"Uhmmm."

Even less decipherable.

He chuckles and nips at the back of my neck.

His fingers move over my slippery skin, honing in on that perfect spot that makes me suck in a breath and bite my bottom lip. My hips move, complementing his hand's decadent dips and soft swirls. Every movement is winding me like a coil.

"Have you thought about me touching you in the shower before?"

His voice is soft in my ear.

"Yes."

He slips a knee between my legs to widen my stance. I press my hands more firmly against the tile and lean into him to increase the pressure. He reads my cues and increases his pace. He grips my hip for better leverage, but the shower's spray hits my chest and it's totally working for me: hard, firm drops landing on sensitized skin.

He grinds his hips against me.

"When? Tell me when."

"After the quarry," I admit.

With his hands on me, I'd divulge just about anything.

Stroke after delicious stroke, sensations build incredibly fast—like cresting a wave.

"I've thought of you so many times." More nips to the back of my neck. "A dozen different ways…long before the quarry." His silky, smooth confession wraps around me, and with it, a rush of pleasure.

I bring a hand down to cover his, making small adjustments: a millimetre shift, a fraction slower.

"*Fuck*," Kent murmurs in my ear. "Always telling me what to do, aren't you?"

What happens next is a detonation—nothing gentle or slow to build. It's surprisingly powerful and intense, and I have trouble keeping my voice contained or my shudders controlled. It's like coming up for air—the first breath when you break the surface.

I ride it out for a few stunned seconds and catch my breath before I turn to face his wicked smile. I run my hands over his goose-bumped skin and pull him back under the water to warm him. I need him close.

"I'm glad I joined you."

He cups the back of my neck with his hand, placing the other on my chest.

"And here you were worried you weren't making good choices," I say, running my fingers down his stomach.

"I think you might be my best choice yet."

My chest tightens as Kent delivers simple kisses like he didn't just break me apart and put me back together.

CHAPTER 21

I'm positively boneless by the time Kent delivers me to my bed. A dozen pink throw pillows scatter to the floor.

He kisses my bare stomach and suddenly I'm as fresh as a daisy, with all the energy in the world. I sit up, attempting to snatch away the towel Kent's wrapped around his waist. It's only right if I reciprocate the orgasmic generosity he's shown me, after all.

I'm such a team player.

Just as I'm about to reach terrycloth, he intervenes playfully, grabbing both my hands. He leans in to kiss me, pushing me back on the bed and holding my arms above my head. My sexual second wind arrives and I'm ready to climb Kent Armstrong like the scaffold on start-up day.

He pulls back, breath laboured, and rests his forehead on mine.

"We need to talk."

Well shit.

I wince. This is the moment I've dreaded, when the bubble bursts and we face the reality of our complicated situation. I just want to luxuriate in our sexual chemistry a little longer—at least for the weekend. Surely that isn't too much to ask.

"Okay…"

Kent rolls away, then settles against my overstuffed white headboard. He runs a hand through his dark brown hair. When it's wet—as it is now—it looks black.

It's almost the same colour as mine. Does that mean our babies would have dark hair too?

Dear lord, woman. Get a grip. It's just sex happening here.

"This isn't just sex that's happening here," Kent says.

Okay, that's weird.

"At least not for me," he adds.

"Okay."

"Is that the only word you've got for me today?" he teases.

"Hold on."

I go to the bathroom and grab my robe before sitting back down on the bed. If I'm going to have this discussion, I need to feel a little less naked.

"I don't think this can be just a one-night thing, do you?" he asks.

"Wait." I put my hand on his delicious forearm, then retrace my steps and return with his Beck T-shirt. "I'm going to need you to put this on if you want me to focus."

He smiles smugly, but complies. Once the T-shirt is on and his smooth, inked chest is no longer calling me like some sort of sexual siren song, I can finally expand my vocabulary.

"What do *you* think this is?" I ask.

I'm so pathetically chicken right now. Unwilling to reveal my hand, I need him to lay his cards down first.

"It's fucking incredible, is what it is."

Unlike my potty mouth, Kent rarely swears. He tends to

reserve it for punctuating specific moments, making strong arguments, or when attending to mind-blowing orgasms—either his or mine. For this reason, his statement lands with a punch to my chest. Miniature fireworks set off in my belly. I want to say *"yes, yes, yes,"* but I'm still too scared.

My phone rings in the other room.

I never get calls. *Who even calls people anymore?* Their timing is absolute shit.

"Sledgehammer ringtone? Nice."

"It seemed appropriate." I give a casual shrug.

Then it dawns on me—my friends are probably worried. I never messaged to tell them I got home because, well, I didn't actually go home.

"Shit, I better get that. Hold on."

I race to my wristlet sitting on the kitchen counter and wrestle with the snap. I miraculously crack the thing open in time to catch the call. It's Greta.

"Hi, G." I'm out of breath and flustered when I finally answer.

"Jesus, woman. Answer your texts. We figured you were dead."

"I'm so sorry. Shit."

"Whatever. Are you okay?"

"Yes, yes. I'm fine. I just haven't been checking my phone."

"Haven't been checking your phone? It's after noon, for Chrissakes…"

There's a long pause.

"Wait a second," she says.

I turn to steal a glimpse of Kent through my bedroom doorway. He's watching me with mild amusement. Gherkin takes the opportunity to jump up and visit with his new BFF.

Brat.

"Soooo…things went well with Kent, did they?" Greta

asks, clearly quite pleased with the situation.

"Um…so…yeah."

I adjust my robe and step out of his line of sight.

"Wait, they're STILL going well? You aren't alone right now, are you?"

"Um, no."

"Did you climb that gorgeous man like the Taylor Building scaffold?"

What is going on today?

"Can I call you later?" I ask.

I walk to my bedroom door and lean against the frame.

"Yeah, fine. Go. I'll tell Sarah we spoke. I'm just glad you're okay."

"I'm so, so sorry. I should've sent a message. How is she feeling today?"

"She's hurting, but she'll make it."

We both chuckle.

We say our goodbyes and I turn to face Kent. He's watching me with a smile on his face and a smug-looking cat on his lap.

"Greta was worried," I explain.

"She knows I'm here, doesn't she?" He scratches Gherkin's chin.

"Is that okay?" I ask.

"Of course. It's not your friends I'm worried about."

I walk over to the bed and sit in front of him. "Who *are* you worried about?"

"Probably the same people you are."

My shoulders fall—deflating—and I look down at my hands. He's right. I've been pushing aside the inconvenient truth of our situation. What's happened here could be a seriously career-limiting move if word gets out. I've always prided myself on having a high level of professionalism, and now I've literally and figuratively slept with the client.

I signed a values and ethics contract—I could lose my job for what I've done.

I rub my face and sigh.

"Don't do that."

I look back up at him and see his sweet smile. He reaches and takes one of my hands.

"Don't own this. We *both* did this," he says.

I squeeze his hand back.

"We can't keep this up—not while I'm working for you," I state.

There it is—decisive and clear. Bandaid officially ripped off. Minimal damage done. Except the pang in my chest tells me otherwise.

Kent's face falls. "That seems a bit extreme, doesn't it?"

He pulls my hand and the rest of my body follows. When Gherkin jumps from his lap, I nestle in against him, resting my head against his warm chest. Kent places his hand on my thigh, smoothing circles over the skin under my short robe. The repetitive movement soothes me but it worsens the ache in my chest.

"I'm not just thinking about me here," I add. "Could you imagine what would happen if the building owner found out their PM is boning the mason?"

That seems to hit home. He retracts his hands and sits up straight. I instantly mourn the loss of our proximity. I want to climb on his lap and beg him to forget the statement.

He runs both hands through his luscious, dark locks and takes a deep breath.

"I'm going to tell you something, and I'm going to need you to *not* freak out."

"Okay..."

I'm worried. *Very* worried. Kind of already freaking out.

"I'm the building owner."

What the...?

Sampson Properties is the owner of the Taylor Building. I googled it when we got the contract and never noticed any familiar names, so this information takes me by complete surprise.

"What the hell, Kent?"

"Correction: Dad is," he clarifies. "But this probably adds even more complexity to the situation."

"Why don't I already know this?"

I'm trying not to panic on the outside as much as I'm panicking on the inside. I'm likely failing miserably.

"Well, less than twenty-four hours ago it was completely irrelevant."

The man makes a good point. Twenty-four hours ago, I hadn't even put on my little black dress yet, let alone removed it.

Another thought occurs to me: his comments earlier about making good choices and feeling pressure to not let his dad down.

Shit. Am I a terrible choice?

I get up and start to pace. "This is not good."

I nervously adjust my robe. I need to think about what this means. I need to breathe.

"You're freaking out," he says.

"Not exactly..."

Yep, totally freaking out.

"Listen to me." Kent stands and approaches me. "This is not a *you* problem, it's a *me* problem. I doubt Dad had 'son boning the mason' on his retirement BINGO card."

Kent chuckles at his own joke.

"How on earth is this not a *me* problem?" I playfully shove him. "And stop making jokes right now."

"My father doesn't even know you, and the likelihood of him finding out is incredibly remote. We just need to keep this quiet until the scaffolding improvements are made and the work is done."

"More than quiet," I reply. "We need to cool things off. Immediately."

"How cool are we talking here?"

"Kent, I could lose my job. You have your own professional credibility on the line. Until this project is done, we need to stop whatever this is." I gesture between us.

"Can we please talk about this?"

"What is there to talk about?"

He takes a step closer, grasping my arms and leaning in to make eye contact. The kind of eye contact that impairs judgment and conjures up fantasy.

"About how incredible *this* is." He leans in closer. "How incredible *we* are."

Dear god. So many feelings.

Most of me wants to stay in our little bubble, to keep this intimacy we've established and protect it. We *are* incredible. I've never felt this kind of chemistry before. But the stakes are too high.

A little voice from deep inside reminds me of another truth: there's an uneven power balance between us. It's a quiet yet persistent alarm bell ringing inside my head.

"Kent, if this is going to work, we need to be equals. Right now, there is no way we're equals."

"I would never take advantage of my position with you."

He holds my arms a little tighter, then surprises me with a hug. All the tension melts away. I feel his hard chest against me; the smell of him fills me up like a sedative, warding off the anxiety I've felt ever since hearing those dreaded words *"we need to talk."*

We stay like this for a moment, as if we know our time is fleeting and something to be treasured.

"Please tell me that once the project wraps, we can revisit this," Kent says, against my ear. Neither of us wants to let go.

"Of course we can," I answer. "We just need to keep our distance 'til then."

"Are we even going to talk?" He pulls away to look at me.

"I don't think we need to completely avoid each other, do we?"

I don't think I could do that, even if I tried.

"Can we message each other?"

"If Larry sees your name on my display he's going to wonder. We'd have zero reason to communicate directly."

"So, then we use other names." Kent steps back, puts his hands on his hips.

"Other names?"

"Yeah, just enter ourselves as contacts with code names or something," he says.

"Code names?"

"Is there an echo in here? Work with me, woman."

"This is a bit much, isn't it?" I ask.

"You can enter me as *Foreman Fuckface.*"

"Oh, then everyone will *definitely* know it's you."

We both snicker.

"But seriously, what name would you give me?" Kent offers a sly grin. "Mr. Long? Mr. Johnson? Maybe just Peter?"

"Dear lord, what is it about men and their need to bring everything back to their dicks?"

I grab a stray pillow and take a frisky swat at him. I'm about to deliver a second but he grabs hold of it, pulling me closer.

Our mouths end up just inches apart. I can feel his breath on my cheek.

"I have a distinct advantage in the name department," he says.

"How's that?"

"I can enter you in my contacts as Bella and no one will ever know it's you."

Hearing him say it again forms a lump in my throat. I'm not sure what it is about hearing him say my name that does these wicked things to me, but it's like an acoustical aphrodisiac that makes my entire body hum.

"I guess you'll just have to wait to see what I come up with," I say.

I inch a little closer, so tempted to close the space. What harm could one more kiss do? One more touch? One more…

"I should go."

His voice breaks my reverie, throwing ice cold water on the moment.

"Okay." I'm barely audible.

He walks to the bathroom. I listen to him dress and I have to stop myself from preventing it. When he steps back into the bedroom, he hands me his phone.

"Put your number in for me, so we can text."

I plug in the numbers and hand it over. We walk together to my apartment door and Gherkin faithfully follows. Kent reaches down for one last affectionate scratch.

"See ya around, Pickle," he says with a bit of a sigh.

"Thanks for bringing me home."

"Yeah, no problem."

Our conversation stalls as we find ourselves staring at each other in the doorway.

"Oh, wait!" I reach over to the table beside my door and grab a lint roller. "Take this—you'll need it," I add with a laugh.

Kent laughs too, then takes it from my hand. I linger, holding it a little longer as he looks at me with those lady-killer eyes.

"Thank you." His words are simple, but filled with so much meaning.

I want to say thank you too.

Thank you for wanting me.

Thank you for lighting me up inside.

Thank you for turning my life upside down.

He leans in one last time and kisses me on the cheek. His nose skims mine as he pulls away, leaving a trail of goosebumps and unfinished business behind.

CHAPTER 22

It takes less than one hour for the first text to arrive.

> Unknown Number: Ok, so what's my handle?

His text is a dopamine hit that puts an instant smile on my face. This kind of clingy behaviour should not be the least bit appealing—anyone else pulling this bold move would be met with radio silence. Kent is a confident bugger who clearly makes his own rules. I want to eat his charm like candy.

Me: Maybe I should enter you in as "Mr. Persistent"

Unknown Number: You say that like it's a bad thing.

Me: Fair point.

I take my phone with me as I nervously putter, putting things away, adjusting pillows, wiping surfaces.

My phone buzzes.

Unknown Number: I would have texted sooner actually, but I've just spent an inordinate amount of time removing cat hair from my clothing.

I laugh out loud, then seek out Gherkin to give him an affectionate scratch. I'm oddly proud of how he's ruffled Kent's buttoned-up exterior.

Me: Sorry.

Unknown Number: No you're not.

Me: 🙂

I pick up Kent's coffee mug and load it in the dishwasher.

Unknown Number: What's up for you tonight?

Me: I think I'll go to the gym. I missed my workout last night.

Unknown Number: You sure about that?

My mouth falls open in surprise. My stomach flips.

Saucy bugger.

I opt to ignore his remark.

Me: I'm in the middle of a 12-week workout plan. I try to stick to it pretty closely.

Unknown Number: Is it leg day?

Me: It's a mix of legs and arms, actually.

Unknown Number: What gym do you go to?

Me: Mr. Muscle on Pine Street.

I head to the bedroom to collect my workout wear but hesitate.

Should I invite him along?

No, Avery. You're cooling things off, remember?

I grab a black tank from my drawer.

Unknown Number: Is that really a gym?

Me: Don't be a snob.

Unknown Number: I'm not a snob! It's a real question, I've never heard of it.

Me: It's not a pretentious gym filled with oiled up dude bros.

Unknown Number: Did you just call me an oiled up dude bro?

Me: It's no frills and has the best staff.

Unknown Number: For the record, you didn't answer my question.

My mind catches on *oiled*…thoughts drift to the yoga studio… to sweaty naked skin…then more sweaty naked skin.

Sweet Jesus.

Me: It also happens to have an amazing smoothie bar next door.

Unknown Number: Yep, totally ignoring me…

I'm chuckling as I enter my bathroom to collect some toiletries, but stop short when I spot it: Kent's Beck T-shirt. It's neatly folded and intentionally left on the counter. There's a small pang in my chest as I run my fingers over the soft fabric. I swear it still feels warm. The temptation to lift and smell it is almost overwhelming, but I resist.

> Me: I'm going now…

> Unknown Number: I guess I'm off to oil up with my fellow dude bros.

> Me: I won't judge.

> Unknown Number: Except you did a little…

God, I love teasing this man.

> Me: Gotta go!

> Unknown Number: Aren't you going to ask me what I'm doing tonight?

> Me: You just told me what you've got planned. Go get oiled, dude bro.

He doesn't text back.

An hour later I'm dressed in my workout wear and my bag is packed. Before I leave, I carefully transfer Kent's shirt to the top of my bedroom dresser. I handle it like an active bomb—as if any sudden movement will set things off. One unintentional shift could release a cloud of musky, manly Kent scent and send me into a sexual tailspin. I need a clear head right now.

A solid workout is all I need.

I don't usually lift on Saturdays, so I'm pleasantly surprised to find Mr. Muscle very quiet when I pass through the turnstile.

"Hey, Sam," I say to the young woman behind the front desk.

"To what do we owe this pleasure?" she replies with a smile.

"I missed my workout yesterday; figured I'd make it up tonight."

"It's nice and quiet, so you'll have the run of the place."

I head to the women's change room and stick my things in a locker, pulling out my Chucks and lacing them up before filling my water bottle at the fountain. I grab my notebook and make my way out to the weight room.

Today's workout is a combination of legs and arms—day five of a five-days-a-week schedule that runs for twelve weeks. I have five exercises on my list, with three or four sets of roughly twelve reps each, depending on the exercise.

I get straight to work on deadlifts, which will target my hamstrings. I load the bar with the appropriate weight, checking last week's notes for reference. I'm about halfway through my second set of reps when I think I spot a familiar-looking figure at the sign-in desk.

No. It can't be.

I shrug it off and complete my set of reps. By the time I take my sixty-second rest break and look back at the entrance, no one is there.

I go back to my bar and finish out my sets, moving on to the next exercise on my list.

I'm starting with good mornings when Sam walks into the weight room with what appears to be a new client. She's pointing out features and equipment as she walks with him on the other side of the room. She bends to tidy a stack of hand weights, and that's when I see him.

Holy shit. It is him.

My stomach pulls a cartwheel. I ignore the tap dancing of my heart.

Kent is dressed in typical athletic wear: a pair of dark grey shorts and a black technical tee. At least this time he's wearing a shirt to cover that lethal chest, but the shorts do nothing to hide his delicious quads and incredible calves.

Without finishing my rep, I set down the bar on the rack with a clang.

When Kent and Sam hear metal hit metal, they turn to face me, then walk over.

"Oh hey, Avery."

The man is pretending he didn't know full well that I was here.

"You two know each other?" Sam asks.

"We sure do. What a coincidence!" he says, laying it on a little thick.

I just stand there looking ridiculous with my eyes wide open.

"Maybe she can show you around?" Sam nods in my direction.

"I'm sure she can."

Even Sam doesn't miss the innuendo, so she flashes me a sly grin and gives me a thumb up behind his back.

We're left alone to stare at each other.

"What are you doing, Kent?" I put my hands on my hips and suppress a smile.

"I heard great things about this place, thought I'd check it out."

"You did, did you?"

"I mean, it certainly generates results."

Kent's eyes trail down my body, over my form-fitting black tank and matching shorts. A line of heat marks the path he takes along my skin. I'm not sure I will ever get used to the feel of this man's eyes on me. I hope I never do.

"I thought we were cooling things down?" I say, perhaps a bit smugly.

I could lift this entire room with the power I feel right now.

"We're just two adults who happened to choose the same gym. It's nothing more than a coincidence." Kent casually peruses the room.

"Well, I'm finishing my workout."

I turn back to the bar and prepare to pick up where I left off.

"I would expect nothing less."

He saunters off to explore the equipment, leaving me to finish out my sets. I try to focus as best I can, but when he glances over, I completely lose count of my reps and end up doing twice the recommended number.

He sets himself up at the squat rack directly across from me. The exercise I'm doing—called "good mornings"—targets the glutes and requires me to rest the bar along my shoulders while I hinge at the hips. Each time I bend forward with a rep, I provide a perfect view of my modest cleavage. I catch Kent stealing a glance and almost laugh out loud when he knocks his head on the rack.

A rack for a rack. Serves you right, buddy.

When I've completed my last set, I replace my bar and feign great interest in my lifting journal, making bogus notes that I will never, ever, look at again. Meanwhile, Kent is finally setting himself up to do his first squat. I can't resist a side-eye glance over at his station.

I watch him set up his foot positioning. It's all wrong—his feet are too close together. He needs to widen his stance.

Whatever, who cares.

I move to my next station to set up for leg extensions, but steal another look. He's got the bar in the correct position, but his back is rounded instead of straight.

No, no, no. He's going to kill his back.

He completes one rep and is about to do another before I decide I can't take it anymore. I march over to intervene.

"Engage your core—you're going to kill your back."

Kent sets the bar on the rack and wipes his hands on his shorts.

"Oh, really?"

I'm not sure of his tone, exactly.

"You need to widen your stance too. Your feet should be shoulder-width apart."

"Shoulder-width stance. Engage my core. Got it," he says.

Is he toying with me?

"Try it again," I suggest.

He walks to the rack and sets up his stance under the bar, lifting to take the weight on his shoulders. He performs the squat flawlessly, core effortlessly engaged and with perfect posture.

"Is that better?" he asks, continuing his reps in front of me.

I enjoy the beautiful view of flexing muscles and physical exertion. He lets out a small grunt with the last rep of his set, triggering several clenches of my own. I wipe a bead of sweat from my brow.

He replaces the bar on the rack and flashes a pleased smile that's all white teeth, tanned skin, and dimple. That's when I realize I've been duped.

I fold my arms, eyes narrowing with suspicion.

"You played me, didn't you?"

"I clearly have no idea what I'm doing. Maybe we need to work out together?"

The expression on his face is an unprecedented mix of innocence and seduction.

"I wouldn't want to pull any muscles," he adds, stepping closer. At this distance I can smell his warm body—a fusion of pheromones and fragrance that makes me take a deeper breath.

"You are incorrigible."

"Big word. Too big for an oiled up dude bro like myself."

A laugh escapes me.

"Fine, but I'm running the show here."

"I'm learning that things work well for us when you're in charge." His eyes turn dark.

Oh lord, help me.

I insist on finishing out my day's exercise plan, which we do together. When we've completed leg extensions, inclined dumbbell curls, and inclined skullcrushers, I bring Kent back to finish out the deadlifts and good mornings I'd started with to complete his workout.

When we work side by side as I demonstrate a deadlift, I get a calm sense of rightness. It's the same feeling I got when we scratched Gherkin together on my couch, or when we've laughed together at a joke. It warms me up inside.

"Do you want to do any cardio?" I ask when we're done, taking a generous drink from my water bottle.

"What do you usually do?"

"About thirty minutes on the treadmill, but we don't have to."

"Don't cut any corners on my account."

"I need to change my shoes." I look down at my Chucks.

"What's with the Converse?" he asks.

"They're the best for lifting—inexpensive and lots of good contact with the floor."

"I'll get started." Kent gestures to the treadmills lined up against the window.

I head back to my locker, stash my notebook, and switch out my shoes for runners. By the time I'm back, Kent is jogging on one of the machines. It's like goddamn poetry in motion watching his body move. I'm not sure how I never noticed in all those months we worked together how fit the man is. I can't *not* see it now.

I'm refilling my bottle at the fountain when Sam approaches me.

"This is new." Sam grins and raises a brow.

I nonchalantly take a sip of water. "What is?"

"I don't think I've ever seen you pair up here before."

I feign indifference. "Really?"

"Really."

"Well…he needed some help."

We both glance over at Kent on the treadmill, witness the precision of his gait, the true athleticism of his movements.

"Yes, clearly he's struggling," she says with a wink before returning to her station.

I walk over to join him, dropping my bottle in the neighbouring machine's cup holder. Kent glances over mid-stride.

"So, obviously you work out," I state, firing up the machine to get started.

"What are you trying to say, exactly?" He flashes me a smile.

"You're technically accurate and you have cardiovascular fitness."

"Stop it with the pick-up lines, woman."

"Seriously though, where do you normally work out?"

"There's a gym near my place. It's pretty trendy, but convenient." He sounds apologetic.

I fall into an easy jog on my treadmill as I think about all the tanned and sculpted bodies he likely sees on a weekly basis. I feel an unexpected twinge of jealousy, but it quickly passes when I catch Kent attempt a casual peek at my ass and he trips over his feet.

I ponder my next move and decide to give the man a show – I set my machine to fartlek training and watch him try to keep up.

Thirty minutes later we're covered in sweat and completely spent. Our legs are like jelly as we reacclimatize to stationary mode. I take a long drink of water and place a hand on one hip. He mirrors my posture, still catching his breath.

"I know I'm using your pick-up line, but I can't help but notice your technical accuracy and cardiovascular fitness." Kent takes a long drink from his own bottle.

I laugh between ragged breaths.

"Thanks."

Mission accomplished.

"I heard there's a smoothie bar next door. Wanna go?" he asks.

"Sure, but I need to shower first."

"Meet me out front in twenty."

I quickly shower, change, and dry my hair (one of the benefits of keeping it short) but Kent still beats me to the front desk. By the time I get there, he's leaning coolly against the counter in a fresh pair of relaxed shorts and a golf shirt, hair still damp from the shower. He's chatting with Sam, who's clearly captivated by the conversation.

Who can blame her?

Kent spots me and smiles. "Ready?"

"I'm telling you, try the Tropical Oatmeal; you won't be disappointed," Sam says.

"Thanks for the suggestion." He grabs his bag and heads to the door.

"Have fun," Sam adds quietly, just for me to hear.

We pop into the smoothie bar and grab our drinks. I get my usual strawberry and banana, and Kent selects some ridiculous green concoction with kale and extra protein. I'm hoping it's because he's feeling particularly depleted after I kicked his ass on the treadmill.

We decide to take our smoothies outside to the summer air. It's one of those beautiful summer evenings where the air is still and warm, but the humidity isn't oppressive. The night is thick with perfume from the flowering shrubs lining the sidewalk. We find a bench and take a seat, dropping our bags on the ground beside us.

"Sam is going to be very upset you didn't get the Tropical Oatmeal, Kent," I tease.

"Next time."

"There's going to be a next time?"

"Oh, hell yes. I've found a great new gym that comes with a personal trainer. Did I mention there's a smoothie bar next door?"

"Probably costs a fraction of the one you're already going to."

"Probably." Kent takes a long pull of sludgy green liquid from his straw.

"That does not look the least bit appealing," I note.

"Hey, I won't judge your pet names if you don't judge my smoothie choices."

His Gherkin reference brings me right back to my apartment, to conversations about cooling off and making good choices. I quietly fiddle with my straw.

Kent clears his throat. "Did I say something wrong?"

"Just thinking about our conversation earlier, about your dad owning the building."

Kent leans back and crosses a foot over his opposite knee. I try not to notice how it emphasizes his quad muscles.

"I'm sorry about that. I try to keep it quiet so people don't act weird with me."

"I'm not mad, just curious. Sampson Properties owns several buildings, right?"

"Yes, and a few of them are classified as heritage properties. Dad wants me to manage any of the heritage rehab projects."

"Makes sense."

"Sampson was my mother's family name. The company is named after her."

"Wow. That's lovely. But seems awfully…heavy—if that's the right word?"

"I certainly feel the weight, yes." Kent looks down at his drink, then takes another sip.

"Do I know any of the other Sampson-owned buildings?"

"Well, you know mine."

"I'm sorry, *mine*?"

"Where I live."

"Of course! That's why you could make it exactly how you wanted it. I don't know why I didn't put that together."

Kent smiles, but doesn't say much. He seems shy about it. I decide to change the subject.

"I still can't believe you came to the gym tonight." I shake my head.

"For the record, you never asked me what I was doing," he notes, turning to face me.

"What if I'd said I was doing something ridiculous or dangerous, like naked skydiving? Would you have joined me then?"

"Anything but hot yoga. Watching you do that nearly killed me last time."

A loud laugh spills out of me and cover my mouth to contain it.

"What? No...at least I had a top on," I argue, spinning in my seat to look at him.

"I would never call that stringy, strappy contraption a top," he states with a smile.

"I was behind you. You didn't have to watch my every move."

"Are you telling me you watched *my* every move?" Kent leans in closer.

"This was very distracting." I gesture to his general chest area.

Kent chuckles, clearly pleased with my confession.

The moment hangs as we take each other in. I've been avoiding looking directly at him all night because of our deal. The shape of his jaw or the dimple in his cheek have been no-go zones, to keep me on my best behaviour and my priorities clear. But now that we're turned to face each other—inches from touching—I feel his magnetic pull. It's that black hole attraction I've been feeling ever since the wedding.

"So, what are you doing tomorrow?" Kent asks, shifting closer.

It comes out monotone, like I'm in a trance. I'm practically mesmerized by his beauty. "Lunch with parents... noon...Urban Roasters."

I'm leaving an opening—like a shower door—hoping he might join.

Kent's arm drapes across the back of the bench; I feel the warmth of him alongside me. From my peripheral vision I see his fingers reach to touch me and I lean into it, instinctively.

"Holy shit—hi, guys!"

We spring to opposite ends of the bench before we've even discerned who's spoken. Once maximum distance is achieved, I look in the direction of the voice. It's Reid, from work.

Remain calm.

"Hey Reid, how's it going?" Kent says, set to max low-key.

Kent is doing a much better job of remaining calm than I am.

"What are you guys doing here?" Reid asks.

"Avery and I just ran into each other at the gym," Kent explains, gesturing casually in my direction, then to our bags.

"Small world, isn't it?" Reid says.

Way, way too small.

"What brings you to this neck of the woods, Reid?" My face is impassive, but my heart might escape my chest.

"My girlfriend had a hankering for some pizza from that wood oven place up the street, so I'm just picking it up." He gestures up the road.

"Oh, nice. Speaking of picking things up," Kent stands and grabs his gym bag, "I have an errand to get to myself, so I better run."

"Goodnight, Reid." He nods in his direction, then turns to me. "Avery." He studies me intensely for a moment, a subtle look of regret on his face. It's gone before Reid can spot it, and then so is he—headed down the sidewalk before I can offer a reply.

"Later, Avery!" Reid shouts over his shoulder as he heads in the opposite direction.

I watch Kent turn down a side street, disappearing into the darkness.

By the time I get home, I'm shaken by the near-miss with my colleague, but surprised to find I'm more upset that Kent and I didn't get a proper goodbye. There's a void left in the wake of his hasty departure that leaves me a little sad.

In the end, I cave like a house of cards: I strip myself naked and slip on his T-shirt. I fall asleep wrapped up in his scent, replaying dozens of shared kisses, but longing for the one I didn't get.

CHAPTER 23

It's risky. It's dangerous. It's a terrible idea.

I repeat this mantra to myself, hoping it finally sinks in.

Last night I almost got caught kissing the client on a public bench, and somehow the risk of losing my job still wasn't enough to throw ice water over the errant flames. Instead, I wake up broody and pining, wishing he would text me.

But he doesn't.

So I don't either.

Looks like being spotted by Reid was enough to shake some sense into one of us.

Pushing aside my unprecedented neediness, I prep for my lunch date with Mom and Dad and keep myself busy. Dressing for Sunday lunch, I choose a yellow sundress and white sneakers. I decide to wear makeup, only because it will keep my hands and mind occupied for a few extra minutes.

At noon, I pull open the door to Urban Roasters and head to our usual table. A few minutes later, I spot Mom and Dad in the storefront window holding hands.

They're always so sweet.

We order our food and make conversation, but I'm completely distracted; I have to ask both parents to repeat themselves on more than one occasion. I realize—mid meal—I've unwittingly selected the chair opposite the door when I find myself doing double-takes each time a dark-haired man walks in. It would seem that my subconscious has already become accustomed to his charming persistence.

It's ridiculous. It's silly to think he'll show. The run-in with Reid was probably enough to keep him away—maybe even for good.

My mother is no fool, so after watching me barely touch lunch and having to get my attention a handful of times, she knows something is up. Aside from several questioning looks, Mom manages to hold back on her inquisition until the plates are cleared. As the server takes the last dish, she makes her move.

"Daniel, I'd really like some scones for my book club meeting this afternoon."

"That's a good idea." Dad drinks from his coffee cup, not taking the bait.

"Would you mind grabbing a dozen from the takeout counter?"

"Now?" He looks over at the take-away line that extends all the way to the entrance.

"Please?" She flashes him a winning smile.

Dad mutters to himself but dutifully stands to join the line. He's barely left the table when she pounces.

"I'm going to cut to the chase...what's going on?"

I'm about to say *nothing,* but she raises a pre-emptive hand.

"Don't say *nothing.* You've been acting weird all through lunch. Why are you watching the door?"

I sit back in my chair and sigh.

"I have no idea. It's pointless after what happened last night."

"Well, this sounds interesting." Mom takes a sip from her teacup.

It's obvious I need to talk to someone about my situation, and my options are limited. At least mom is removed enough from the key players to provide objective advice. Sarah is too closely connected to Kent through Tom, and Greta will just tell me what she thinks I want to hear.

This calls for motherly advice, and maybe some of her tough love, so I proceed.

"Mom, have you ever had a workplace romance?"

"What are we classifying as *romance*?"

"Exactly what it sounds like," I say, a bit confused.

"You need to be specific…is it hanky panky or an actual relationship?"

"For the love of god, Mom, did you really just say *hanky panky*?" I laugh, which feels like such a relief.

"It makes a difference," Mom states.

"How?"

"If it means nothing and you're risking your professional reputation for a roll in the sack, then it's silly. But if there's more potential, there's nothing silly about it."

I'm surprised by my mother's assessment. I figured a woman of Mom's experience and professional status would be quick to dismiss any romance that jeopardizes career goals. I urge her to elaborate.

"I will make this quick, in light of our time constraints, but when I worked for my first engineering firm out of college, I met a very handsome and charismatic man who ended up reporting to me due to my seniority at the time."

I lean in to hear my mother's story. "I'm intrigued. Tell me more."

"He was charming as hell…" She looks off a bit dreamily, remembering. "We had a lot of chemistry. There may have been a copy room incident…" She takes another drink of her tea, suppressing a smile.

"Oh my god!" I giggle, a little shocked by her admission. "What ever happened to him?"

"He's waiting in line for scones."

The air thins, the room stills, my jaw drops.

"Why didn't I know this?" I ask, absolutely shocked.

"When and why would I have told you?"

The woman has a point. My parents have a right to their own private backstory.

"How did you get from the copy room to married? You're being intentionally cryptic. I need details."

"Well, we realized two things. One: we needed to remain professional and cut the office antics. Two: it was more than just physical. So we talked to our direct supervisors and had him removed from my supervision. Not long after that, I got a better job offer and that permanently solved our problem."

Settling back in my chair, I think for a moment, wondering how this information applies to my own situation. I take a look over at Dad, still waiting patiently in line as the woman three customers ahead dawdles over pastry choices.

The man is a saint.

"Okay, Bella. Your turn."

I think about what I should tell her, and decide to be selective.

"I've recently become involved with someone from work."

"Does he report to you?" she asks.

"No."

"Good. Do you report to him?"

"Not exactly, but there is an uneven power dynamic, for sure, which tilts in his favour."

"Okay…" She looks thoughtfully. "Has any funny business happened at work?"

"God, Mom—no."

From *hanky panky* to *funny business*. What a day.

"I wouldn't judge you if it did. These things happen, you know."

I'm blown away by this new side of my mother. My fondness for the woman has only deepened today.

"We were out last night and someone else from work saw us," I explain. "We claimed we'd only run into each other. It was terrible. He ran off as fast as he could."

"Wait, isn't this job almost done? Do your circumstances change when you move on from this building?"

"Yes, everything changes."

Please god.

"Then just keep things on the downlow," Mom suggests.

I find it immensely charming that my mother uses the term *downlow*.

"In theory, this project should be finished in a couple weeks," I explain.

"Then just keep a lid on things and remain professional at work. It's only a matter of days—this isn't rocket science, hon." Mom punctuates the sentence with a generous swig from her cup.

Her words have more weight than they would for most, given that my mother *is* in fact a rocket scientist. Well, more specifically, an aerospace engineer.

Dad finally makes it through the queue and heads to the cash register with his wallet open. Mom leans in to say more.

"If this is something you want, you shouldn't feel guilty about going after it. Generations of women have put limitations on themselves for all sorts of wrong reasons." She points a finger in my direction. "You've done it too. I've seen you talk yourself out of doing things because you hold yourself to some unfair moral standard." She pauses for a beat. "Professional and personal success aren't mutually exclusive. You deserve to be happy, Bella. But be smart about it. As long as the two of you respect each other, everything will work out in the end."

Moms have a unique way of cutting through the crap and providing clarity even in the most challenging circumstances. I want to stand and hug her, but I settle for squeezing her hand.

"Who needs to respect each other?" Dad asks as he approaches the table.

"We're just talking about someone from work," I reply.

"Is it that PM? That guy still riding you?"

What an unfortunate choice of words.

Mom catches my pink cheeks but holds back her smile. She finishes her last swallow of tea with a raised brow. If she didn't already know it's Kent, she certainly does now.

"Let's head home; I have to tidy before the gang comes over." Mom stands, grabbing her purse and sweater.

"I paid up at the register. We're good to go."

"Thanks for lunch, Dad." I collect my things and stand.

Mom pauses, attention on the door.

"Well, well. Look who's here," she says quietly.

I follow her gaze to the entrance.

My heart starts to dance.

I'm an odd mix of fear and felicity as he walks over to join us. We look at each other briefly and smile.

"Mom, Dad, you remember Kent."

"We certainly do," Dad says. I'm a little worried what he might say next, but he seems to be exercising some restraint.

"Kent, you remember my parents from the wedding? Victoria and Daniel."

"Yes, nice to see you again." He scratches the back of his head.

Mom examines him carefully, mouth turned up in a knowing smirk. "Pleasure to see you. Unfortunately, we need to run." She flashes a silent message to her husband.

"Yes, we do," Dad agrees, "Go easy on our girl, Kent. The Taylor Building is lucky to have her."

Cringe.

"Oh dear, if you think Bella wants anyone to go easy on her, you really haven't been paying attention," Mom mutters to Dad as she loops her arm through his and drags him toward the exit. She glances back at me and winks. Dad looks confused.

I turn back to Kent. I'm not sure what to say, so I decide to keep up the ruse and pretend I haven't wished upon every single door jingle that it would be him walking in.

"What are you doing here?"

He sinks his hands in his pockets in a gesture of acquiescence. "Come on, you knew I'd show."

My chest tightens.

His face is serious and I'm having difficulty interpreting his emotions. It's putting me off my game. I can't even throw out a clever retort, which is my go-to coping mechanism.

"Can we walk?" Kent gestures to the door.

"Yeah, sure."

"Just let me grab a coffee."

I use these moments to step outside and compose myself, taking several deep breaths.

This is it.

It's the verdict I feared was coming: he's going to cut through all the bullshit and tell me he's not just cooling things down, he's putting us on ice—indefinitely.

By the time he meets me outside, I've worked out an exit strategy, a way to save face and back away gracefully.

I speak before he can get a word out. "I know what you're thinking. Reid was a wake-up call, and we can't let that happen again."

"I hated that." Kent takes a sip from his paper cup.

"I know. It never should have come to that."

"Agreed."

My stomach drops, anticipating what's coming next. My body heats nervously. I turn to collect my thoughts and lead us to a shaded spot under a tree.

"I felt like a bloody teenager last night. I'm a grown man, for Christ's sake."

Yes, you certainly are.

He scratches the back of his head with a contemplative look on his face.

"How I reacted—" he begins.

I interrupt. "You reacted how anyone would've under those circumstances."

I'm giving him his out: absolving him of responsibility and untangling anything that might be keeping him twisted up with me. I can at least make this easy for both of us.

"I don't want to have to run with my tail between my legs every time I get caught kissing the girl," he states.

Here it is. The death blow. I brace myself for what's coming.

"I want to touch and kiss you any way I choose—any way you ask."

Wait, what?

"Bottling this up so we're ready to burst every time we're together in public isn't the answer. We need to be free to do what we want—be whatever we want—behind closed doors and under wraps so we aren't taking chances like we did last night."

This is not the direction I thought things were headed.

I turn and lead us farther up the sidewalk, away from

the few people who are congregating by the cafe entrance. We stop under another tree.

"I can see the confusion on your face, Bella. I know you have your concerns. I know you're worried about *power dynamics* and some sort of perceived inequality between us, but can't you see you've got me on my knees? If anyone has the upper hand here..."

His sentence trails off. He runs a hand through his hair and looks down at his feet. I'm surprised by the vulnerability he's showing me and it's rendering me speechless. My belly flutters. I'm managing to keep them contained, but a mix of powerful emotions threatens to spill over my edges.

"I thought we were cooling things off?" My words are barely audible. Empty, contrived words that feel like someone else is saying them.

Kent steps closer, feet firmly planted, posture straight.

"I can keep this a secret, but I want you to know—for the record—that I have no interest in cooling anything off between us."

Sweat drips down my back.

I'm stunned by the bluntness of his words and floored by the conviction behind them. A subtle buzz of nervous excitement starts to build inside me.

"I will wait as long as I have to, as long as it takes for you to be comfortable. But no, I don't want to *cool things off*. I want us to melt every surface of that fluffy white apartment of yours, and set fire to my fucking teak."

His eyes linger on my lips, and then meet mine. The intensity of his gaze and the words he's just spoken sucks the air from my lungs.

He slips his sunglasses on like a fucking movie star and turns to leave.

"Call me when you're ready."

He slips a hand in his shorts pocket and determinedly

walks away. Instinctively I take a step to follow him, but I stop myself short.

I need to be sure.

The joy I feel from hearing what he's said has thrown me off kilter.

It occurs to me for the first time that I'm not only risking my job with Kent, but I'm risking my heart too. Maybe that's the scarier thing to lose.

CHAPTER 24

 Monday morning, we're all summoned to the site trailer for a meeting. Larry has an update on the scaffolding situation and a work completion plan to share with the team. It's the first time Kent and I will be together in a work setting since, well, being together in a non-work setting.

I've spent a fair part of my Sunday night running through everything in my head.

There's no question in my mind what I *want* to do.

"I want to touch and kiss you any way I choose—any way you ask."

Fuck, yes.

But I need to think about what I *should* do.

"You deserve to be happy, Bella. But be smart about it."

It's easy to act impulsively when immersed in a fog of lust. It's difficult to act sensibly when a man tells you he wants to *"melt every surface"* of your apartment with you.

Sweet Jesus.

By the time I'm treading up the stairs to the site trailer, I've decided that I'll heed my mother's advice and be both smart and careful. I will wait this project out before revisiting my relationship with Kent. It's the sensible thing to do.

What's a couple of weeks?

I arrive a few minutes early, coffee in hand and armed with a dogged determination to put my professional and personal lives back in their well-established and separate compartments.

I absolutely can do this.

I push open the trailer door and bravely step inside to find Kent.

Alone.

I freeze.

He's seated at the meeting table, thumbing away at something on his phone. The two of us alone together in the trailer has literally never happened before.

Of course it would happen today.

He looks up and shares my surprise.

"Hi." His face softens into a gentle smile.

My resolve pops like a helium balloon.

"Hi."

My voice is soft and weak. Definitely not professional me—not assured and confident. I clear my throat and try again.

"I mean, hello." I stand up straighter, then grab a seat opposite him and settle in, eyes avoiding his general direction.

We're spared from further awkward silence when several others arrive. I open my notebook and start to doodle in the margins, sipping too generously from my fresh cup of coffee and burning my mouth in the process.

Reid and Luke talk about weekend projects and pull out their phones to share photos. The thing about working with handy mason types is that everyone always has a household project on the go. Sometimes we even chip in time on each other's renovations to help out.

"So, we've put in a watertight system, redone the tiles, installed multiple heads. It's going to be awesome," Luke explains to Reid, who leans in to examine the photos.

"That's gonna look amazing, man. Can't wait to redo ours. There's nothing like a good shower."

That comment gets our attention.

I reflexively sit up straighter, eyes shooting over to Kent. He's already looking at me, clearly having heard the comment. He redirects his gaze to his phone and covers his smile with a scratch to his upper lip.

"Good pressure?" Reid asks.

"*Really* good pressure," Luke replies.

I swallow back another large gulp of volcanic coffee and wince.

"But it's not just about the pressure. The position of the heads—"

"OH MY GOD, LUKE. Do we really need to hear all about your fucking plumbing?" I exclaim.

"Holy shit, Avery. Why are you so cranky this morning?" Reid asks.

"What's gotten into you?" Luke adds.

"Yeah, Avery, what's gotten into you?" Kent repeats from across the table, his mouth turned up on one side.

I fire a glare in his direction, and he bites back the smile on his lips.

I shift in my seat and desperately try to avoid looking at him.

I definitely try to avoid thinking about showers.

Or pressure.

Or positions.

Fuck.

He clears his throat, and I glance up in a moment of weakness. He makes adjustments in his seat, then casually crosses a foot over one knee. That's when I spot it: one single rogue Gherkin hair at the bottom of his pant leg.

The intimacy of a single cat hair causes a pang in my chest.

I sigh in resignation.

This is not going according to plan.

Thankfully, the arrival of our other team members serves as a distraction. Larry shows up a few minutes later, stomping on the hollow floor and dropping his messenger bag loudly on the conference table.

"Hey, everyone." Larry sets up his laptop and connects to a large monitor that's installed on the wall. "Sorry I'm late."

"All good, Larry," Kent replies.

"I've got some updates on the scaffolding situation and a revised timeline to share with the group."

Larry fires up a slide deck that shows a photograph of one steel part of mysterious provenance.

"This single part is the root of our challenge right now." He gestures to the monitor and slides a hand in the pocket of his distressed jeans. "Thanks to supply chain issues, we're having some difficulty procuring this thing, and it's wreaking havoc on our project schedule."

"How much havoc are we talking?" I ask.

Please say little havoc. Baby havoc.

"Unclear at this point, but my parts guy is doing his best to sort it out."

"Are we talking days here or weeks?" Kent asks.

"My rep in TechScaff's parts division—Rod Johnson— has been getting creative."

Rod Fucking Johnson?

A squeak of a laugh escapes me, and I try to mask it with a cough. I avoid looking in Kent's direction, knowing full well that it would send me into fits.

Damn you, Kent, and your clever pseudonym suggestions.

"Yes, yes…his name is *very* funny," Larry comments with an exaggerated eye roll. "Come on, Avery."

"No, no, it's not that!" I insist. My face grows hot with embarrassment.

But what else can I possibly tell them?

"I expect better of you than that." Larry shakes his head and turns back to the monitor. "Anyhow, moving on."

Great. Now the entire team thinks I have the maturity of a twelve-year-old.

Yet another sigh in resignation.

Larry is discussing the pros and cons of working with said Mr. Johnson and the TechScaff crowd when my phone buzzes. I turn it over and notice a new message.

> Unknown Number: Good thing you didn't use that name—you'd have even more explaining to do.

I sit up straighter and glance at Kent. He's still looking at his phone. I mask my grin with another sip of coffee; Kent finds something incredibly fascinating to read in his notebook.

I return my attention to Larry.

"So, given the supply chain issues and expected delays, I'm going to walk us through our likely scenario." Larry fiddles with his cursor. "To manage your expectations, we're likely weeks out on the completion date."

Kent and I immediately look at each other in abject horror.

"Okay, before you say anything, I can see it on your faces." Larry holds his hands up in capitulation. "I know we're all sick of each other and want to move on. We'll do everything we can to expedite."

Oh, we're wanting to move on, alright… but not at all for the reason he assumes.

Weeks? Weeks?

"Shit, Larry. This is ridiculous," I say.

"Let's just stay calm. First, let's review the six-week look-ahead that I've prepared for today." He flips to a Gantt chart that confirms our worst nightmare.

"Six weeks?" I mutter under my breath.

No, no, no…

I glance at Kent. His expression of dread has been replaced by one of defeat.

We can't wait six weeks.

Six torturous weeks.

My stomach turns. My chest aches. The walls of the small trailer seem to close in.

The rest of Larry's presentation passes in a blur. When he finally finishes, the group scatters. Kent lingers at the conference table, but I slip out the trailer door. I need air and space and time to figure out plan B.

CHAPTER 25

Four restless nights.
Four solo workouts.
Half a dozen revisited conversations.
Multiple second-guesses.
Zero text messages.
Still no plan B.

grab my gym bag and head to Mr. Muscle for a lonely Friday night workout. Something en route makes me turn right instead of left, and before I've consciously thought about things, I'm standing on the sidewalk outside of Kent's apartment.

What I'm doing here, I'm not exactly sure. But I know I can't spend one more night tossing and turning without having a conversation with him about our situation. If I'm being honest with myself, maybe it's also time to acknowledge the void he seems to leave every time he walks away.

Fragments of conversations float in my head.

"…if there's more potential, there's nothing silly about it."
"Professional and personal success aren't mutually exclusive."
"This isn't just sex that's happening here."
"Call me when you're ready."

Before I lose my nerve, I slip inside the vestibule and find a large vintage buzzer panel to my left. After a quick search of the name plates, I find "Armstrong" at the very bottom. I take a deep breath and press the button.

There's a long pause.

The intercom crackles, and he speaks.

"Hello?"

I hesitate. I'm so happy to hear his voice, so glad he's home, but I need to dig deep to find the courage to take the next step.

"It's Bella."

There's another long pause. The air seems to still in anticipation.

"Come on up. Top floor, if you don't remember." His tone is impassive.

How on earth could I forget?

A buzzer sounds and the door clicks to allow my entry.

I find my way to the elevator, remembering wet floors and rushed steps the last time I entered these halls. The ride up is spent taking deep breaths and administering a pep talk. By the time the metal doors open, Kent is already waiting at his apartment door.

I want to run to him like the leading lady in my own black-and-white movie. He certainly looks the part: grey T-shirt, worn jeans, tanned bare feet. He is most definitely leading man material. But his body language is off—he's standing in a defensive pose.

I decide to keep things light.

"Hey, bet you're surprised to see me."

He holds the door open and allows me inside, avoiding my eyes before heading to his kitchen.

"You're right. I didn't think I'd see you for at least another six weeks."

He returns to the counter, pulling a knife from the block.

"If at all…" he adds.

He starts chopping vegetables.

I recognize this version of Kent from our early days on the scaffold: abrupt, inflexible, dismissive. I resist the urge to go back to my own default settings.

"You're angry with me?" I ask.

The knife hesitates, hangs in the air.

He continues.

Chop, chop, chop.

"I'm not angry," he says, but his tone is stiff and emotionless.

"You don't exactly seem happy to see me."

Silence.

"Maybe I should just go." I turn toward the door.

"Stop. Wait." He puts the knife down loudly on the counter and rounds the island.

I face him, hands on my hips.

"I'm frustrated." He sighs loudly. "I laid all my cards on the table, and I got nothing back."

"*You* walked away—I didn't. You didn't even give me a chance to reply."

"The radio silence I've had these last few days said enough." He scratches the back of his head. One of his nervous habits I've only started to learn.

"Don't you dare. You told me you'd wait. *As long as it took,* you said." I take a step closer.

"I'm only human, alright?" He takes a deep breath. "Pride and all."

He leans against the kitchen island, folding his arms protectively.

"Look, I didn't come here for a fight." I mirror his defensive position.

"What *did* you come here for tonight, Bella?" His words are laced with vulnerability, like he's bracing for heartbreak.

"I just came...I came to..." My words are trapped on my tongue.

I wanted desperately to see you.

I look at his beautiful face, his furrowed brow, his broad shoulders, how his shirt sleeves strain over his folded arms. My hands squeeze tight, wanting to touch him.

Kent takes one more unguarded glance at me and I remember...

"Can't you see you've got me on my knees?"

It cracks through my indecision.

I close the distance in three steps and take his face in my hands, planting a hard kiss.

It's a certain kiss. A firm kiss. Nothing unsure about it.

He unfolds and wraps himself around me, one hand bracing the back of my head, fingers grasping the short hairs at the nape of my neck. The other spreads across the middle of my back and pulls me in.

Suddenly everything is clear and all the bullshit fades away. Every stroke of my tongue is a message delivered with urgent and immediate effect.

I need you, I want you, don't walk away.

We pull apart, short of breath, and our foreheads rest against each other.

"Are you sure?" he asks.

I nod. "I can't wait. I don't want to wait."

My words flip a switch, drawing us back together. We're a messy tangle of hands and lips and desperate need.

Kent pulls away and takes a breath.

"I'm sorry I was angry. I had no right to be."

I flash back to a dozen heated moments on the scaffold, the rush of the arguments, the exhilaration of the fight. The flow of blood to my cheeks right now feels as hot as they always have in the middle of our verbal sparring matches. A flicker of unexpected fire ignites in me.

"I think I like making you angry."

I'm as surprised by the admission as Kent is.

His eyes turn dark. My confession leads to fervent kisses: hard lips and biting teeth. I pull away long enough to tug off his shirt. I run my hands down his smooth, tattooed chest. I've craved this for days. I slide my hands along his strong pectorals as I kiss him again.

He steers me toward his couch, never breaking contact with my lips, holding my face in his hands. Just before we get to the butterscotch leather, he steps back and in one motion pulls the loose-fitting sundress I'm wearing up and over my head, tossing it aside. I kick off my sandals, leaving me standing in just a pair of pink polka dot boy-shorts.

"Polka dots? Sweet Jesus, woman, you're going to be the death of me."

I smile and go back to kissing him. Reaching down, I blindly work at his belt, but stumble with the buckle. I try again without any luck.

"Take your pants off," I command.

"I'm under no misconception that I'm in control here," he begins, opening his belt buckle, "but it might be nice if you occasionally let me take charge. Who knows—you might even like it."

"Stop talking," I tease.

I move in for another enthusiastic kiss. He pulls away.

"See, right there…" He's having a hard time focussing as my hands wander and find his incredible ass. "Maybe you *want* me to do the talking."

He grinds his hips against me, sending new warmth to my thighs.

"Upstairs," I order. I'm doing it on purpose now.

"No, no…I'm taking the lead this time…and I will not be rushed."

His words cause a flutter in my stomach.

"Next you'll be pulling out the clipboard and orange highlighter."

"You mean this orange highlighter?" He pulls it from his back pocket and holds it out in front of me, his pants finally undone.

There's a devilish look in his eyes.

He walks me backwards toward the couch and gently coaxes me to sit, leaning me into the cushions. He settles in to kneel between my legs.

He takes the highlighter, lid on, and lazily traces it up one arm, across my collar bones and down the other. The feel of the hard plastic leaves goosebumps on my skin. My chest rises and falls. He looks at me intensely before drawing the highlighter back up my arm and slowly— torturously—circling each nipple.

I draw in a ragged breath and shift my hips instinctively.

"Marking all of my mistakes?" I ask nervously, my nakedness suddenly feeling vulnerable.

"Annotating the best parts." He smiles.

He leans to replicate the movement with his tongue, taking each nipple in his mouth. My head falls back to rest against the cool leather. I arch to give him better access, to show him not to stop.

"So good," I whisper.

He moves quicker, harder, and heat builds between my

legs. I move my hips in response, trying to make contact with him. I might lose my mind soon if he doesn't touch me there.

Kent pulls away and looks down at my hips. He takes his orange highlighter and makes one light sweep over the outside of my shorts, grazing the fabric along my crotch. Heat turns to raw ache with the unhurried motion. I suck in a breath.

It's a love-hate relationship I have with that highlighter now.

Just as I'm developing a fondness for it, he tosses the instrument aside and grabs the waistband of my underwear.

"Can I take these off?"

I love that he's being so respectful, but in this moment I want him to tear them to shreds. I raise my hips off the couch to help, and Kent slides the polka dot fabric off the rest of the way.

He settles between my legs and pulls my hips toward the edge of the seat. My legs fall open and I think I know what's coming next, so my stomach flutters in anticipation. I watch him examine me reverently, and my need for his touch reaches a new peak.

He pauses and looks up at me. If he's searching for permission, he must find it in my expression, because in the next moment he leans down and delivers a long, slow stroke of his tongue that makes it difficult to breathe.

I gasp, my head falling back again, grabbing at the cushions, but there's nothing to hold. My fingers find Kent's hair.

I glance down at the vignette in front of me—his dark hair and tan skin against my pale thighs—and it sends a shot of lust through me that starts at my lower belly and radiates.

Each long sweep of his tongue inspires a gasp for air.

"Too much?" he asks.

He's reading my body.

"Don't you dare stop."

He offers me a wicked smile and goes back to work, lingering in the places that elicit the greatest response.

I'm thinking about how no one has ever managed to bring me to orgasm this way when Kent reaches up to run his thumbs across my nipples while working magic with his mouth.

Everything changes.

No one has ever done THAT before either.

His persistent, rhythmic circles make me moan and I reflexively press into him. I'm definitely not in control now. He responds to my cues with a gentle rake of his teeth and I let out an involuntary hiss.

"Ohmygod."

It's like he's found an archived copy of the Isabella Avery code spec and tapped into the sexual configurations in my programming.

We go on like this for minutes. He casts a spell on me with alternating strokes and sexy nips that straddle the line between pleasure and pain in the most wonderful way.

My legs begin to shake. I grab at his forearms, needing to get my bearings, as the sensations build. I can't stay quiet, I can't stay still, and I can't take a full breath of air.

When I come, it hits like rolling waves: just as it recedes, another knocks me over and sends me swimming. When I finally catch my breath, I ride out the gentle ebbs and flows. I bring a hand to my face, feeling wrung out and spent.

Kent places kisses on my stomach as it rises and falls.

"Is that what you came here for, Bella?" he asks, wearing a satisfied smile.

I nod as all my nerve endings spring back to life.

He plants one more kiss on my belly. "Now we can go upstairs."

CHAPTER 26

 I wake in the darkness hours later and scan the room. I love how the city light enters through the historic building's clerestory windows, falling on the floor and creating shadows. I settle on my back, adjusting the pillow and shifting under the crisp duvet.

Kent moves beside me.

His warm hand slides up under the covers, along my naked stomach, making circles. The gesture is so sweet, so tender, it fills me up with warm contentedness.

"You okay?" His voice is soft and drowsy.

"Can't sleep." I roll over to face him, mirroring his position.

"You've been fidgeting all night. Carving stone in your sleep."

"Sorry."

"You don't have to apologize." He rests his hand on my hip.

I see the outline of his face in the moonlight and I'm drawn to it. I feel for his lips, kissing him gently when I find them. The sound our lips make together in the silence is as beautiful to me as birdsong in springtime.

"You worried about Pickle?"

"No, I fed him before coming over."

"Someone was feeling optimistic," he teases.

"Stop it." I give a playful poke to his stomach. "I was on my way to the gym and acted on impulse. I had no idea I'd end up here."

He runs his hand up my rib cage, stopping just below my breast. I love the warm weight of it on my side.

"I'm really glad you did."

"Me too."

There's a long silence.

My stomach hasn't stopped doing cartwheels since I showed up here tonight, so it's no wonder I can't sleep. I think about what I should say, how much I should divulge. I consider what he said earlier; he's played all his cards. Am I ready to lay down a few of my own?

"I'm nervous," I admit. I need to say it fast.

His hand smooths down my ribs. He grips my hip and squeezes.

"That's why you can't sleep?"

"Maybe?"

Definitely.

I tuck my hands under my cheek; my arms cover my chest protectively.

"Talk to me." He gives my hip another affectionate squeeze.

I hesitate.

He trails a finger along my arm. "Are you afraid we made a mistake?"

"No!"

Please don't think that, for even a minute.

I take a deep breath in through my nose, out my mouth. A cleansing yoga breath.

Do I tell him?

"Just a lot going on in my head right now," I say.

And my heart.

"Lots of feelings, that's all," I add.

He nestles in closer. The white of his smile is visible in the low light.

"Me too."

"Yeah?"

"Yeah."

My stomach performs one more advanced gymnastics move for good measure. I inch even closer.

"Tell me," I say, placing a hand on his chest for gentle encouragement.

I know it isn't fair to ask him to share more, but I selfishly want to hear it.

"I'd rather show you."

Before I get the chance to answer, he finds my lips, rolling on top of me and caging me in with his forearms. The weight and warmth of him sets me alight.

I shift my legs to wrap them around his waist, feeling his length grow with each new kiss. I run my hands up and down his strong back as he kisses a trail along my neck—his favourite part. I lean my head back, offering myself up to him and suck in a breath when he stops to lick the hollow of my throat.

He hitches up one of my legs for better access, teasing me with circles of his hips. A moment passes between us as we look at each other intensely in the relative darkness.

The light spilling across the room creates a beautiful backlight for his torso. I gently trace his cheekbones, then skim across his stubble. I explore his Cupid's bow with my fingers, and when I pass a thumb along his bottom lip, he turns his head to follow, kissing my palm.

There's an electricity buzzing between us. The feel of

him between my legs makes me heavy and needy. I shift my hips, rubbing against him for relief.

"I better get a condom," he says.

The heat that's building between us is a sweet kind of torture. I need to move but I want to stay. I don't want him to pull away either.

"I have an IUD." I run my hands down his smooth back, stopping at his firm ass. I pull him towards me and push up with my hips.

It's an evil ploy, really.

"I haven't been with anyone else for months," I continue. "What about you?"

I deliver one long and languorous kiss.

Kent pulls away and rests his forehead against mine. Our breathing is laboured and hot.

"Do you honestly think I could have been with anyone else after meeting you?"

I do the math behind that statement, and I'm astounded.

My throat tightens. "That's a really long time."

"You're telling me."

One more deep kiss.

He pauses to run his nose along my jaw, stops to nip at my ear. I can't hold back the smile that emerges from deep inside me.

"I don't like thinking about you with someone else," he growls. "I know it's ridiculous, but I didn't enjoy hearing you say that."

"Well, we've all got a past, so I don't know what to do about that."

"I do."

In quick, efficient movements, he sits up and pulls me to his lap. My legs straddle him—hip to hip, chest to chest. He holds my face and kisses me, slow and gentle at first, like I'm a treasure in his hands. But they quickly change to something different: urgent and intense.

He brings his hands to my thighs, smoothing over my skin before gripping my hips. I roll them while my nipples rub against his hard chest. We both let out a low moan.

The ache that's building between my legs is excruciating. I need more of him. I reach between us and move him to the right position.

"I want to feel you so bad, but are you sure?" he asks.

"Yes." I don't hesitate before lifting my hips and lowering slowly, taking him in, inch by incredible inch.

The two of us settle together for a few sweet seconds, savouring the connection and the intensity of the moment.

"You feel so good," he says, his warm breath against my throat.

I wrap my arms around his neck and kiss him, slipping my tongue past his lips as the instinct to move takes over.

Movements are slow and languid in these first few minutes with nothing between us. Each sink of my hips is matched by my mouth. My teeth catch Kent's bottom lip as I pull away, letting him know I want to go harder, I want to be rough.

He reads me so well, fluent in all my signs and signals. Helping, he lifts his own hips to meet mine with each fall. It's equal parts giving and taking with each delicious turn.

There's something about our position—our physical connection—that's incredibly intimate. Working together like this feels like we're in sync. The boundaries between our bodies become a blur: it's unclear where his ends and mine begins. The effect is surreal.

"Tell me that you feel this too," he says.

He wraps his arms around me.

I take his face in my hands and look at him. Even in the low light I can see the intensity in his eyes.

My chest tightens. "I do."

His relief is palpable as he kisses me hard until the

sensations in the rest of our bodies become too much to ignore and we need to move again.

Our pace quickens. I arch my back, letting go of him so I can reach behind myself and grab one of his strong thighs for better leverage. My other hand rests on his chest, his heart pumping against my palm. His hot hands return to my hips, helping me move, ensuring that I hit perfectly each time.

My legs begin to shake, and before long my entire body tremors from exertion but I can't stop, I won't stop.

"I'm so close," I murmur.

"Tell me." It's his turn to be greedy.

"So good...oh god." My head falls back, face fixed with tension.

He pulls my hips toward him even harder, his strong arms focused on coaxing me over the edge.

This time it hits like a jolt of electricity, my entire body shuddering with the shock.

Kent holds me in place as deep as we can go while my body vibrates and hums.

"It feels so good inside you," he says softly.

Seconds later I see him come apart, his own body shaking, eyes closing tight as he completely loses himself in the moment.

His eyes flutter open and we share an exhausted smile. He kisses me gently between heavy exhales, head coming to rest against my thumping chest.

We fall back and lie in a tangle on top of the sheets, letting the loft's cool air chill our sweat-dampened skin.

"You have no idea the things you do to me," he says, breath still laboured.

"Oh, I think I do."

CHAPTER 27

 Eventually the need for food and water drives us from our nest. I head home early to feed Gherkin, but Kent isn't far behind.

Two hours later he arrives at my door. I find him deliciously leaning against the frame, hair wet and tousled, muscular legs exposed by athletic shorts. I pull him in for a kiss, making no attempt to hide the bold sniff I take of his cleanly shaven neck.

"What a welcome," he says, grabbing my ass with both hands.

"You smell incredible."

"Do I?" he asks with a chuckle.

"Always."

He runs his fingers through the damp hairs at the nape of my own freshly showered neck.

"I'm a little disappointed that you already showered. I'm rather fond of joining you in there."

My stomach flips and I contemplate tearing every stitch of clothing from his body with my teeth, but I exercise some self-control. It would be easy to fall back into bed right now—and who would blame us? But I've been down this road before, where no one's thinking clearly or even thinking at all. Two people caught up in a Blitzkrieg of banging where someone inevitably comes out a casualty. While I don't consider Kent enemy forces, I still hear a protective little voice saying *make sure this time is different—don't get caught up in the barrage.*

Kent and I have most definitely established that we have an abundance of sexual chemistry. The question is: do we have enough of everything else?

I reluctantly pull away from him and head toward my kitchen. Kent pauses to pat Gherkin, who purrs loudly and rubs against his shins like the man has salmon in his pockets.

The true love affair here.

"I thought we could make some brunch," I suggest.

"I'm starving. I guess we burned a few calories last night."

He comes up beside me at the island and slips a finger in the waistband of my cropped leggings, pulling me in close to plant a light kiss. He follows with a gentle rub of his nose against mine before taking a playful nip at my bottom lip.

Sweet Jesus.

"Pancakes!" I say with disproportional enthusiasm.

It's going to take a lot of carbs to tamp down this fire.

Kent watches on as I start to pull ingredients from the cupboards.

"Sure. What do you want me to do?"

"Cut up some fruit." I place a cutting board and knife in front of him and head to the fridge to see what I've got.

As I pull strawberries and blueberries from the produce drawer, he grabs an apple from a large fruit bowl on the counter, tossing it in the air and catching it in the opposite hand.

"I can handle that," he says.

"Yes, you've proven you're quite a proficient chopper." I make a chopping action with my hand, mimicking his posture from the previous night.

He raises an eyebrow.

"Too soon?" I tease.

He flashes a crooked grin. "That's okay—I can take it."

We both get to work; I assemble the batter and Kent washes his hands before setting up his cutting station. We settle into a calm domesticity without skipping a beat. I glance over at him as I'm pulling out a pan and catch him stealing a look back at me. We smile at each other, still not saying a word.

I set up at the stove.

"I'm surprised you aren't assessing my batter mix, Mr. Armstrong. Making sure my constituent parts are adequately measured."

"Oh, believe me, I'm checking out your parts."

I relish the sparkle in his eyes.

"Is this an approved mix?" I say, failing comically to imitate his voice.

"Don't make me pull out the orange highlighter, woman."

My face flushes as he gives me a wink.

Oh, lord help me.

I will never look at that writing instrument the same again.

As Kent transfers sliced berries into a bowl, I realize that aside from toast and coffee and maybe the odd donut in the site trailer, we haven't really eaten together before.

"Shit, I should have asked if you even like pancakes."

"Who doesn't like pancakes?"

"For all I know, you're vegan or gluten intolerant." I'm pretty sure he's not gluten intolerant after the toast we ate the other day, but I don't recall seeing him actually eat any of the donuts at work.

"No, I'm good with gluten. I'm not vegan or vegetarian but I do try to eat less meat than I used to because of its impact on the environment."

He grabs a couple of bananas from the fruit bowl and peels them.

"Not to mention the health benefits," he continues, chopping the bananas into coins. I watch his large, tanned hands and how deftly he handles the knife. The veins in his forearms move with each slice.

I realize I'm staring at him when the first batch of pancakes in the pan starts to burn.

"Oh shit," I say, quickly flipping them.

"Distracted?" he asks, never looking up from his work.

"Maybe a bit."

He chuckles.

We linger at the table with our cups of coffee, long after the large stacks of blueberry pancakes have been eaten.

A heap of work materials has been pushed aside to make room for us. Kent lifts one of the many stone-related periodicals from the pile and studies it, turning to the flagged page.

"Laser cleaning of stone buildings," he reads aloud.

I'm quite shy about it, so I don't mention that I've submitted an abstract on this topic for consideration at an upcoming international conference. I've been doing extra research to know what my peers have been saying recently about the technology.

"Some light reading," I joke.

"What you know about stone conservation is seriously impressive." He returns the journal to the pile.

I lean back in my chair and take a drink from my mug. "You think so?"

"I *know* so."

I pretend his statement doesn't make me positively buoyant with validation.

"We haven't talked shop in a while," I note.

"We've had other things to talk about." He smiles, waits a beat. "And *not* talk about."

The electricity that's ever-present when he's near starts to build its charge again and it feels like we're two clouds ready for lightning. I need to change the wind direction.

"We do need to spend *some* time together clothed."

"Bah, highly overrated."

I laugh. "We need to get to know each other."

"We've known each other for months." He sits back and rests an elbow on the back of his chair.

"Correction: we've known misrepresented and misinterpreted versions of each other for months."

He hesitates before responding. "Fair. What do you want to know?"

My mind swims with potential questions. Kent takes another drink from his coffee cup, waiting as I deliberate. I consider my options. There's so much I want to know about the man in front of me, but where on earth do I start?

"You always seem to be alone at work—the lone Sampson Properties soul among our motley crew. You arrive alone and leave alone. It kinda feels lonely. *Are* you lonely?"

I'm not sure why I opt for such a long-winded and serious question. I guess my subconscious self has been fretting about Kent's happiness a little longer than I realized.

His brow furrows, clearly as surprised by my question as I am.

"Not at all. Sampson Properties has a great team: admin staff, facility managers and other PMs. I just decided to handle this project on my own."

"Why's that?"

"Maybe I want to keep it all to myself."

His single dimple makes a delightful appearance.

An unexpected sense of relief follows.

"Good." I take a drink of my coffee. "Your turn."

Kent flashes a devilish grin. I can practically see his mental wheels turning as he ponders his next move. His question comes more quickly than I'm expecting.

"Why did you freak out so badly when we ran into each other at the wedding?"

The wedding. God, it feels like a lifetime ago.

"You think I freaked out?"

"You *know* you freaked out, Bella."

I look down at my cup and wipe at a drip that's run down the side. If we're going to get to know each other, I need to be honest.

"I don't know, I guess it felt like worlds colliding. Don't you agree?" I pick at a callus.

"I was more distracted by you in that dress."

My heart swells.

"I suppose it was quite the change from my usual look."

"For the record, your *usual look* completely does it for me...but seeing you in pink, that slit up your thigh...it nearly killed me." He grabs my hand across the table, threading his fingers through mine.

I lean in closer. I take a long look at his handsome face—his bright eyes drawing me in.

"That charcoal suit of yours was pretty spectacular too," I admit.

I grab his other hand and squeeze it tight.

"I wanted to watch you dance," he confesses.

"Of course you did, you little perv," I tease. "You eventually did anyway."

"I sure did." His eyes turn pitch black. "Worth the wait."

He pulls me in closer, I'm practically leaning over the table now.

"Why didn't you dance at the wedding?" His voice is soft, his tone a bit sad. "You just sat alone at the table while everyone else danced."

I shrug, considering my words. "I guess I wasn't ready to show you that side of myself yet."

"What side?"

"The one who's clearly nothing like the person you know...or at least knew then." I sigh. Talking like this makes me feel raw and laid bare. Being naked right now would be less exposing.

"I want to see it all, Bella," Kent says.

"Back then I was just Avery."

His chuckle stirs me from my introspection.

"Um...there's never been *just Avery*. You're a dynamic powerhouse. Don't make it sound like you've been shrinking yourself down to size."

"But here's the thing: maybe I have?" My confession leaves me feeling weak. I try to read Kent's face; all I see is tenderness and care. He feels safe.

I decide to go all in.

"Maybe I've been packaging myself for specific audiences, thinking I need to be what people expect of me." I hesitate. "Or what I *think* people expect."

"What, like Stone Mason Barbie?"

"Complete with mallet and chisel," I joke, but it misses the mark.

"I hope you never think you need to package yourself up for *me*." Kent tugs at my hands again, looking at me intensely.

I hesitate, not sure how I feel. The conversation has turned unexpectedly serious. My pancakes sit like granite in my stomach.

I look down pensively at our interlaced fingers.

"Well, there's really only one solution," Kent announces. He drops my hands and pulls back his chair to stand. I'm startled and confused by the abrupt shift.

He pulls out his trademark charcoal-cased phone from his pocket and selects his music app. I watch curiously as he touches the screen.

The opening synthesizer of NSYNC's "Bye Bye Bye" pipes from his iPhone speaker, full of tinny distortion.

Oh, Christ.

Kent starts moving his hips.

"Come on, let's do this. Let's hammer one out right now." He shifts in time to the music.

Dear god, it's adorable.

"When you say *hammer one out*, this is not the type of dancing that comes to mind."

I stay solidly fixed to my seat.

"We can do the horizontal hokey pokey later; right now I want you to cut a rug, get jiggy with it, show me your moves." He does the distinct Timberlake-style fist pump, body bounce combo and I almost choke on my coffee.

Oh god. It's cringey. And fabulous. And so fucking sweet.

He takes my hand and pulls me to stand.

With his hands on my hips, he works me into a funky rhythm and sway. I'm not cooperating.

"We don't need to do this," I insist.

"Yes, we do. You need to know you can dance in front of me."

When he throws in some shoulder shrugs, I cover my mouth to hide my laugh.

"Okay, okay. I can dance in front of you. Point made." I pull back and try to sit, but he grips me harder and locks me in an embrace, still moving to the music.

After a few seconds, his face turns serious and the swaying stops.

He takes my face in his hands.

"Don't ever feel like you need to keep parts of yourself hidden from me, okay?"

I swallow back a lump in my throat and nod.

"I don't want some curated version of Bella Avery; I want the whole package."

"You want to collect the whole set?" I ask shyly, hoping a joke will help break the tension.

"Don't forget all the accessories," he says with a soft smile.

My heart feels way too big for my chest.

He leans his forehead against mine. I plant a soft kiss on his lips.

"Wait." He pulls away suddenly.

These abrupt shifts are an entirely new side of Kent I've never seen before; nothing like the restrained PM I've shared a scaffold with. The buttoned-up spreadsheet soldier has made room for a relaxed Romeo. Let's face it, they're both irresistible, but this playful version of him I'd like to get to know.

"If we're getting do-overs, I want this one again." He thumbs through tracks on his phone, smiling when he finds the one he's looking for.

The first notes of the Beck song we danced to at the wedding kick in and a strange flood of nostalgia washes over me. So much has changed in just a few short weeks—it's wild.

"This is how I really wanted to dance with you that night," he says.

He pulls me in close and fondles my ass.

"You did now, did you?" I laugh. "Are you sure you didn't still hate me?"

He pulls back to look at me.

"Do you listen to a single thing I tell you? I was totally into you." He burrows his face in my neck and takes a playful nip at my ear.

"Lusting after my construction tees and safety boots, were you?"

He swings me to the music, spinning me once before bending me into a swoon-worthy dip that makes my panties heat.

"I've told you, that completely works for me. There's no side of you I don't lust after."

"Oh, I'm sure when my years of manual labour leave me too old and decrepit to dance in our kitchen, you won't find me so lust-worthy."

It's out of my mouth before I can stop it.

Shit, what have I done?

My stomach drops.

I've ruined everything.

My face burns, red hot with embarrassment.

He looks at me, quiet and pensive for a moment. I see him swallow.

Backpedal.

Think of something.

Anything.

Quick.

Kent breaks the silence.

"I think I'd like to see that, actually."

The air thins, and I find it hard to breathe.

I'm still paralyzed with humiliation when he pulls me close to kiss me, taking my jaw in his hand. His kiss tastes like a mix of sweet maple syrup and coffee; his tongue feels like velvet in my mouth.

I wrap my arms around him and my body charges on

contact, like I'm electrified by his power. With each stroke of his tongue, he takes another step, backing me up against the closest wall. We press into each other, my gaffe abandoned for ardor.

"Can we get naked now?" Kent asks between kisses.

I step away from him to pull my cropped sweatshirt over my head, tossing it on the floor. He licks his bottom lip.

I turn to walk towards my bedroom, peeling off my pants as I go.

"Are you coming?" I ask when he doesn't immediately follow.

"Pretty much halfway there."

CHAPTER 28

Never wanting to stay idle, the Fleming Stone Service team meets at the Taylor Building site trailer for a demo of the project BIM tools. Building Information Modelling isn't new by any means, but it is to most of our team. Taking advantage of the project down-time, we've pulled in the IT folks early on Monday morning to show some of the group what it can do.

Reid and Trevor just about lose their minds when our lead BIM specialist zooms in on a 3D rendering of the building façade and tilts the angle for better views of the turrets.

#architectureporn.

I think they might need a moment alone when—with an effortless click—they see how the model gets up close and personal with the asset database. And who can blame them? That shit is hot. Well, it is to heritage building nerds like us, anyway.

We're chuckling over Larry's third Keanu-Reeves-style "whoa" of the morning when the door to the trailer pops open. I glance over my shoulder as Kent walks in with an older gentleman.

Our brief eye contact causes a full cartwheel in my stomach and heart palpitations. He turns to offer a wide smile to the group.

My face flushes as I'm reminded of the last time I saw that smile—just three hours earlier—and the very hot shower that precipitated it.

I take a deep breath in through my nose and out through my mouth.

Keep it cool, woman.

Kent's dressed in his go-to plaid shirt, but it looks completely different to me this morning, because this time I'm the one who buttoned it.

I swallow hard.

I get a warm flush thinking back on the weekend. The delicious body soreness I'm feeling is my naughty little secret and the only real evidence that the events of the last forty-eight hours even took place. If not for the aching muscles and phantom nibbles still haunting my skin, I might believe they were just a dream.

"Mr. Armstrong, this is a surprise," Larry comments.

At first, I think Larry is being oddly formal with Kent, but then I take a closer look at his companion. The resemblance is striking: ice blue eyes, sharp jaw, pronounced cheekbones. It's like I'm catching a glimpse of the future—the same handsome Kent, but with grey hair and deep lines on his face.

"Dad's made a surprise appearance," Kent tells the group, flashing a look of warning that has everyone sitting up straighter.

"Hello everyone," says the senior Armstrong. "Hope I'm not interrupting."

"You're just in time to watch the BIM demo." Larry gestures to the oversized monitor on the wall.

"Ah, yes. Kent's been telling me about this."

I note the scepticism in his voice.

The trailer is small and the heat of approximately a dozen bodies and the hard-working IT equipment was already making my upper lip sweat. Throw in an unexpected meeting with *the dad,* and I'm finding it hard to breathe.

"I'm not convinced these tools are worth the heavy investment." Kent's dad slips his hands in his pockets. The resemblance really is uncanny.

"Come a little closer and see for yourself." Larry waves him over to the screen.

As the IT team takes him through the demonstration again, I watch Kent shift nervously on his feet.

The team slips back into enthusiastic observer mode and Larry points out key features he found impressive in the earlier demo.

"It certainly seems like a very attractive tool, no question about that." Mr. Armstrong crosses his arms across his wide chest. "I'm just not convinced it's really going to be useful. We've managed fine without jumping on technology trends before."

I can't help weighing in.

"The digital as-builts that we hand over at the end of the project will be extremely useful. Not only will the facility manager be able to see beyond the walls to find problems, like a leaking water valve, they'll be able to find the manufacturer of that valve for a replacement and its warranty information from the safety and comfort of their office."

Kent's father turns to me, eyebrow raised in newfound interest.

"I don't believe we've met." He extends a hand out to me.

Kent begins, "This is Av—"

"Isabella Avery," I interrupt. "But you can call me Avery."

It's out of my mouth before I've really thought it through. The revelation is oddly liberating.

"Greg Armstrong," his dad replies. His handshake is firm and brief.

The look of surprise on Kent's face almost makes me giggle. I take a quick pan of the group and they all look extremely confused, except Larry, who knew full well what my name is. Reid and Sam have matching furrowed brows and I spot Trevor in the corner mouthing *"Isabella"* with a look of utter bewilderment.

"Avery is our best heritage stone mason," Larry explains.

I catch a few eye rolls from the guys, but I give them the amount of attention they deserve. I take the opportunity to explain the value of BIM further.

"It can help with clash detection later on when planning future projects, which can now be designed on a desktop rather than starting from scratch with 2D blueprints, saving time. Time equals money."

Greg looks intrigued, so I continue.

"When you see how much it helps with building-maintenance activities and ties into sustainability and building life cycle management, you'll want it for the rest of your portfolio."

I've been avoiding Kent's face throughout this exchange. I decide to take a quick look to gauge things.

Have I said too much?

He's smiling—up until now, a relatively rare thing here at work when I'm speaking.

Phew.

I consider my next words carefully, but decide to forge ahead. "Kent made a good choice implementing it on this project."

The entire group freezes and stares, clearly shocked by the unprecedented compliment. Reid and Sam look at me like I have five heads.

I steal another glimpse at Kent when the group's attention shifts back to the monitor. His face is filled with pride. He gives me a wide smile before catching himself and looking away.

Good choices. I want Kent's dad to know about all his good choices.

I really hope I'm one of them.

Eventually the crowd thins, and Kent's dad is among several who leave. Just our core group lingers, chatting casually. No one has said a word to me since hearing me refer to myself as Isabella, or since seeing me defend one of Kent's professional choices.

I worry that I've made a mistake, that I've given up the plot. As curious looks are shared and eyebrows begin to raise, my paranoia kicks into overdrive. The instinct to restore the old dynamic overtakes me—the need to throw everyone off our trail. I start to look for a route back to normal, whatever the hell that is.

I see an opening when Reid raises the controversial topic *du jour*. It's like he's served up a ball for me to hit out of the park.

"Those sill repairs we identified on level two…are we gonna use dutchmen or just use mortar fills?"

Thank you, Reid.

This one is easy because I know it's something we completely disagree on.

"They're skyward-facing and subjected to a lot of water and weathering; they need to be dutchmen," I chime in.

I wait for Kent to take the bait.

"They're small; they can just be mortar patches." Kent says it out loud, but to no one in particular, distracted by something on his phone.

"They won't hold up to the elements—they need to be natural stone," I counter.

"The mortar only has to last as long as the rest of the front point mortar. It'll be fine."

He's looking right at me now; his face is serious.

"So you want to build in maintenance issues from the start?"

I'm trying to provoke him, to get him worked up now.

"Calm down, Avery. Front point mortar lasts over fifty years. I'm not creating a maintenance problem."

Nothing gets me worked up like a man telling me to calm down. Kent knows this and has chosen these words intentionally.

"It holds up that long when it's a thin mortar joint, not a wider surface prone to precipitation run-off. A stone dutchman is the best approach."

I say the words like the decision is final, but Kent has other ideas.

"I'm not spending the money. They're going to be mortar fills. My decision is final." He looks back at his phone and scrolls across the screen.

His dismissiveness sets me off. The verbal sparring I'd intended for the benefit of the crowd crosses an invisible line and legitimately annoys me. Kent's always known how to push my buttons.

"Here we go again, ignoring the subject matter experts." This time the words feel childish and leave a sour taste in my mouth. I pick at something on my high-visibility vest.

"Here *you* go again, making it personal." He tucks his phone in his back pocket.

The team exchanges resigned looks. They know the drill.

We've run out of things to say, but I need to keep it going. Letting the topic drop would be incredibly off brand.

I lean in just for emphasis. "Maybe if you got those pretty little hands dirty on occasion, you'd know why this is a terrible decision."

Pretty little hands? What the hell am I even saying?

Kent's eyes grow in surprise, then narrow in anger.

"What the hell is wrong with you?" he demands before striding out the door.

I turn to find Larry's angry face.

Shit.

I knew as the sentence escaped me that I'd taken things too far. That was really unprofessional. If I'd said the same thing to a woman, I'd be pulled in front of someone for harassment charges.

"That was too far, Avery," he growls.

My stomach turns.

"I know."

I'm the last one to leave the trailer that night. I've kept myself busy doing research for the potential conference presentation and trying to keep my mind off my colossal fuck up.

I don't get a single text from Kent for the rest of the day, so he must be pissed. I can't blame him; I'm pissed at myself.

I lock up and head home. Once I get to my apartment, I

snuggle Gherkin for a few extra minutes. I'm needy and feeling sorry for myself. Only cat therapy will do.

Normally I'd grab my workout clothes and head to the gym, but instead I take a long shower and change into comfy clothes, then settle in on the couch with a book and beer and try to escape from my own world for a little while.

I've reread the same paragraph at least a dozen times when there's a knock at the door. Assuming it's a neighbour, I don't even check the peep hole before swinging it open.

It's Kent.

My heart cracks open.

He's still wearing his work clothes, and looks up from his phone and smiles.

He's smiling?

My stomach does its usual Kent-associated flip-flop, but today it's mixed with fear-induced nausea.

"I'm so sorry," I blurt out, stepping closer. I lean against the open door, crossing my arms protectively. The need to make things right between us fills me with an unexpected urgency.

He seems surprised and doesn't say anything for a few seconds.

"I'm sorry too…that I didn't buzz up. The front door was propped." He gestures behind him. "It looks like someone's moving in."

"I'm so, so sorry," I repeat. I seem unable to move forward with our conversation until I'm sure he's heard me, until I'm sure he understands.

He sees the seriousness in my face and steps over the threshold. He puts his phone down on the entryway table and comes closer, taking my face in his hands. I stubbornly stand in place, propping the door open.

"Hey, hey. What's wrong?" He rests his forehead against mine.

"I was horribly unprofessional today. You have every right to be pissed."

"That was just some crap you needed to spout. Who the hell cares?"

I pull back reflexively. "*I* care! Women have been putting up with that type of vitriolic bullshit for generations, and I just sank to that level." I take a deep breath.

"Bella. Stop. It's fine."

"I won't—it's *not* fine. I have so much respect for you, Kent. I hope you know that. Please tell me you do."

"Of course I know that. It was just our usual sparring. It's okay."

"I can't do that anymore." I surprise myself with the statement.

"Okay," he says.

"When I didn't hear from you, I was sure you were pissed."

"Shit. No, I was just busy with Dad. He wants to implement BIM across all properties." He laughs. "Looks like you made a compelling argument."

He smooths his thumbs across my cheeks.

"What you did today...that was...I know what you risked by doing that. What you risked supporting me in front of the others." I see his Adam's apple bounce as he swallows, trying to piece his sentences together.

"It wasn't a big deal."

I shrug it off, feeling incredibly vulnerable all of a sudden.

"Are you going to let me in?" he asks.

It's a loaded question—the double meaning isn't lost on me.

I grab hold of his forearms and squeeze, then step back to let the door close behind us. As soon as it clicks shut, I'm backed up against it, but Kent is slow and tender, mending my breaks with each kiss.

He unexpectedly starts to chuckle, his laughter vibrating against my lips.

"What's so funny?" I ask. I can't help but chuckle too.

"*Pretty little hands.*" He breaks into a full laugh.

"Oh god, it's terrible." I bury my face in his chest, hot with embarrassment.

"I've been accused of a lot of things, but that was a first."

"I'm so sorry," I say directly into his shirt.

"You think my hands are pretty, do you?" He starts to smooth them over my back and the motion is delightfully comforting, especially after the stress of the day. I lift my face to look at him and he's giving me a beautiful smile.

"Everything about you is pretty." I adjust his collar, nervously.

His expression turns slightly wicked. He grazes my ear with his lips.

"Do you want to see what I can do with my pretty little hands?"

Well, this has escalated quickly.

A shot of adrenaline surges through my system, making my extremities—and more intimate parts of me—tingle.

He kisses a trail along my neck to the other ear.

"You want to see these pretty little hands of mine get dirty?"

It's my Mary Shelley moment: *Dear lord, what monster have I created?*

I manage one full breath before Kent kisses me long and deep. His hands—indeed, very pretty hands—fall to my waist. One slides up my loose-fitting cropped shirt and slips under my lace bralette. His warm hand covers my bare breast and my nipple stiffens against his palm. He lingers, passing his thumb across my sensitive skin, coaxing it to grow even harder from his touch.

When I moan into his mouth, Kent brings his second hand up to join the other.

I think I could die exactly like this and feel completely satisfied with my time on earth, but Kent isn't going to stop there.

He pulls away to look at me, more of the devil in his eyes.

"You aren't complaining about my pretty hands now, are you?" he asks, clever grin on his face.

"Uhmm." I'm completely inarticulate.

He pinches one hardened nipple between his fingers, and it sends a jolt of electricity right between my legs. Grabbing the waistband of my leggings, he pulls me closer. The act of being handled, him moving me into position, makes me ache. I widen my stance.

It's hard to know if I opened my legs anticipating his next move, or if his move comes after reading my signal, but he turns his hand against the stretchy spandex and slips it down the front of my pants. Two firm fingers run along the outer gusset of my underwear, teasing me as he watches me squirm.

"That good enough?" he asks. There's a glint of mischief in his eyes.

He knows it's not.

He does it again, slower. It's torture.

He wants me to say it.

There's another pinch, another pass of his hand. I shift my hips and arch my back.

He murmurs in my ear. "Tell my pretty hands what you need."

"I need them on my skin," I whisper, oddly shy about saying it. Despite what outward appearances may suggest, I've never been great about telling partners what I need. I'm more *show* than *tell* in this context.

"Like this?" he asks, slipping his hand inside my panties.

He slides his fingers against my hot, slick skin and I sigh with relief.

My knees slightly wobble, so I wrap my arms around his neck for support. He buries his face in my neck, nipping at my ear.

"You're so wet," he whispers, sending a pang to my belly and more heat to his hand.

I'm unravelling, each slippery movement of his fingers pulling at imaginary threads, one by one.

My head falls back against the door as he slips one finger inside. The burst of sensations practically has me climbing the wall.

"Another," I beg.

He slides another in and the force of it brings me up on my toes.

Each intense push forces me stalk straight, legs taut with tension. Not a stitch of my clothing has come off, but I'm coming completely undone.

When my legs start to shake, he props me up, taking my weight against him. Changing up his movements, he slows down to make gentle circles with his thumb between strokes. He rakes his teeth along my neck.

"I want to feel you come on my pretty little hand."

That's the secret combination that cracks my code, breaking me open.

The silence of the room is broken by my sounds. They're raw and guttural, punctuated with throaty moans. My eyes squeeze shut as my mouth falls open in surprise.

Kent holds his hand in place as I come down from my high and melt into him.

When my breathing returns to normal he pulls his hands out from under my clothes and rests them on my hips.

"Sorry if I got a bit carried away with the dirty talk."

"Are you seriously apologizing to me right now?" I'm still only half lucid after my mind-blowing orgasm.

"Well, I *am* half Canadian."

The joke takes me by complete surprise and when I look up, we break into giggles.

"It's true," he adds. "On my mom's side."

There's a thump from the living room—Gherkin leaving his post on the couch.

Kent plants a long, slow, deep kiss on my mouth and I run my hand along the bulge in the front of his pants. He pulls back with a hiss.

"Pickle better cover his eyes, because we're about to get really naughty here."

"Oh, he can handle a little sleepover," I say.

"I assure you, there will be no sleeping here tonight."

Kent flutters his fingers along my rib cage, making me giggle.

There's a jarring knock on the door behind us.

"Think it's Mrs. Allen from down the hall?" Kent whispers. "She's the fondle police."

I'm grinning as I turn to look in the peep hole.

My stomach falls.

It's Larry.

The penny drops as I flash back to an earlier conversation: before the demo, before the drama. *"I'm going to be near your place tonight—I'll drop that hard drive off so you can start prepping for the next project."*

Shit.

In all my angst I'd completely forgotten. What a complete fuck-up.

"What's wrong?" Kent whispers.

I put my fingers over his lips. *"It's Larry,"* I mouth silently.

Kent immediately starts to back away from the door, his face mirroring my expression.

I escort him to my bedroom and give my hushed demands. "I forgot he was coming. Stay here."

Once the door is shut behind him, I take a fortifying breath and consider my options. I quickly come up with my strategy: deny, deny, deny.

Yep, that'll work.

I check myself in the mirror next to the front door and try to put on a game face. Jesus Christ. Two minutes ago, I had Kent's hand down my pants. The change in direction is like sexual whiplash.

A second series of knocks sounds just as I open the door.

Larry has a sheepish look on his face and is wearing a stylish pair of dress pants and a button-up shirt. All polished and cleanly shaven, it'd be hard to recognize him if not for his shock of red hair and trademark freckles.

"Sorry, Lar. I forgot you were coming."

"No, the apology is mine. I should have buzzed up, but the front door was propped and three people were fighting with a mattress. I wanted to get out of their way."

"It's all good," I say, trying on an extremely casual expression and hoping it fits.

It's cool. Everything is cool.

"I have to run, but here's the hard drive." Larry hands over the small black box.

"Thanks."

"Now you'll have the photos and data to start work planning for Bryson House."

I look down at the device, feeling a bit guilty that I just want him to leave. Larry is such a kind person and wonderful boss, and here he is trying to help me out so I can work from home a little easier. It's not his fault I just had an out-of-this-world orgasm literally at the hands of his client.

I soften a little and try to make conversation.

"So, you're in the neighbourhood tonight?" I ask.

"Yeah, I have late dinner plans." His face flushes pink. Larry obviously has a date—so sweet.

"Nice," I reply.

"I don't mean to trouble you, but since I'm here, do you think I could borrow that stone reference book you mentioned the other day?"

"Oh, yeah, sure. Step inside—it'll just take a sec."

Larry enters my apartment and lets the door close gently behind him. As with everything about Larry, his actions are calm and controlled. A steady hand.

I drop the hard drive next to my laptop on the dining room table and head to my bookshelf, looking for the one he's requested. It doesn't take long to find it, but in the few short seconds it's taken me to return to him at the door, Larry has focused his attention on the entryway table.

"Isn't that Kent's phone?"

He looks down at Kent's signature charcoal case.

Shit.

I feel the blood leave my face and a shiver pass through me.

Come up with something quick, you idiot.

"Oh, is that whose it is?" I hope that my voice isn't shaking. "It was left in the trailer today—I grabbed it when I was locking up."

Remain calm.

"Lemme check." Larry pulls his own phone from his pocket, finds a name in his contacts, and hits the call button.

Kent's phone lights up.

"Yep," Larry confirms.

"Oh, well...mystery solved." I add a fake laugh for good measure.

Oh god, this is terrible.

"It's strange, I swear I saw him put it in his pocket before he left today."

I look down at the phone where it sits like a live bomb. I swear I hear it ticking on the table.

What do I do?

"Here, you might as well take it," I say, handing it to him forcefully, keeping up the ruse. "You'll see him *long* before I do."

Larry takes it and puts it in his pocket, I hand him the book too. He hesitates for a moment, looking like he wants to say something, lingering like he doesn't want to leave.

Oh god, does he know?

The moment hangs between us.

He looks at me expectantly, giving a nervous scratch to his chin.

Or is it me who's supposed to speak?

There's a seemingly endless span of silence until I catch a slight shake of his head.

"Have a good night, Avery."

Larry turns and walks out the door.

"You too!" I say with more enthusiasm than necessary just as the door clicks shut behind him.

As quickly as he arrived, he's gone, and I'm left staring after him. My brain feels just a few seconds slower than reality right now, like when the sound and video are out of sync on a television broadcast.

What the hell just happened?

I try to process everything as I walk in a dazed fog over to my bedroom door. When I open it, I find Kent sitting on my bed, elbows on his knees.

"You gave him my phone?" he asks.

"Shit, I'm sorry. I panicked."

He starts laughing.

I fail to find the amusement in the situation. "You think this is funny?"

"I'm sorry I left my phone out there. I wasn't exactly thinking clearly after having my hand down your pants."

"Well, that makes two of us."

"You handled that well, all things considered." He stands and approaches me. "You okay?"

"Fuck, Kent. That was close."

"I know."

He wraps his arms around me in a supportive hug and I finally take a full breath.

"It's all good. I'll get my phone back tomorrow. A digital detox might be nice, actually. Let's just order in some food and spend time with Pickle."

"Sure."

My body temperature drops along with my blood pressure. I shiver. Kent pulls me closer to warm me, running a hand up and down my back.

"It's all good," he repeats.

Bless his heart for trying to soothe me, but it's not working in the slightest to settle my nerves. I nestle into him for comfort, hoping his warmth and scent can work their usual magic.

I glance over Kent's shoulder to where his phone should be on the table, and my stomach turns.

I know what I need to do.

CHAPTER 29

Larry agrees to meet me at a boring chain coffee shop across town first thing the next morning. I've chosen PPE-free, neutral territory, with no nosey colleagues around or staff that we love, so it won't matter if this location is forever ruined by association with what's about to happen.

By the time Larry arrives, I've worked myself into a bit of a state. I'm needing deep yoga breaths to keep myself centred and calm.

Three counts in, three counts out.

The café's air conditioning is giving me goosebumps, but then again, my internal body temperature always seems to drop when nerves set in. Despite my feelings, the moment I spot Larry I know I've made the right decision. I owe this to him and to myself.

We settle in with our coffee. I cut straight to the chase.

"Larry, I'm meeting you this morning to offer up my resignation."

Silence.

He gives me nothing but a blank stare. I need to fill the

empty space, so I keep talking. I look down at my hands wrapped around my paper cup so I can't see the disappointment in his face.

"I've violated the values and ethics policy in my contract."

Larry noticeably relaxes.

"Oh, is this the Kent thing?"

WTF.

"You haven't been poached by another company, have you?" he quickly adds.

"No..."

"Thank god." He sits back, shoulders dropping to their normal position, and takes a casual sip from his cup.

"Larry, did you hear what I said?"

"Of course I heard."

"Why aren't you freaking out? And why did you mention Kent?"

Larry gives me the kind of look my mother used to give me when I told her I didn't eat the chocolate chips in the cupboard.

"What?" I press.

Larry leans in, resting his elbows on the table.

"There's always been a pretty high baseline tension between the two of you, but when Reid mentioned in passing that he'd spotted you on a bench somewhere, that was the clincher."

Dammit, Reid.

"Throw in the general recent weirdness with you, and then the phone last night..." Larry hesitates, "I figured things had finally come together. I mean, so to speak." He blushes with the gaffe.

He takes a larger drink of his coffee and adjusts in his seat. Larry has never been a talk-about-your-emotions type. He's always super supportive and kind, always there if you need him, but not a dig-deep kind of guy. This is uncharted territory for us.

"Ave, these policies are in place to protect *our business*. If I thought for one second Kent was getting an easier time of it because of your relationship, that'd be one thing but…I somehow doubt that's the case." He laughs one of his awesome full-body laughs, making his shoulders shake.

I'm gobsmacked.

Speechless.

"Look, I didn't exactly do things to discourage it." He looks down at his hands, "I could have sent someone else to the quarry."

"Nothing happened at the quarry."

"It's none of my business." He throws up a hand to shield further discussion.

We sit for a moment in silence. I absorb what he's told me. Has Larry been playing matchmaker?

"You're my best mason, Avery. Quite frankly, I'd be lost without you. You're not resigning on my watch."

I breathe deeply for the first time in hours. I feel physically lighter. I want to jump to my feet and embrace him, but that's not how we roll.

"Thank you, Larry. That means a lot to me."

He sits back again, relaxing now that the intensity of the moment has passed.

"I do think you guys can sometimes get a little…heated. Screaming in the trailer isn't your best look, Ave."

"I know." I cover my face with a hand.

"Would it be better if I took you off the project? Reid and the guys can finish this up; we're only days away anyway."

I sink into my chair. I don't want to abandon the Taylor Building. It feels counterintuitive to walk away, and I'd love to see it through to the end. But upon further reflection, I concede that what Larry is suggesting is best and the most professional approach. I think about the advice my mother gave me: *"You deserve to be happy, Bella. But be smart about it."*

I need to step away.

"It's best if I do."

I feel the weight of a masonry wall lift from my shoulders.

"Okay, I'll let the guys know that we're moving you ahead to Bryson House. They don't need to know why. We should be getting mobilized on site soon anyway."

"Thanks, Larry."

"It's nothing."

"Seriously." I look him squarely in the face. *"Thank you."*

He offers a kind smile that reaches his green eyes. "You know, I'm not upset by these developments, Ave. You guys are both great people. It's nice to see you end up together. Quite frankly, it's about time."

Who knew Larry was a little romantic at heart?

For the first time I consider what that means.

Us.

Together.

Like, really together.

A dozen scenarios come to mind. Meals at restaurants, hand-holding in the street, impromptu coffees at Urban Roasters. A relationship no longer under house arrest. I'm surprised by how excited this makes me.

"Who would've thought, hey?" I ask with a shy laugh.

"The trailer is going to be a lot quieter now," he teases.

I wince.

"It's okay, you can make it up to me."

"How?" I ask with trepidation.

"One last assignment for the Taylor building." Larry takes a generous swig of coffee. "I need you to go with Reid to the Sampson Properties warehouse to pick up a crate of ornamental iron. It's being reinstated. It's been at their warehouse for safekeeping. He'll need a hand."

"Sure, I can do that," I say. Easy peasy. Super straight-forward.

"Consider it your last official duty on the project. Reid's made arrangements. They should be expecting you."

One last thing to do before I walk away from the Taylor Building and Sampson Properties. One last thing before I close one chapter and open another. Nervous excitement works in my stomach.

Larry stands to go, so I follow suit. I spring to my feet, filled with unbridled enthusiasm for what lies ahead. I'm about to walk away, but he stops me.

"Wait…Avery." He zips open his laptop bag and reaches inside.

"Wanna give him his phone?"

Turns out Reid *didn't* make arrangements, and when we arrive at the Sampson Properties warehouse they *aren't* expecting us.

Thanks, Reid.

We park by the loading dock and make our way to the main entrance. I'm eager to get this over with so I can get to Kent and share the good news. I'd text or call him, but with his cell phone sitting in my bag, that obviously isn't going to work.

We find an older gentleman who appears to know his way around the warehouse and enquire after the crate. The man thankfully knows exactly what we're talking about when we tell him what we're after. He takes us to a shelving rack at the back of the tidy, small warehouse. It's on the third shelf, so a pallet jack isn't going to do the trick; we need a forklift.

"I don't have a valid forklift license anymore; I let the young kids handle the heavy machinery now. Rhonda does —she's out back in the yard," the warehouse guy tells us.

"No problem, I'll go track her down," I volunteer.

I leave them behind and make my way outside. I'd have Reid do it, but I can't stay still right now. I need to keep one steel toed foot in front of the other to get to the end of this day and over to Kent's apartment.

I'm mentally comparing first date options as I walk out to the yard. The thought of going public is making me equal parts excited and edgy. I'll admit, it's been thrilling keeping things under wraps and having our little secret— the rush of not getting caught—but the notion of taking this to the next level and giving it a proper shot in the light of day excites me more than I even expected.

I follow the sound of reverse signals coming from a Quonset hut. I peek inside and spot a woman in PPE on a ride-on lift, shifting around pallets. I wait until she's stopped (health and safety 101) and shout over for her attention.

"Hey, are you Rhonda?"

"Are you here for the crate?"

Aha. Reid redeems himself.

"Yeah, I hate to trouble you, but we need the forklift."

"No problem."

Rhonda steps down from the machine and strides over.

"Nice to meet you," she says, holding out her hand.

"Isabella Avery, but everyone calls me Avery." I'm still getting used to using my full name at work, but find I'm feeling more comfortable each time I do.

"We have another forklift inside—just let me park this one and I'll be right with you." With that, she hops back on and turns the key. Rhonda capably maneuvers the machine to the back of the hut, pulling my eye in that direction.

That's when I spot it.

A familiar stainless-steel cage on a wooden pallet, tucked in behind several others and partially covered with a tarp. I walk closer to investigate. While Rhonda is still occupied, I pull back the tarp and confirm my suspicions.

It's our pallet of stone, missing for weeks… inexplicably tucked away at the back of the Sampson Properties hut.

She spots me pulling off the cover and approaches.

"We've been looking all over the place for this," I tell her.

"Really?" she asks.

The look she gives me makes it clear that not only has this pallet of stone been sitting here for a while, but she has no knowledge of its significance.

"This is stone for the Taylor Building. What on earth is it doing here?" I say more to myself than to Rhonda.

"Mr. Armstrong told me to put it there."

Dread starts to rise in me, like a filling tank.

"You mean Greg?" I ask with my last reserve of optimism.

"No, Kent."

CHAPTER 30

The rest of the afternoon is an out-of-body experience. I go through the motions of loading the crate into the Fleming truck, driving back to the city center with Reid, and dropping it off at the work site. All the while, I run through various scenarios and possible explanations for why that pallet of stone ended up where it did, and why Kent would've been responsible.

Maybe Rhonda has it all wrong.

To this point in my life, I've read dozens of romance novels, and nothing incites rage and paperback-tossing in me faster than when the main characters of a story jump to conclusions and don't talk to each other. I refuse to be a miscommunication trope cliché, so I'm doing my best to reserve judgement until I can speak with Kent and clear the air.

I really hope Rhonda has it all wrong.

I drag out every task and still manage to finish work early. I haven't managed to connect with Kent to give him his phone back, but I know—based on our early morning conversation—that he won't be wrapping up at work until late today, so I go home and shower and throw on a favourite sundress before heading to his place.

I try not to feel too stalker-like as I read a romance novel —appropriately titled *Chaos Is My Brand*—on a bench outside his apartment and try to organize my thoughts.

"This sure is nice to come home to."

I'm taken by surprise. Immersed in some intense character dialogue, I'd been distracted from Kent's arrival. I look up at him from my perch, and he's backlit by the late-day sun.

He looks like a bloody angel.

I sigh wearily.

Please let Rhonda have it all wrong.

When I gather my things and stand, Kent looks over his shoulder reflexively. That's when I remember he still doesn't know about my conversation with Larry—that we're free to be whatever we want to be, free to kiss hello on the sidewalk. My chest tightens, sad that the amazing news I'd wanted to sing from the rooftops just hours before has been overshadowed by finding the pallet of stone.

Kent picks up on my tension.

"Everything okay?" he asks.

"Let's just go inside."

He leads the way, holding the door open for me and unlocking the main door. We ride the elevator in silence, from opposite sides of the cab. He watches me closely, trying to read my mood. When I make brief eye contact, he delivers a solar-flare smile that does dangerous things to me and almost makes me forget what I'm here for.

Damn dimple.

We arrive at his floor and make our way inside his apartment.

Kent heads straight for the kitchen.

"Something to drink?" he asks.

"No, thanks." I unzip my bag and reach inside. "Here's your phone." I set it on the kitchen island while he gets himself a glass of water.

"Wait…how did *you* end up with it?" He takes a long drink from his cup.

"It's a long story, and we'll get there, but I need to talk to you about something else first."

"Okay…"

"Reid and I went over to the Sampson warehouse today. I went inside the Quonset hut. Why is our pallet of stone in there?"

Open mind, Avery. Open mind.

Kent's face falls.

My open mind starts to close.

"Kent…" I urge him.

He stays silent, running a hand through his dark locks, stopping to scratch the back of his head. He looks down at the glass in his hand.

"I put it there." His voice is so quiet I can barely hear him.

"*What?*"

My voice, on the other hand, can be easily heard.

"Why?" I ask when he remains silent.

"It's hard to explain." His voice is just above a whisper.

"Try me."

Silence.

"How long has it been there, Kent?"

"Since before the quarry." He takes a ragged breath, expression pained.

"Why?"

More silence.

"Tell me what's going on."

He takes a deep breath and stands tall before speaking.

"I put it there so no one would find it."

What the fuck?

My open mind officially slams shut.

"Why on earth would you do that?" I demand.

"To delay the project. If we didn't have the stone, we couldn't make the repairs and… the project couldn't wrap."

"That only costs you money. I don't get it."

He pauses, then looks me straight in the eye.

"If the project couldn't wrap, I couldn't lose you."

Now I'm the one who's rendered speechless.

Kent rounds the island to stand beside me, but seems to read my body language and maintains a reasonable distance.

"From the very beginning of the project, all you wanted was the exit door. You couldn't get away from me fast enough. I needed time." He takes a step toward me. "Time to get to know you, for you to get to know me. To give us a chance."

I flash back to the myriad of project delays and stumbling blocks and it registers: every single one of them was because of Kent. Mortar patch deficiencies, repair problems, stone supply—all client-directed changes or scope additions.

My stomach sours.

"You lied to me," I say with a laboured breath. "You lied to Larry, to the entire team. What the hell, Kent?"

"I've told you, sometimes I make terrible choices. This was one of them." He folds his arms in front of his chest. "I fucked up."

Thing is, it isn't as simple as one terrible choice. This is a *series* of terrible choices, the manipulation of an entire team of people in almost diabolical ways. The thought makes my stomach twist.

Then I remember the quarry, and my heart sinks. The turning point in our relationship was just a fabricated scheme.

My hurt flips over to anger.

"The quarry…" It comes out like a whisper.

Kent moves in closer. I can tell he wants to touch me, but he thinks better of it.

"The quarry wasn't even my idea. It was Larry's, remember?" He leans in to make eye contact, begging me with his own to listen. "I didn't mean to take it that far. When we got back—after our time together there—I let all of the stone repairs go; we didn't even need the materials in the end."

"How magnanimous of you," I spit out.

I pick up my bag and make for the door. I can feel a rush of emotion coming over me and my self-preservation instincts take over: I need to get out.

"I'm sorry," Kent insists, following me.

I turn back, his words igniting a spark that flashes to hot rage.

"You're only sorry you got caught."

He shakes his head. "That's not true."

"Then why didn't you come clean, at least with me?"

"I could never find the right time to admit what I'd done."

"Maybe between dances in my kitchen?" I lean in closer for emphasis. "Or how about before hand-jobs against my front door?"

My harsh words land exactly as intended.

He winces, raking both hands through his hair and taking a deep breath. "I knew I had to tell you. But how do you tell the woman you'd turn your entire life upside down for that you've deceived her?"

His words nearly do me in. I need to look away to keep the tears from coming.

He must know he's making headway, because he comes closer.

"I just wanted to get lost in you for a while. Lost in *us*."

"It was all lies," I declare. Judgement passed; no jury required.

"Nothing I feel for you is a lie."

"Don't." I hold a hand up.

"And if not for this fucking scaffold delay, we'd be telling everyone that we're together," he continues.

The scaffold.

Something in my mind clicks.

"That was you too, wasn't it?"

He doesn't even try to hide it.

"I panicked the night at the pub. You backtracked after I was sure we'd finally connected at the quarry. You were going to bail. I called in a favour with a friend at the Ministry…but I refuse to feel bad about that. In the end, people's lives were at risk. I feel *good* about what I did there."

Points to Kent.

"Yeah, it feels good to toy with people's jobs," I retort.

I approach the door, but he steps in front of me.

Wrong move, Kent.

"Do *not* stop me," I command.

"Please don't go. You're moving too fast. We need to talk this out."

"There's nothing to discuss."

He looks at me with sad eyes, glassy with unshed tears. I can see his chest heaving from stress. If I'm honest with myself, half of me wants to smooth his furrowed brow with a kiss, the other wants to run for the hills.

The two sides battle it out in my heart. How do I trust a word he's saying when our entire relationship is built on deception?

"I was foolish. I know that. Let me make this right," he pleads. He's as close as he can get without touching me.

I almost do it. I almost stay. Instead, I turn away and reach for the handle.

"I saw you at the McKinnon House." Kent's words land as my hand does on the metal.

I freeze.

"We wanted to check out other Fleming projects to see comparable work before we awarded the contract," he continues. "You were tearing a strip off a mortar supplier for getting your sand ratio wrong. You were a force to be reckoned with, Bella. Your spirit, your intelligence. It's like a film came off my world and I finally saw in colour." His words spill out like he's in a confessional.

I keep my eyes fixed ahead; I'm still gripping the lever.

"You wrecked me. I couldn't stop thinking about you. I had to have you."

At that, I flip around to face him.

"*Have me?* What the fuck, Kent? I'm not some prize. What kind of toxic shit is that?"

"That's not what I meant. My words aren't coming out right. I had to *know* you. I needed you in my life."

He tries to get closer, but I step aside.

"Just like now, every time I opened my mouth, I ruined it. You hated me. The only way I could keep you near was to do these stupid things."

I say nothing.

"Please Bella, don't go. Stay."

The fact that I'm considering it only makes me angrier. Angry at him, angry at myself.

"Don't pull your swoony '*stay*' shit with me. I fell for that once and only once—that will *never* work again." I point my finger at him furiously.

The version of Kent that looks back at me is distressed and disheveled, but as handsome as ever, and I feel the first fracture in my heart. His hair is a mess, and his eyes threaten to overflow.

He drops to his knees.

"If you want me to beg, I will. No hesitation. Please, Bella, give me a chance. Give *us* a chance."

I shouldn't be surprised that he's laying it all on the line like this, but the shock of his forthrightness might undo me.

He tentatively places his hands on my hips, smoothing them over my cotton sundress. I don't resist his contact because I know this might be it—the last time he ever touches me. I sigh against the bittersweet softness of his caress and swallow back my tears.

I summon the last of my courage, stand tall and strong to face him.

"You've done exactly what you said you never would—taken advantage of your power over me. You made my career some sort of game to toy with and you played with my heart too. I will never forgive you for it."

It feels like leaving part of myself behind me when I pull away from his grip. I block out the sound of him calling me as I walk out the apartment door.

Like a tracer and sledge cracking through stone, I feel the last break in my chest as the elevator doors slide shut after me.

CHAPTER 31

Nothing gets a person out of self-pitying fetal position faster than the sound of a cat barfing up a hair ball.

The next morning, I go from blissful unconsciousness to bolt upright in the time it takes to register the sound of three Gherkin gags. In the end, I'm one gag too slow. By the time I've made two determined strides to move him to the hardwood, he's thrown up on the rug.

Fucking cats.

Once I've cleaned the mess, I'm so wide awake from silent rage that heading back to bed would be a pointless exercise. I head out to the kitchen and stick a high-caffeine pod into my coffee machine and make the groggy walk to the bathroom.

When I catch myself in the mirror, I'm horrified by what I see: dark under-eye circles, bloodshot eyes, and perhaps the worst bed-head of my life. I release a defeated sigh and splash cold water on my face.

So far I've managed to keep my shit together. No crying myself to sleep, no wishing he would chase me, no second-guessing myself. I refuse to cry over this man who has clearly maneuvered me in unacceptable ways.

I'm making a clean break, and the healthy choice to move forward and not look back.

Dragging myself to the kitchen to collect my coffee, I curse at the mess that awaits me. In my sleep-deprived fog I forgot to put a mug under the spout and my full-octane sanity syrup has spread clear across the counter.

Fucking coffee.

Once I've cleaned up mess number two, I make another cup. I slip into a chair with the warm mug in my hands and lean into the distracting task of reviewing the documents on the hard drive Larry dropped off two days ago.

Two days. So much can change in two days.

I shift from downloading documents to reviewing spreadsheets to checking emails, but absolutely nothing holds my attention. I consider taking a break to read my book, but in my present state I'd only end up rereading the same page over and over.

I pull my chair back from the table and view my space objectively. Like my mind, it's a total mess. Scattered papers, stacks of books, random tools and trinkets. Cleaning has always been my distraction method de choix.

A clear workspace makes a clear mind, right?

I collect the books first, neatly returning them to my shelves. Then I carefully sort the papers, tossing the unneeded scraps and scribbled notes left over from drafting my abstract. The restored order is remarkably satisfying.

I move to the collection of miscellaneous items that have been cluttering my workspace for weeks. When I pick up a toolkit to remove it from the table, I miss an open latch. The bottom starts to fall out from under it, but I manage to catch it before it falls. In the struggle, one single item slips out and skitters under the table. Getting down on hands and knees to find it, I catch a shiny piece of plastic wedged between a chair and the wall. I reach over and grab it, then hold it up to see what fell.

Fucking French curve.

A whimper escapes when I involuntarily picture the solid black outline of the same shape across Kent's perfectly formed chest. I resist the urge to fold in on myself.

It's the crap cherry on top of my shit sundae.

I stand and grab my phone, dialling Greta's number. Thankfully, she picks up after the second ring.

"Hey, Bells. I can't talk long—I'm running cable."

I sigh in relief just hearing her familiar voice.

"G, I'm going to need your help."

"Please take this and have Tom return it to Kent." I hold out the Beck T-shirt to Sarah and prompt her to take the garment. "I need to get it the hell out of here."

I practically toss it at her like it's contaminated. And maybe it *is*—filled with dangerous chemicals that could make me second-guess every single decision I've ever made.

Pheromones are a bitch.

She stuffs it in her oversized purse. A sad sound escapes me when the blue fabric disappears from sight, but I mask it with a cough and head back to the kitchen to grab my wine.

Greta has mobilized the troops. She's assembled a small team equipped with plenty of food and drink and enough unfailing loyalty to help me through the night.

Along with Sarah, Greta has brought along our friend Violet—a badass commercial diver who just happens to be on leave from her current contract making repairs to an offshore oil platform. Greta, Violet, and I are just three of a larger group of formidable females who are dear friends and have bonded closely from being fellow women in trades.

We're convened in my living room, spread haphazardly across my overstuffed couch and surrounded by a teenager-worthy junk food pile and rim-defying drink pours. I've done my best to get everyone up to speed on the situation and while glasses are being topped up, the gang is still processing the information I've given them.

Since the relationship was kept under wraps, no one had been aware of the latest developments. While they certainly weren't surprised by the news—least of all Greta—they're still awkwardly at the starting line when Kent and I are clearly at the finish.

I'd been worried about how Sarah might take the news. We're so close, and I wasn't sure how she'd feel about being left in the dark. Plus, with Tom and Kent being such good friends, it adds complexity to the situation. I don't want her to feel caught in the middle.

"How are you holding up?" Sarah asks.

It means a lot to me that this is her primary concern.

I grab her hand and give it an affectionate squeeze. "I'll be fine."

Clearly I'd fretted needlessly.

"Well, shit. Thank god you're off the project," Violet remarks.

I sigh with relief. "Yes, that's rather serendipitous." I take a generous drink from my wine glass.

"But wait, what *are* you going to do?" Violet asks, tucking a lock of her silky platinum hair behind her ear. "Someone should be telling your boss that Kent pulled this shit." I'm taken aback by the uncharacteristic harshness of her tone. "He should lose his job over this."

I've already given this some thought and decided I'm

not going to say anything to Larry. I mean, I *could* tell Larry. I could even tell Kent's father. I could probably do some pretty significant damage to him professionally and personally. But I won't.

All feelings aside, I still oddly respect Kent professionally. While his decisions were extremely short-sighted, and hurtful to me personally, I don't think he intended to damage the Fleming business or harm anyone.

Besides, what would I even tell them? That in order to keep me—Isabella Avery—he deceived an entire team with a string of false delays and bogus deficiencies? I still hardly believe it myself.

I realize I haven't answered Violet when I find three sets of eyes staring back at me.

"No, I'm not going there. I just want this behind me."

"What's next then?" Greta asks.

"I'll do what I always do—dust off a few feminist T-shirts and wear them passive-aggressively at work for a few weeks." I give them a smug smile.

Weaponized feminism—the best kind of therapy.

"My fave is your Cyndi Lauper *Girls Just Wanna Have Fundamental Human Rights* shirt." Sarah chuckles and takes a generous swig from her beer.

"No, no, no, her best is the Hillary Clinton *Nasty Woman* tee," Greta says.

"Come on, how are we even debating this? *Smashing the Patriarchy Is My Cardio* wins, hands down," Violet insists.

I do have an impressive collection.

It's admittedly a relief to be making light of the situation. I settle back comfortably in the couch.

Sarah shoots a knowing look at both Greta and Violet, and after a few quiet seconds, leans in to speak. "Well, professional matters aside, how are you actually feeling about this?"

Well, that didn't last long.

"I've gotta say, all things considered, you're remarkably composed," Violet adds.

The women exchange cautious looks.

"How should I be?" I ask. "I refuse to fall apart over a man who clearly manipulated me. I won't waste my tears, thank you very much."

I take a large drink from my glass, enjoying the slight alcoholic burn from the dry wine as it slides down my throat.

"You're only human, Bells," Greta says softly.

"It's okay if you fall apart a bit. It's okay to be sad." Sarah reaches over to squeeze my leg.

"I know." I sigh. "And I know you're all here to help me pick up the pieces if I do."

"Admitting that you're heartbroken isn't going to threaten your feminist ideals, you know," Greta says, between handfuls of popcorn. "Strong and successful women get their hearts broken too."

Don't I know it.

"I'm not feeling very strong or successful these days." My body sinks further into the couch.

My words elicit an unexpected and categorical response in Violet.

"Don't do that, Bells. You're letting shit that you had no control over steal your power."

Being slightly older than the rest of us, Violet has always filled the big sister role among the group and been a steady hand when the rest of us show less restraint. Her disproportionately angry statements today are leading me to wonder if my own trials and tribulations are hitting a personal nerve.

"Sometimes forgiveness is power." Typically bullshit-proof Greta doesn't seem herself tonight either.

Is Mercury in retrograde?

"I'm not going to forgive him," I say decisively.

"That's the spirit." Violet raises her glass to toast me.

"Stop that," Greta says, pushing Violet's drink away. "I'm just saying that while you absolutely don't *have* to, it's still okay if you *want* to. The power lies in having the choice. Not in stubbornly refusing to do so."

Greta grabs the gummy worm from Violet's hand and shoves it into her mouth.

Violet shakes her head. "Why are you being so bloody rational? I want to be a stubborn asshole. I want *Bella* to be a stubborn asshole."

"What's going on with you?" I ask Violet.

"Is this because of your breakup with Charles?" Greta asks.

Bingo!

"No, Christ. That's history," Violet replies with a swat of her hand. "Completely irrelevant. This has nothing to do with Charles. Moving on." The expression on her face tells otherwise, but she's not talking.

A conversation topic for another day, it would seem.

"I can't believe he begged," Sarah says, eyebrows raised in surprise. To this point she's remained rather quiet about the situation.

"Yeah, wow," Greta says. "But I'm not surprised. I mean, how far gone does a man have to *be* to go to *these* lengths to keep a woman?"

The room goes silent.

Until now, Kent's side of things has neither been considered nor discussed. I feel a pang in my chest as I remember the sight of him: distraught and on his knees. I see his sad blue eyes willing me to stay. I feel the traces of his warm hands on my hips, gripping my smooth cotton dress as I pulled away.

I stop myself and shake my head.

"I refuse to believe this kind of shit is a sign of his affections. It's the grownup equivalent of telling me that the kid who pulls my hair likes me. It's fucking toxic."

With that, all discussion about Kent's side of the story comes to an end.

The girls leave around midnight—by our standards, very late. Work starts early for women in trades. It had been obvious they were reluctant to leave me, and their sacrifice of precious sleep to care for me means more than they could ever know.

I feed Gherkin a snack and head to the bathroom to get ready for bed. I'm exhausted, but when I finally climb into bed, sleep eludes me.

I toss and turn, trying hard but failing disastrously to block out moments and memories.

"It's like a film came off my world and I finally saw in colour."

I roll to my back and squeeze my eyes shut, blocking out the mental images of us together—hot and hurried moments and intensely intimate ones too.

"I'd rather show you."

I end up on my side, knees up protectively. I rub at my chest, desperate to wipe away the ache that's settled there, pretending not to notice in the empty silence of the room that a part of me is missing.

CHAPTER 32

Lying starfish in my queen-sized bed, I stare at the ceiling. The apartment is eerily silent. Once again, I've beaten the alarm by hours, so the comforting morning sounds of the neighbourhood haven't started yet. No traffic coming in through the windows, no neighbours shutting doors or drivers starting their vehicles. I pick up the rhythmic sound of my fridge motor from across my apartment. In the relative quiet it's conspicuously loud.

So are the voices inside my head.

Ninety-nine percent of the time I love living alone. Right now—this very minute—is the one percent I don't. The lonely hour.

A thought sneaks in before I'm lucid enough to stop it: Is Kent lying awake and alone in his bed right now too?

I cover my face with my hands.

Stop it. Don't do this to yourself.

But I spiral.

My mind goes straight for the worst-case scenario: What if he's not alone?

I hate that, despite best efforts not to, I linger on this

question. I hate the way my chest squeezes when I do. But what I hate the most is that even after telling myself again and again that the shit he's pulled is toxic—that I'm doing the right thing by walking away—an ounce of regret remains.

At least I'm not cleaning up cat puke this morning.

I roll myself out of bed and go on autopilot. I start my morning ritual: feed cat, insert coffee pod (with mug this time), hit the bathroom, grab brewed cup, head to the table.

I decide that today *must* be the day I finally leave the apartment. I cannot stay holed up in this place indefinitely, despite the temptation to do so. Working from home makes it dangerously easy to slip into the shut-in life. I'm not quite ready to head back to Mr. Muscle, but I think a yin yoga class would do me some good.

Once I'm settled with my morning coffee, I pull up the Zen Den app and pre-register for Dana's evening yin class. A slow and meditative practice is exactly what I need.

Next, I check my work email for urgent items. Sadly there's nothing for me. Not a single note from Larry or the rest of the team to offer a pleasant distraction. All is silent on the work front, but I suppose it's to be expected. At this point, they know I've been transitioned to the next project and won't be bothering me with the minutia of project wrap-up.

I scroll to the bottom of my unread messages, and amongst the spam I spot an email with the subject heading "Invitation to Participate." I check the sender address. My heart flutters when I see it's from the International Conservation Council's abstract review committee.

From: abstracts@icc.org
Subject: Invitation to Participate

Dear Ms. Avery,

Your abstract titled Adopting Laser Technology for Cleaning Exterior Masonry Buildings: Illustrative Examples from the Taylor Building has been accepted by the review panel. We would like to extend a formal invitation to participate as a speaker at the upcoming ICC annual conference.

Please reply with confirmation of your acceptance as soon as possible. We look forward to seeing you.

Sincerely,
ICC Review Committee

I let out a squeal.

This is amazing news for me professionally, but equally positive for Fleming, who will get a boost from the publicity. It's such a great opportunity to feature the work done by all of us on the Taylor building.

I jump to my feet and clap my hands together.

I can't wait to tell Kent.

My heart sinks the moment my mistake registers.

Dammit. I just broke my own heart.

By the time I get to yoga, I'm so tired.

I've been stumbling through life since my world blew up on Tuesday. It's been one foot in front of the other as I push through to the end of the week. Friday, sweet Friday:

when I can fetal position under the covers and hide away from the rest of the world for a couple of days.

One more day. I can do this.

I run into Dana in the change room. She fills her water bottle at the sink while I'm taking off my hoodie. Her trademark soothing voice pulls me from my thoughts.

"Are you alright, Bella? You look a little sad."

I want to crawl into her supportive arms and speak my truth.

Seems Dana is the heartbreak whisperer.

"Work's just been a lot lately."

I'm not exactly lying.

"Take care of yourself. Listen to what your body is telling you during class today. Don't push too hard."

Her words settle around me like a warm, fuzzy blanket. They're like medicine for my soul.

"I hope tonight is exactly what you need." She twists on the cap.

"Thanks, Dana."

What is it about other people being nice to you that can crack your façade? Dana's kindness threatens to undo me, and I have to breathe through it to maintain composure.

"See you in there." She walks away and greets other students at the door.

The extent of my exhaustion finally hits me—fatigue from days spent wearing a mask of acceptance and pretending I'm not coming apart at the seams.

I sit on the change room bench and rest my face in my hands. I close my eyes and try to work through the unexpected wave of sadness that threatens to overtake me. After a few minutes, I find the energy to collect my things and head into the studio.

Once I'm on my mat, the warmth of the hot studio soothes my aching muscles and the familiar scent of essential oils helps to settle me.

Dana presses *play* on a beautiful playlist of hammered dulcimer. A sense of calm falls across the studio.

"Welcome to your sixty-minute yin class, everyone."

Dana leads by example, taking a deep breath in and long breath out, prompting the rest of the class to do the same. She doesn't even have to try; her presence is enough to still the room. Zen is her superpower.

"Today's practice is intended to challenge us mentally, physically, emotionally. We will be holding our poses for several minutes. The challenge will be in maintaining our focus and breathing through the intensity of each pose."

Dana walks slowly and lightly through the room, speaking as she weaves through the yoga mats and everyone sinks further into their calm.

"These positions are a metaphor for life. In mastering the ability to breathe through these sometimes unsettling holds, we will learn to breathe through the challenges in our daily lives."

Breathe in, breathe out.

I mimic her breaths. One deep breath in, hold it for a few seconds, then let it out. We haven't yet moved from the restful pose on our backs, and I'm already finding it difficult to stay present and not let my mind drift.

"While your practice is meant to challenge you, if at any time a pose doesn't serve you, causes you pain, or simply isn't working today, please feel free to modify or skip it. This practice is yours and meant only for you. Let it give you what you need."

A lump returns to my throat. Dana's kind voice is threatening to undo me again.

"Today's practice will be a hip-opening yin practice. Our poses will be focused on the hips, which hold a lot of tension in our bodies."

My hands instinctively go to my hips, as if willing them to relax.

"By working the hips through yin practice, we aim to break that tension and bring peace to our minds, bodies and souls."

Dana's voice continues to soothe the class. Warm and soft, punctuated with exaggerated breaths that remind everyone to just breathe.

We're in good hands.

Eventually Dana guides us to a reclined butterfly—our first long hold. While the pose is simple and passive, I notice immediately how difficult it is to relax and be present in the moment. But I maintain a disciplined practice; each time my mind drifts I bring it back to the studio and refocus on what's around me.

The sounds.

The sensations.

The smells.

"The hips are associated with the sacral chakra, which houses our creative energy and sexuality and is connected to how we relate to our own emotions and the emotions of others," Dana explains. "Don't be surprised if you find yourself feeling emotional today as we break through tension in the hips and unblock the sacral chakra."

I begin to worry I've made a terrible mistake.

It wouldn't be the first time I've underestimated the power of yoga.

Despite what my sacral chakra might need, I manage surprisingly well to block the memories of Kent and his beautiful body working through his own poses masterfully here in the studio. It helps I've chosen the opposite side of the studio to practice today.

But as we shift from pose to pose, other memories creep past the barriers of my focus. By the time I'm stretched out in reclined swan, they've infiltrated completely, playing through my mind like a bittersweet highlight reel.

The deeper I stretch, the faster they seem to play.

Haphazard and disparate, each frame is a painful study of our connectedness and chemistry.

It's just noise.

I concentrate again on my posture, my breathing, my practice.

I listen closely to Dana's voice and let her centre me for a few minutes until the intrusive thoughts sneak back in. This time the pictures are different, snapshots in time that frankly take my breath away.

His dimpled laugh.

His hand against my pale skin.

My fingers tracing black lines along his chest.

They're a collection of ordinary moments that felt nothing less than extraordinary and made my heart glow, incandescent.

I'm stretched out in pigeon pose, head resting passively on my forearms when the memories culminate with close moments and honest words spoken in the dark.

"Tell me you feel this too."

A phrase so intensely intimate and exceptional that it finally does me in.

I don't fight it when the undertow of emotions pulls me in. I surrender completely as it draws me down, awash with poignant remembrance as the current takes me with it.

I begin to sob on my mat as the sense of loss sets in.

Ours was a fleeting and fiery relationship that was over before it even had the chance to begin. With us having to keep to the confines for discretionary purposes, I'm left with nothing tangible to show for it. Not a single photo, not a dried flower, not even a hand-written note scribbled on a piece of paper. Just phantom kisses and spectral scenes that destroy my inner peace.

I don't know that she's approaching until I feel Dana's warm hand press against my back. I sink further into the mat. She makes soothing circles in a clockwise direction as my body shakes in a vain attempt to contain my cries.

"That's it, Bella. Let it out," she whispers. "Let it give you what you need."

I spend the rest of the session in wide-legged child pose on a tear-soaked yoga mat. Class continues without me and I'm too much in crisis to care.

CHAPTER 33

I seek comfort in the company of my mother at my parents' kitchen table. It's the backbone of my childhood. The place where no problem can't be solved. World leaders could broker peace deals at this beat up old chunk of wood.

Having managed to scrape through the work week, I surmise that something's gotta give. I'm allowing myself the weekend to sort out my proverbial shit and get on with the business of living.

And let's face it. When shit's getting real, it's time to talk to Mom.

I'm clinging to a very strong gin and tonic that's been lovingly prepared from my mother's latest boutique bottle. I'd suggested a cup of tea, but once my mother laid eyes on me, she said, "We're going to need something stronger."

I guess I look just as bad as I feel.

We've worked past the niceties and are approaching the topic at hand when my phone's trademark ringer sounds. I glance at the display and see it's Larry calling. It's late, and on previous occasions I may have been tempted to let it go to voicemail, but my lack of productivity these last few days makes me want to overcompensate.

"Hey, boss."

"At ease, soldier. I'm just calling to congratulate you. Awesome news about the conference, Avery."

"Thanks, Lar."

"It's good news for all of us. We'll send a small delegation to do some networking and ride your coattails."

I chuckle. "Walk two paces behind, minions."

"I went ahead and made a formal request to Kent to publish documentation and other Taylor building information, you know, on behalf of Fleming. He got back to me within minutes. Formal approval granted, no questions asked."

"Oh!" Hearing his name completely throws me. I pause.

"Avery?"

I pull myself together.

"That's great. Thanks." I'm honestly relieved he had the foresight to do it. In all my excitement it hadn't even occurred to me that we'd need his permission. It spares me one very awkward email.

There's another moment of silence as Larry undoubtedly wonders what's going on.

I feel the need to end the phone call. "Listen, I better go. I have tons of data to get through before we mobilize at Bryson next week."

Then I remember it's seven p.m. on a Friday night—there's no way I'd be working this late.

Shit.

Well, I'm committed now.

"Thanks for calling," I add, staying on message.

"Later, Ave."

I hang up and put my phone down on the table. Mom's curious face awaits me.

"Want to tell me what that was all about?"

I cross my arms on the cool wood surface in front of me and I let my head fall on top of them. Where do I even begin?

"Bella?" Mom urges.

After a few seconds I sit up properly in my chair, take a fortifying swig of my drink, and try to summarize the entire complex situation in one sentence.

"Kent and I decided to give it a go, but I found out he manipulated me in diabolical ways and so now it's off again."

Mom remains silent. I study her face for reaction, but it remains blank.

"You're going to have to start at the beginning." She takes a generous slurp from her own glass, like she knows she's going to need it.

I recount the highlights, focusing on how we'd decided to try a relationship, how I'd spoken with Larry and stepped away from the project, and how I'd found the pallet of stone. I don't provide every detail of my confrontation with Kent, but I do mention it had been quite emotional and fraught with tension.

When I'm done speaking, I finish my drink in one last, medicinal gulp.

"Okay," Mom says.

"That's it? That's all you're gonna say?"

"I'm reserving judgment."

"Why?"

"It's what mothers do."

Fair point.

Mom grabs my empty glass and steps over to the counter to mix me another.

"How are you holding up?" she asks over her shoulder.

"I'm pissed. I think what he did was an enormous abuse of power. I think some of the things he said to me are red-flag-level toxic, and I think it's a damn good thing I found that pallet when I did."

Mom returns to the table, hands me my second drink, and takes a sip from her own.

"Have you heard from him since?" she asks.

I feel a small pang in my chest when I consider that he's not even tried to call or text, but it's a little late now for me to backtrack on wanting him to respect my boundaries.

"No, and I think that's for the best. I think a clean break is smart. I'm drawing my line."

"I've been hearing the word *think* an awful lot in your sentences, Bella. You're telling me all about what you think, but what about how you feel?"

It's the question I've been dreading. The one my dear friends were probably too cautious to ask. Leave it to Mom to cut straight to the chase.

Up to now, I've skillfully draped a sheet of irate intolerance over my greyer feelings and tucked in the edges neatly like little hospital corners. Quite frankly, I don't want to lift my cover. After last night's breakdown at yoga, I'm afraid of what's underneath.

I look at my dear mother across from me and make a silent agreement with myself: in the safety of her love and support I'll take one peek, explore what might be hidden.

The moment that I do, my mind snags on something he said.

I look down at the lime floating in my glass. "He said that when he first saw me, it was like he finally saw the world in colour."

When I say it, the power of my emotions overwhelms me, and I have to blink away tears. I look up from the drink I'm clutching and catch the sad sympathy on Mom's face.

"Wow, Bella. That's beautiful."

"Yeah." I take a ragged breath.

"Powerful," she adds.

I mask my emotions with a casual laugh and shrug, feigning indifference.

"Whatever. He was probably just saying that to make me stay."

"Is that what you think?"

I need to shut this down. I'm foundering.

"Putting what he said aside, putting what he *did* aside, it was way too much too fast, Mom. I wanted him to join us for lunch, for Chrissakes. What was I thinking?"

"Maybe you *weren't* thinking for a change—you were just feeling?" Mom suggests.

I don't respond. I wouldn't know what to say if I did.

Mom takes a slow drink and sets her glass down.

"The word *diabolical* may be a titch overdramatic, don't you think?"

Of all things for her to fixate on.

I quickly make a mental list of his offences:

Hid a pallet of stone. *Bad.*

Dragged a self-professed stone geek on an all-expenses-paid trip to a stone quarry. *Okay, less bad.*

Had a hissy fit over some mortar patches, made me redo several stone dutchmen to improve their overall appearance and ensured work was performed to an incredibly high standard. *Okay, maybe he's not quite the devil.*

"Do you honestly think I'm judging him too harshly?" I ask.

"I don't think it's *him* you're judging here at all."

My brow furrows. "Do you remember how confused you were when Gerard and I started collecting Pokémon cards?"

"Yes…" Mom shoots a curious look in my direction.

"That's how I feel at this moment. Speak English to me."

"Ah yes, here it is. Your signature sarcasm and humour, wielded as a deflection tactic."

"I wasn't actually trying to be funny just now. I guess I just *am*," I quip.

"Always easier to laugh and play everything down than talk about difficult subjects. But here's the thing…*you* came to *me*, Isabella. Clearly you want to talk about it."

Whoa, she's giving me the full *Isabella* treatment.

I know she isn't scolding me, but I can't help feeling a little smaller as she calls me out on my crap. And she's right. I did come to her. I'm not even sure why I'm having such a hard time being real with her right now.

This is my mother in front of me, someone I've always been forthright with. Someone who—aside from the more intimate details, because *eww*, she's still my mom—I've always been able to discuss my relationships with. Why not now, after my complete meltdown last night?

I consider my next steps, then lean in.

"I may or may not have completely fallen apart at yoga last night."

"What do you mean by *fallen apart*?"

"What do *you* mean by it's *not him I'm judging here at all*?" I counter.

Mom sits back with a satisfied smile. She seems to think she's getting somewhere. It only confuses me more.

"You're your own worst critic. Always expecting yourself to follow some set of unwritten and ever-changing rules," she begins. She takes a sip from her glass and the lime slips to the bottom. "Now—your turn," she prompts.

I rip the Bandaid off.

"The emotions of our unceremonious split came to a head last night and I ended up crying into my yoga mat. I mean that literally, by the way."

A weight comes off my shoulders with the admission.

"I'm not surprised. It's a lot to take in. I get the sense that you two had really connected. You know, it wouldn't break any *rules* if you wanted to talk things out with him."

I try not to bristle at the tone Mom uses as she verbally underlines the word "rules."

"Are you seriously telling me that you would have tolerated this kind of crap from Dad?"

"I've tolerated worse from your dad. You just don't know about it." Mom swirls the ice in her glass as she waits for her words to sink in.

What?

"What does *that* mean?" I ask.

"No relationship is perfect, Bella. You have no idea what people have faced either alone or as a couple."

"Are you telling me that Dad has..."

I don't even get to finish my sentence. Mom cuts me off with a raised hand and firm voice. "That's between me and your dad. Just as you didn't know all aspects of our origin story, you don't know—or *get* to know—every detail of our day-to-day relationship." Mom pauses and finishes her drink. "And for the record, your father has tolerated worse from *me* too."

I can't argue with what she's told me. What we see on the outside is just the weathered face of the larger stone—there's no telling what types of faults are inside.

"I'm sorry if maybe we were too successful in compartmentalizing things and keeping you kids out of it. Maybe that was a disservice to you, if your key takeaway is that every relationship has to be flawless."

I'm speechless.

I guess I know where my compartmentalization skills come from.

"I don't even know what to say," I finally admit.

"I've always worried a bit that you've idealized our relationship. Maybe I was right to worry."

"I have *not* idealized your relationship."

Wait. Have I idealized their relationship?

I've totally idealized their relationship.

"There's something else you need to consider," Mom begins.

Oh boy, what now?

I brace myself for the next revelation from Victoria Avery.

"In Kent's defence, he might be just as upset at *you* for talking to Larry about your relationship without speaking with him first."

My belly takes a nervous dive.

"What if Larry took the news poorly? What if you really did end up resigning? What if the news made the rounds? You didn't even give him the chance to get ahead of it."

Mom mops up the ring from her glass with a napkin while I consider the various scenarios.

Shit.

There were two of us to consider, but I operated unilaterally. That's not me. I'm a team player. How did it never occur to me to check with him first? And if it was this easy for me—Little Miss Standards and Guidelines—to lose the plot, it's no wonder Kent did.

"Didn't think of that, did you?" Mom asks with a raised brow.

"Shit, Mom. I totally messed up."

My realization is enough to tip the balance. A flood of emotions washes over me. My mom grabs my hands from across the table.

"Oh hon, you've always been so hard on yourself and those who try to love you. Holding everyone to some unattainable standard—worst of all yourself. Have you ever considered maybe you do that because it's safer?"

"What? How?" My words come out high and squeaky.

"Zero risk. But here's the thing—also zero reward. Relationships are all about risk, Bella. Calculated ones that make you dig deep and listen to your gut."

"Well, my gut's a bloody idiot if it's telling me to go to Larry without talking to Kent first," I grumble.

"You're not perfect, okay? Don't expect yourself to be. But maybe also go easy on others if they aren't either." Mom's smile is kind, and she grips my hands harder. "What's your gut telling you now?"

"It's telling me to run."

"Nah, that sounds like fear talking." Mom nudges me when I remain silent for too long.

"It's telling me this could be the biggest risk I've ever taken."

My heart races just recalling the events of recent days. The excitement of being together, the adrenaline rush of nearly getting caught.

"And?" Mom prompts.

"Maybe…the biggest reward," I nearly whisper.

With that acknowledgement, my emotional scales tip over and the tears finally start to fall. Mom stands and rounds the table to sit next to me, stroking my back.

"Oh, Bella."

I lean in for a hug, comforted by the familiar warmth of my mother. The smell of her timeless perfume grounds me with each breath.

"What do I do?" I say into her shoulder.

"I can't tell you that. You need to decide for yourself. But the good news is that—despite what you might think— there's no wrong answer."

Mom's shades-of-grey response isn't the answer I need.

I pull away and wipe the tears from my cheeks. "I want it black and white, Mom. I need cut and dried."

"Bella, relationships aren't rehab projects. You don't get to tie everything up with neat little reports and spreadsheets. You can't tear down the tarps and sweep up the debris. We're all messy and full of deficiencies. People make mistakes. I do, you do, Kent does. In the end, we're all just projects always under construction."

With that, I see them: my false expectations of myself and others. Bars set ridiculously high. Why hadn't I ever noticed this before?

The fatigue of several days without sleep and the effect of two generously poured drinks sets in and my eyes feel unprecedentedly heavy.

Mom places a hand on my shoulder. "Go rest on the couch for a bit. You're tired. Dad'll be home from grocery shopping soon. We can watch a movie or something."

"Okay," I say, heading to the familiar couch in the family room.

My thoughts return to Kent and his list of offences.

Do I talk to him? Do I let him explain? Do I take the chance that it will lead to our reconciliation? The thought both terrifies and thrills me.

Is reconciliation truly what I want? Do I accept him, deficiencies and all? Or is letting him back into my life a deficiency of my own? What if he does something like this again?

I'm so, so tired.

Paralyzed by fear and doubt, I simply don't know what to do.

So I do nothing.

CHAPTER 34

Five weeks later

"Thanks very much!" I close the back door to my Uber and head to the hotel's main door, wheelie case dragging behind me.

I'm more than a little flustered after a frustrating twenty-four hours of flight delays and cancellations. I'm cutting it close to my presentation time, but I'm thankful to have my luggage with me and still enough time to snag my early check-in and clean myself up before it's showtime.

After registering at the front desk, I scurry off to the elevator, hands loaded with a generous swag bag, my room key, and luggage. I head up to floor twelve where I locate my room and awkwardly stumble across the threshold.

I let out a relieved sigh as I throw off my jacket and slip off my shoes.

Time to get my head in the game.

I take a quick pan of the room and find an unexpected

mass of stunning pink flowers on a mid-century inspired credenza in the corner. I move closer to examine them. They're peonies—my favourites—in shades of light pink, with almost no greenery added to the vase.

I lean down to smell them and get a sweet hit of their incredible fragrance. I hunt for a card and find it wedged between the stems. There's no envelope, just a simple die cut of heavy stock that says "congratulations" across it. I flip it over to examine the back, searching for clues about the sender, but find none.

Probably just a gift from the committee.

As I'm heading toward the bathroom, a wine bucket catches my eye next to the large television monitor. Inside is a bottle of pink champagne chilling on ice.

"Wow, the ICC is really rolling out the red carpet!"

I'm feeling very much like a spoiled princess by the time I hit the shower.

The team has never seen me in anything but work clothes and safety equipment, so it feels a little strange as I select my outfit. I brought a few things to choose from. They're mostly blazers and dress pants, but I did bring along one dress for social events and even a pencil skirt if I want to pair it with a blouse. I consider my options.

I've been working on myself these past few weeks. Thinking about all my compartments and why I have them. Some are justified boundaries—a desire to separate "work" Bella from "play" Bella—and totally fair. But I've realized that some have been the result of expectations set on myself, the product of being too concerned about how I could be perceived by others.

I need to relax. Just be me. That's one gift Kent has given me: making me more comfortable in my own skin.

Kent.

I've done my best not to think about him.

Working my butt off on my presentation and all the

related materials has been the perfect distraction. I've thrown myself at the task entirely, and I'm one hundred percent ready for this.

Going bold, I decide to wear the grey pencil skirt and a matching blazer. I punctuate the outfit with a muted pink sleeveless blouse that's silky soft and incredible on my skin. It's a bit unexpected for me, but it'll make me feel like a boss when I'm standing at the podium.

I dress and put the final touches on my short hair and makeup. I use the last minutes I have to run through my speaking notes and make sure I have my USB stick safely tucked in my pocket.

I loop my name tag lanyard over my head, take one final look at myself in the mirror, and stand in a wide, confidence-building stance for just a few extra seconds before I make my way to the door. I take deep, filling breaths. *I've got this.*

I head to the elevator.

Larry and the rest of the Fleming gang are congregated in the atrium outside of the main presentation room when I find them. They're all looking a little uncomfortable in dress shoes, starchy dress shirts, and anti-wrinkle pants as they huddle together awkwardly.

"You're not going to get much networking accomplished like that," I say as I approach. "Allow me to introduce the concept of mingling."

The group turns to look at me. I brace myself for awkward glances and maybe a few teasing comments about my appearance.

They don't come.

"Hey, Avery," Reid says, like it's any day on the scaffold. Given his indifference, I might as well have a Carhartt shirt on and a pair of jeans.

I wait for others to notice, but they all just look genuinely happy to see me—like I brought a fresh dozen to the site trailer on a Monday morning. Leave it to a group of dudes to not even notice a transformation that's standing right in front of them.

Typical.

"You made it!" Larry says, adjusting his tie.

"What a trip! Thank god I'm here on time."

"You're going to kill it, Avery," Luke adds.

I smile, touched by the encouragement. "Thanks."

I check my watch; it's fifteen minutes before my time slot. I need to get to the podium and meet with my moderator before it's officially go-time. I say goodbye to the team and agree to meet them at the poster session later.

Inside the presentation room the air is cool, the AC cranked to accommodate the hundreds of warm bodies that will soon fill the seats. The chill and my nervous energy combine to make me shiver.

I shake hands with my moderator—a soft-spoken architect from a firm I've never heard of before. I make a mental note to google him later.

My belly starts to churn, but I remind myself that I know my stuff and could probably present this material in my sleep. The room begins to fill. I'm grateful when the Fleming guys occupy the front row—it will help having their familiar faces right in front of me.

I load my deck on the conference laptop and test out the remote control. The chairs quickly fill, and before long, the moderator has taken his position at centre stage.

It's a bit of a blur as he reads my bio and makes the introduction. Before long, he's handing the reins over to me.

It's too late to bail now.

I step up to the podium and glance down at Larry before I start, looking for gentle encouragement. I'm met by a loyal and friendly face who urges me, with a simple smile and nod, to proceed.

Using the notes in front of me as a guide, I jump right in with both feet.

"While relatively new, laser technology is quickly becoming the method of choice in architectural rehabilitation and conservation projects."

I transition through a couple of introductory slides and then continue to highlight the benefits of the technology.

"While being just one tool available to the mason, it represents the least invasive method of stone cleaning currently available to specialists. Laser is also an environmentally responsible choice, having little to no by-product and requiring zero chemical use." I pause for effect. "All factors considered, laser provides an alternative that is preferable to traditional abrasive or chemical cleaning methods."

I'm encouraged by the appearance of interest on the faces of the crowd, so I continue with renewed confidence.

"As you will see from our examples at our recent project, the Taylor Building, laser has been highly effective in cleaning wide expanses of flat stone expeditiously. When used in the early stages of the project, it can aid the team in assessing the true condition of the stone."

I quickly hit my stride, gesturing to photographic documentation on one slide before lab test results on another. All information has been carefully selected to show the crowd the advantages of this approach and the efficacy of the treatment.

Running on little sleep due to my red-eye flight, I think I might be hallucinating when I first spot him in the crowd.

I avert my gaze, keeping on-track and on-script, flipping to the next slide.

"See here how the laser has been highly effective in removing the heavy atmospheric pollutants from the building's façade." I gesture to the images on the large presentation screen.

After a couple more slides I instinctively pan to where I think I spotted him in the third row. When my eyes identify him conclusively—his dark hair and sharp jaw—it hits me like an adrenaline rush straight to my heart.

I stumble on my next sentence.

Fuck.

I examine the notes held tightly in my hand. They temporarily blur in front of me, obscuring my crafted script.

Get your shit together, Avery.

I look back at Larry and thankfully his ever-present smile works to reset my focus.

I'm spurred on.

Twenty-two slides later, I find myself at what is intended to be my dramatic conclusion. I look up high and tall into the audience, proud of what I've done, and wrap up my thorough analysis.

"In the end, we're left with a building with restored architectural legibility, improved water vapour transmission performance, and thorough repair. While removing potentially harmful and disfiguring soils, laser still leaves behind the material's distinctive patina and respects the historic building's passage through time."

I step away from the podium and fold the papers in my hand. "Thank you."

A generous round of applause erupts from the crowd, and I feel colour rushing to my cheeks. My heart swells with their approval.

The moderator steps up to the microphone and engages the audience, giving me a moment to take a few breaths.

"Audience members are welcome to approach the microphones located at the sides of the room, or you can place your questions and comments in the conference app chat feature. Do we have anything for our speaker?"

I field several inquiries about the technology. Someone asks about the cost of the equipment and training required to operate the laser.

A man wearing bold blue glasses steps up to the microphone to ask a final question.

"I've heard that laser machines have automated settings and practically operate themselves—anyone can use them. Can you speak to this?"

"This notion is a fallacy. Lasers require a knowledgeable and skilled operator, and putting a machine like this on 'preset,'" I pause to use air quotes, "takes the control of the unit away from the user. A professional needs to maintain full control over every tool they use."

I pause for a moment before elaborating further.

"As for who should be using them? Well, the laser is only as effective and as skilled as the person using it."

I don't think I mean to do it, but my eyes shift over to Kent as I'm speaking.

"The mason needs full control over their choices. When this control is lost, damage can occur that is both harmful and potentially irreversible."

The metaphor just spills out of me; I don't even catch it at first. There's a message I'm trying to send him as I finally brave eye contact. Bright and beautiful blue eyes stare back at me—his face is thoughtful and serious. The intense look Kent delivers leaves me with no doubt that he knows exactly what I'm saying.

Our connection only holds for seconds, but an unspoken exchange passes between us.

You took my power away from me.

I know.

The moment is lost in a flash as the moderator steps in between us. We transition to goodbyes and thank yous, leaving me to wonder if it happened at all.

I'm quickly encircled by a small group of participants offering me congratulatory messages and handshakes and —of course—I'm buoyed by my success. But after a few minutes pass, an opening breaks through the crowd and I can't help but look toward his seat.

He's already gone.

CHAPTER 35

I'm a bit rattled by the Q & A when I finally catch up to the guys at the poster session. I plaster on a fake smile and go through the motions, feigning interest in half a dozen subjects while subtly scanning every face in the crowd.

I'm lingering at a vendor's tool display when Larry approaches.

"We're gonna head out to grab a bite. You coming?"

I distractedly survey a set of handmade chisels.

"Honestly, Larry, I'm exhausted. I think I'm just going to go back to my room." I point my thumb over my right shoulder, attempting to appear casual, like the sight of Kent hasn't sent me spinning.

"All good?" he asks. "I spotted Armstrong in the crowd."

I shouldn't be surprised that he's noticed, but somehow I still am. Larry has proven himself time and time again to be an incredibly observant and astute person. He's a successful businessman in large part due to his people skills. I guess I've been so head-down in my own bloody business that I hadn't expected anyone to notice.

He takes a step forward and slides his hands in his pockets. Looks like he's trying to keep things casual too. "I don't know what's happened there—and it's really none of my business—but I'm here if you need to talk."

Oh, Larry. He's the best.

"I'm fine, Lar. Really. But thank you. I'm just having a bit of a post-travel and post-presentation crash. It's nothing some room service and sleep won't cure."

Days of sleep. Pounds of hotel cheesecake.

"We still have all day tomorrow to group bond," he says, leaning in slightly as he speaks. "Go put your feet up, Avery. You've earned it."

"Thanks. Keep those kids in line." I gesture to where Reid, Luke, Trevor and the others are standing in an awkward huddle. One's extracting a wedgie from his butt; another is using a piece of folded paper to pick food out of his teeth.

"They're a handful," Larry admits with a shake of his head.

I give his shoulder a pat. "Good luck with that."

I head to the main lobby before anyone can slow me down. Nothing is getting between me and this hotel's trademark feather bed.

I'm the first one on the elevator when it arrives at lobby level. I hit number twelve and settle at the back corner leaning against the railing, the full extent of my fatigue finally setting in.

It's been an emotional roller coaster of a day. No wonder I'm completely sapped.

A boisterous group of businesspeople get on at restaurant level three. They smell like beer, spirits and pub food, and have clearly had more than just a couple. The vibe they're giving off is innocent fun though, and I smile as they squeeze in together, all laughing as they accommodate the crowd.

Just as the doors are about to slide shut, someone holds the elevator. A tanned hand and exposed forearm reaches between the brass doors, stopping them just in time. A man slips in and takes the last space available in front of the button panel.

I freeze.

I watch his hand through a gap between occupants as it hits number eight.

My heart stops.

I'm too stunned to move.

I catch another glimpse of him through the shifting bodies. He's looking at his phone. My eyes pan the length of him. Through the sliver of view I'm afforded I see he's wearing navy-blue dress pants and a powder-blue button-up shirt that's pressed to perfection.

His choice at first seems odd: I don't think I've ever seen him wear blue.

His shirtsleeves are rolled up, exposing his beautiful familiar forearms and a stylish, large watch. He slips his hand in his pocket, the movement straining his tricep against the shirt's fabric. The sight of it sends a shot of chemicals through me. I grasp the railing harder, taking one step back so I'm flush with the mirrored wall.

I'm torn between wanting to shrink down to nothing-ness and wanting to jump up and scream.

The elevator moves so quickly. Before I've decided between options A or B, the entire group of tipsy profes-sionals file off at level seven and the door shuts behind them.

We're left alone.

Kent still doesn't realize I'm behind him.

I want to speak, but my voice isn't cooperating.

The elevator keeps lifting and lifting. I need to decide.

Do I let him go? Do I intervene?

What's the risk?

What's the reward?

I squeeze my eyes shut and take in a breath.

I'm not a big believer in fate. Quite frankly, I think we make our own fate. But being caught on an elevator alone with Kent in some surreal full-circle moment feels like a sign from the universe. It's telling me *this is your chance.*

Before I've had the chance to work out my strategy, the moment decides it for me. The elevator chimes and comes to a stop.

I'm still speechless.

Kent stashes his phone in his pocket and moves to make his exit as the elevator doors slide open.

I panic.

Before my brain registers what I'm doing, I grab his forearm. It's warm and strong and deliciously familiar. Heat rushes through me.

Kent spins around to face me.

I watch as the recognition hits him, as confusion and shock flip over to something kind and sweet.

His face lights up. The doors slide shut behind him.

"Hi," he says.

A single syllable.

A simple word.

It's everything.

A sense of calm washes over me.

"Hi."

It's all I can manage to say back.

CHAPTER 36

I drop his arm when I realize I'm still holding it.

"I'm sorry I grabbed you, I—"

"It's okay," he says eagerly, taking a step closer.

The moment hangs between us as the elevator starts to move. We just keep looking at each other in silence like neither can believe what's in front of us.

"Your presentation..." he says, pausing mid-sentence. "It was amazing."

"I stumbled a few times." I fiddle with my lanyard.

"Stop it, you did a great job. I'd hire you," he teases.

His playfulness makes me smile.

And just like that, a smile so bright and disarming crosses his face that it feels to me like summer sunshine after weeks of winter cloud. I survey his features: the light in his eyes, the white of his teeth and that indescribable dimple.

God, that dimple.

I refocus.

"I forgot to mention the—"

He doesn't let me finish.

"Each time you make a negative comment I'm going to counter with something positive."

"I mispronounced laser in my first sentence," I state, testing him.

"You handled those questions like the pro that you are."

Heat rushes to my cheeks.

"I can do this all night," he warns flirtatiously. His confidence as alluring as ever.

His bold choice of words causes a rush of unexpected heat. I swallow hard.

The elevator chimes and the doors slide open on my floor. We both stand in place, unsure of what to do next.

He glances at the display panel.

"Looks like I missed my stop." He doesn't look too upset about it.

"This is mine."

We switch positions, so I'm nearest the door. The cab is probably eight by eight, but we're acting like it's two feet deep. His hand grazes my hip in the shuffle, and he pulls it away reflexively.

Just the feel of his thumb brushing my skirt makes my skin hum and I find myself wanting to lean back into it.

I stand frozen at the threshold.

We stare at each other in silence as the seconds tick away, until the sound of the door's buzzer startles us out of our daze.

I know I shouldn't do it. I should just turn my back and walk away. But I can't let him go.

I grab his hand and pull him after me. The doors slide shut behind us and the elevator moves to another floor.

I look up at Kent, who's fixed with a surprised yet delighted expression.

"I'm sorry, I need to stop doing that." My face flushes with heat.

What the hell am I doing?

His eyes darken. He gives me a crooked grin.

Butterflies move in my stomach.

"We should talk," I declare. Then I lose my cool and backpedal. "If that's okay?"

"Yes," he says. "Of course."

Oh, god…I haven't thought this through.

"Where?" he asks.

Shit. Where?

Bringing him to my room seems completely inappropriate. If we go back down to the bar, we'll be surrounded—hard pass. The roof-top pool is a rumoured pick-up joint and jammed with singles at cocktail hour, so that's not a great choice either. If I suggest *his* room, he'll think I'm fishing for a booty call.

I quickly apply my conservation-standard risk-based decision-making and arrive full circle at option one.

"My room," I say flatly.

Kent's eyebrows shoot up.

"There's nowhere else to go right now that won't be socially awkward or impossible for us to hear," I explain.

His face returns to normal. "It's fine," he says. He gestures to the hall in front of us. "Lead the way."

I turn and walk toward my room, concentrating on my steps in my kitten-heeled shoes. It would be just my luck to snag one on the hotel carpet and land on my face right now. I take it one determined stride at a time until we're in front of my door and—with just a slide and click—we're walking inside.

Thankfully there is an anteroom of sorts with a seating area. It's not quite a suite, but it's a larger room, made for professionals who need to do business throughout their stay.

I busily remove things from the chairs as Kent surveys the surroundings. His eyes stop at the vase of pink peonies in the corner and I think I see him blush. When he spies me looking over at him, he covers his smile with a hand. There's a scratch to the upper lip and a rub of his nose.

I glance back at the flowers, and it clicks.

"They're from you."

He shrugs and slides one hand into a pocket. The other scratches the back of his head.

"How did you know I like peonies?" I ask.

"They're the same as the ones you caught at the wedding. I knew you liked them because you picked them up to sniff them after they'd fallen to the ground."

"I didn't realize anyone was watching me."

He turns to fully face me.

"Of course I was watching you. I couldn't take my eyes *off* you."

My chest tightens. The air feels thin.

"You knew what kind of flower they were?"

"Well, yeah." He shrugs nonchalantly. "I took a couple of landscape architecture courses."

I look over at the pink champagne still sitting in the bucket.

"Did you send that too?" I point at the foil-topped bottle.

"Maybe." He smiles. "Seemed on brand."

Holy, shit.

The man knows me well.

"Thank you."

"You're welcome."

I sit in a chair and motion for him to take the other. I'm desperate to get my shoes off, so I slip out of them and tuck my feet up underneath me.

I try not to notice how the fabric of his navy pants strains against the muscles of his thighs when he takes his seat beside me. I fail on that front epically.

"I'd offer you something to drink, but there's only tap

water or bad hotel coffee. We could open the pink champagne…"

Kent smiles. "I'm good, thanks."

He leans forward, elbows on his knees, and tents his fingers in contemplation. It's surreal to see those hands in front of me. I try not to think too much about them.

"So…" I start.

Kent jumps right in.

"I want you to know how sorry I am. I'm sorry for deceiving you, for hurting you. I never wanted anything other than honesty between us. I made a terrible mistake, and I've been thinking a lot about it these last few weeks—"

His words bring me instantly back to his apartment, to raw wounds and stinging hurt. I don't want to revisit that, so I jump in to change tack.

"I've been thinking a lot too," I interject.

He seems taken aback by my admission. "Yeah?"

"Yeah." I mirror his posture. "My mother thinks I hold myself and others to too high a standard."

He furrows his brow in confusion.

I shouldn't have done that—framed it like it's an accusation against me from my mother and not the honest truth. I take a deep breath and try again.

"She's right. I do. I think that's why I always compartmentalize so much. I have real hangups about how I should act around certain people—preconceived notions of what people expect of me. In turn, I expect too much from others. I'm not being fair to anyone, least of all myself. But I'm working on it."

"I'm working on things too." He sits back in his chair, relaxing into the cushions. I follow his lead and tuck my feet back up on the chair.

"God," he says, rubbing a hand across his forehead. "My issues have sub-issues." He takes a deep breath and continues. "I think that working for my father has been a terrible mistake. I felt pressured to take over the family business like a loyal son, but in the end, it just made me feel like I was under his thumb—a perpetual teenager."

"I never considered that."

"I never said *no* to him of course, because why on earth would I? It was easy. Want a job? Here you go. Want an apartment? Here's that too. The only time I really said no and did things my own way was after we lost Mom, and that was a complete over-reaction. Nothing healthy about it. In the end, it scared me right back onto my current path. There has to be something in the middle."

"Why didn't you ever tell me about this?"

"I was too busy living on autopilot, punching the clock and checking my boxes."

He winks and it makes me smile.

"Besides, what could I have possibly said that *wouldn't* have made me sound like a privileged, obnoxious asshole? 'Poor me, who has an amazing job and everything I'll ever need.'" He winces from his own words.

"Fair point."

"But what's way offside is how things have translated to my other relationships—both professional and otherwise. I think I need to be in control to feel like I have any autonomy over my life." He pauses for a moment. "I take it too far...like what I did with you."

His face is sad and weary.

What he says makes total sense. This is *his* list of deficiencies—we've all got them. It's okay that he has a long list; god knows I have one myself. I don't need to know he's perfect, but if I'm going to give this another go, I *do* need to know he's trying not to perpetuate the cycle.

"So what do you think you're going to do?"

"I'm working on a way out of the family business. It's not truly mine and not what I want to do for the rest of my life. I want to get back to architecture—do something more creative." He scratches the back of his head thoughtfully. "Mixing business and family hasn't been great for my dad and me either. I want a chance to reset that relationship too."

"This is big."

"Yeah, it is." He nods. "But I'm ready."

"You said 'that relationship *too*,'" I note.

"I did." His smile is coy.

"You said it like there are other relationships you want to reset."

I'm blatantly fishing.

"Because there are." His eyes twinkle. A flicker of hope, maybe? Or promise?

"Such as?"

I want to hear him say it.

"Bella, you know I'd do anything for a chance to make things right with you. I'm a total work in progress and I know I'll make mistakes. I'm just asking for a chance...to see where this could go."

"Under construction," I amend. A little chuckle escapes me.

"What?"

"Not a work in progress. You're just under construction," I say with a shrug.

He chuckles too.

Someday I'll properly explain it.

I look at the man beside me and know exactly what I want. It scares me how much I do. But as much as my feelings rock me, it's my own deficiencies that trip me up now.

"You really want to try this again, knowing that I'm a hot mess who has a head full of hangups and a boat load of unreasonable expectations?"

"Stop talking about my girlfriend like that."

My jaw drops in delighted astonishment.

The nerve.

"That's awfully bold, Mr. Armstrong."

I cross my arms, feigning indignation.

"Like I said before, every time you say something negative about yourself, I'm going to follow it with a positive."

"Oh, really?"

"Remember—I like highlighting your best parts." He shoots me a devilish grin.

Fuck, this man is saucy.

Heat rushes to my face. I'm shocked by the nerve of his comment—that he's made it so soon—but of course I'm fucking thrilled.

"Kent Armstrong, mind your orange highlighter," I tease right back.

He leans forward.

"I've moved on actually." He licks his bottom lip deliciously. "I'll have to underline and circle you now."

I lean forward too.

"Keep talking..."

"Maybe a few of those sticky flags."

"I think stationery is my new favourite position."

We laugh.

This. This is what I've missed most. The chemistry. The way we banter, playing off each other and making the other person funnier, smarter, brighter.

Life in spectacular colour.

In an instant, his words come back to me, and I stop to really look at him. His lapis-faced watch, the rosy colour of his cheeks, the powder-blue shirt that matches his eyes. It's like a charcoal-coloured filter's been pulled from the frame.

It all makes sense to me now.

"There's one more thing I need to address," Kent says, breaking my reverie. His face turns serious. "I've been examining and re-examining everything that happened between us..."

Where is this going?

My stomach twists ominously.

"I thought that showing up everywhere you went was funny and charming, but it was an invasion of your personal time and space. I'm sorry about that."

My heart lifts.

"But I loved it," I admit, my voice breathy.

"You did?" He seems legitimately surprised.

"Some might not have, but I did. And for the record, I don't think anyone else could have gotten away with it—you charming bugger."

"I should have asked," he insists.

"Now you can."

I grab his hand and squeeze. The gesture feels so natural to me, the fact that it's our first real affectionate contact in weeks doesn't immediately register.

When he threads his fingers through mine, it sends a slow wash of warmth up my arm and lights me up inside.

We sit in silence for a minute and luxuriate in our glow.

"Come here," he says, tugging on my hand.

I rise and join him, sitting sideways on his lap.

We watch together as his hand slides up my thigh and when we look up at each other a powerful surge of emotions comes over me. The same look is in his eyes.

"God, I've missed you," he breathes.

"I've missed you too."

The look on his face makes my chest ache. I've never seen him so serious or overcome with emotion.

"I'm going to be a better man. The kind of man my mother would have been proud of. The kind of man you deserve."

"Kent..." My forehead falls against his. I draw in a ragged breath.

"I'm a bit afraid to touch you."

"What? Why?" I cup the nape of his neck.

"Afraid you'll disappear, like some sort of mirage." He smiles nervously.

That's when I truly understand how much our time apart has hurt him. I'd only seen my side of the pain.

I pull back and rest one of my hands on his cheek. His eyes close as he leans into my palm, seeking comfort. His dark lashes close and reopen and I enjoy every handsome detail of his face.

"I won't. I'm real," I whisper.

I hold his face and kiss him like he's fragile in my hands. Tentative, gentle kisses that barely seem to land. The feel of his lips on mine is everything I remember, but this time they're truly precious—soft and safe and sweet.

When my hands move down to his chest—eager to feel his warmth and strength against my palms—he hitches his breath in response and parts his lips in invitation. Quickly we're lost in languid strokes that feel like we could kiss forever.

The tension builds. I shift restlessly on his lap. Things turn needy and wild as we try, with hot and bruising kisses, to make up for weeks of deprivation and angst-filled lost time.

Kent pulls away first, flushed-cheeked and rosy-lipped.

"I need to get access." He pans down my body and back up. The eyes that find me are dark and eager—exactly how I expect mine to be.

He slides off my blazer as we take our first daring step, planting one warm, reverent kiss over the silky fabric of my blouse where shoulder and neck meet.

His favourite part.

I feel drunk on my power, knowing what he's missed.

We step apart for just a moment, long enough for a silent message to pass between us.

You can have me—I'm yours.

As if to confirm understanding, he leans in to whisper, lips touching my ear.

"Let me show you what you mean to me, Bella. Please."

Goosebumps erupt on my skin; heat rushes straight to my thighs.

It feels like slipping off to sweet oblivion when our bodies finally come together on a hotel feather bed.

We're literally miles from where we started, but this is where we begin.

CHAPTER 37

Stretching to place my crystal flute on the bedside table, I clumsily spill a few drops.

Shit.

I mop up the pink, fizzy liquid with a discarded sock I find strewn on the floor, then burrow deeper under the sheets.

We've brought the pink foiled bottle back with us from the conference and finally popped the cork at Kent's place. We were in the mood to celebrate.

And celebrate we did.

Kent emerges from the bathroom, leaning against the door frame, full beautiful body on proud display. He's wearing only a pair of dazzlingly white briefs and a self-satisfied smile.

Oh, Christ—the tighty-whiteys from the wedding!

They're clearly at least one size too small, but the bugger can't look bad in anything even when he tries. The white of the cotton only enhances his lingering summer tan, the snug fit only highlights every gorgeous…um…*muscle.*

I giggle and pull up the sheets to cover my massive grin.

"Where the hell did you find those? The Armstrong archive?"

"At the back of my drawer. Aren't they spectacular?" he boasts. I think I spot a hip wiggle.

"Oh, they're *something* alright…"

"Come on, woman. They're tight. They're white. They're *right*."

Three bounds and he's on the bed with me, diving under the duvet and finding all my tickles. I squeal in unreserved delight.

The light from his smile is incandescent—a familiar burst of brightness supplied by striking blue eyes and white teeth against tanned skin.

He's a ray of golden sunlight and warm as the summer sun.

My sun.

The very centre of my orbit.

The end.

ACKNOWLEDGMENTS

I hope when you read these pages you can smell the lime dust from the mortar, the rattle of the scaffold is felt under your feet, and maybe—just maybe—their kisses bring a rush of heat to your cheeks. (I won't specify which ones.) Thank you, readers. That you took the time to read my book—when you could've chosen any other—means more to me than you'll ever know.

Who knew that a cup of tea and a simple conversation could lead to this? Amy Lea thank you for asking me "have you ever considered writing your own book?" Clearly it did something on some sort of subconscious level to rattle the creative thoughts loose and they sprang free.

Josie. Josie Juniper. Where do I even start? When I told her I'd imagined a story about a female stone mason and a project manager, she said "you need to write it!" Then she held my hand every step of the way and became the type of mentor and editor that most can only wish for. Thank you for your friendship. Thank you for making me a better writer. Thanks for helping me make the chapters as tight as Kent's ass. What fun we're going to have on our many adventures together.

To mom, who we lost in 2020. Much like Victoria Avery, she often surprised me with an unexpected story that seemed to tell me something I never knew about her or myself. As a true lover of books, she would have been so excited for me. I'm going to be excited for me on your behalf, Mom. I love and miss you.

Thank you to the four men in my life. Dad, thanks for always cheering me on. Please don't read this book. To my boys, who make me so proud every single day. I hope you never read this book. To Dave, for being my partner in every sense of the word and not only supporting my outrageous goals, but doubling down on the domestic front to make sure I can achieve them. You simply make me a better person. P.S. I encourage you to read this book.

To my sister Pam and my sisters from other misters— Heather, Emily and Jen. You are my rocks. The love and support you show me is endless. I hope the love and gratitude I feel for you is as obvious as the lust in Kent's face.

Beta readers probably don't realize how incredibly important they are to a debut author. By the time a book reaches these people, a new writer is both thrilled and terrified to share their first work. Thank so you much to my beta readers for their kindness and honesty and for helping me polish this story into what you see today. Sarah, Gen, Tara, Sam, Dani, Danielle, Heather, Monja and Eeva, thank you for sharing in my joy.

Social media can often feel like a weight on the chest, but sometimes it can bring happiness to your heart. I've found so many amazing authors and bookish people on Bookstagram who have become friends and given me so much of their time and sage advice. My editor and friend Josie is one of those people, but there are so many others. Jenni Bayliss, you are a treasure. Thank you for always answering my random questions and for being such a wonderful human being. Dani McLean and Heather McPeake, I hope I can one day return the many favours and kindnesses you've bestowed. Heather, your advice throughout this self-publication journey has been essential to my success. You're reading this—either on paper or device—because you shared your knowledge with me. I will be forever grateful and will do my best to pay that kindness forward.

Paige Moreland, thank you so much for patiently working with me to make a cover that stands out on the book table. I love it. Thanks for going out of your comfort zone.

To Erin and Phil who not only enthusiastically supported me when I told them about this project, they jumped in with legal advice that had me cashing in some serious karma points. (I owe you, large!) Thank you to Francois Larose for walking me through the copyright and trademark process. IP is no joke, folks. Protect yourself.

When it comes to friends, I have an embarrassment of riches. The love and support given to me when word spread I'd written a book warmed my heart. There are too many to mention by name without fearing I've missed someone essential, so I will just thank you all for enriching my life. Thank you, friends.

Lastly, to yoga for saving me. Yes, yoga has literally saved my life. Nicole and the gang at Yogatown, I love you.

We all wish to leave a mark on this world, to maybe leave a little love behind for others. God knows I've been on the receiving end of love invested that continues to pay dividends. From my mother, from lost friends, from previous generations. I hope that when I'm long gone someone might stumble upon this silly story about a boy and a girl who fell in love and feel delighted—even if just while reading the spicy bits.

ABOUT THE AUTHOR

Since meeting Mr. Darcy in English 101, **Kate Cole** hasn't managed to shake her obsession with all things happily ever after. A sucker for romance, this Canadian bibliophile is a woman in construction in the street, spicy romcom writer in her desk seat. When she isn't reading or writing, she's also a wife and mom in suburbia who can't get enough of Duran Duran or pedicures that match her current reads.

Under Construction is the first novel in Kate's Women in Trades Romance® series.

instagram.com/katecoleauthor

www.ingramcontent.com/pod-product-compliance
Lightning Source LLC
Chambersburg PA
CBHW061649190726
48289CB00006B/1802